DEATH OF A SAHIB

The long, drawn-out squeal of pain which roused him at daybreak ended with an animal-like grunt. He was still puzzled to know what a pig was doing in a hotel run by a Hindu when someone kicked the door open. The intruder who stormed into his room was wearing a khaki shirt under a thin, long-sleeved pullover and a pair of KD slacks. The chevrons on the sweater indicated that he was a sergeant or Havildar, but the Springfield carbine pointing at him hadn't been drawn from any police armoury. As Beardsley got to his feet and slowly raised his arms in surrender, the intruder was joined by a wiry, younger man. It didn't need a Mensa intellect to deduce that the bloodstains on his clothing belonged to some-one else and had dripped there from the serrated cutting edge of the combined fighting knife and home-made knuckle duster he was clenching in his right hand.

About the author

Clive Egleton is widely regarded as one of Britain's leading thriller writers. He began writing in 1969 after a distinguished army career and a life spent travelling abroad. He is the author of seventeen highly acclaimed previous novels, including THE RUSSIAN ENIGMA, A CONFLICT OF INTERESTS, A DIFFERENT DRUMMER, PICTURE OF THE YEAR and, most recently, GONE MISSING.

Death of a Sahib

Clive Egleton

CORONET BOOKS
Hodder and Stoughton

The characters and situations in this book are entirely imaginary and bear no relation to any real person or actual happenings.

First published in Great Britain in 1989 by Hodder and Stoughton Ltd.

Coronet edition 1990

British Library C.I.P.

Egleton, Clive, *1927–*
  Death of a sahib.
  I. Title
  823'.914[F]

  ISBN 0-340-52031-0

Printed and bound in Great Britain for Hodder and Stoughton paperbacks, a division of Hodder and Stoughton Ltd., Mill Road, Dunton Green, Sevenoaks, Kent TN13 2YA (Editorial Office: 47 Bedford Square, London WC1B 3DP) by Cox & Wyman Ltd., Reading.

For our good friends and near neighbours
Phyll and Peter Brough

CHAPTER I

FOR SHEER squalor the Excelsior was in a class of its own. The lavatories were housed in a tin shack and consisted of a row of wooden 'thunder boxes' positioned over a deep latrine that had been dug out of the sun-baked earth behind the hotel. The nearest thing to a vanitory unit in Beardsley's room was a wash-hand stand with a metal bowl that had to be filled from a cold water tap at the far end of the corridor. The final touch was provided by the greyish sheets on the charpoy which looked and smelt as though several previous occupants had slept in them.

Ordinarily, Beardsley wouldn't have gone anywhere near the place but the Excelsior was the only hotel in Patna and he'd had to spend the night somewhere. Yesterday evening, while still some eight miles from the village, the taxi driver he'd hired to take him to Etawah had been forced off the road by an oncoming truck and had fractured the differential casing on a rock embedded in the uneven verge. With the lubricating oil steadily draining away, they had managed to reach the outskirts of Patna before the red-hot bevel pinion and crown wheel had finally seized up on them.

Obtaining the necessary spares hadn't been a problem; Tata dominated the motor manufacturing industry in India and the only model they produced was a 1958 version of the Morris Oxford which they built under licence. With the help of Lal, whom Beardsley had also engaged in Agra, they'd had no difficulty in finding a replacement prop-shaft and rear axle in what, at first sight, had appeared to be a junk-yard near the railway station. The one thing Beardsley hadn't been able to resolve was the fact that the repairs wouldn't be completed until late the following morning at the earliest. If the last train to Etawah hadn't already departed, he would have paid off the Sikh driver there and

7

then; as it was, he'd been forced to stay the night at the Hotel Excelsior.

Beardsley had taken one look at the charpoy and decided the rickety wooden chair was infinitely preferable. Convinced he wouldn't get a wink of sleep, he had sat there in the chair smoking his way through the last packet of duty free cigarettes until finally he was just too damned tired to worry about the fleas, bedbugs and cockroaches which came crawling out of the woodwork.

The long, drawn-out squeal of pain which roused him at daybreak ended with an animal-like grunt. He was still puzzled to know what a pig was doing in a hotel run by a Hindu when someone kicked the door open. The intruder who stormed into his room was wearing a khaki shirt under a thin, long-sleeved pullover and a pair of KD slacks. The chevrons on the sweater indicated that he was a sergeant or Havildar, but the Springfield carbine pointing at him hadn't been drawn from any police armoury. As Beardsley got to his feet and slowly raised his arms in surrender, the intruder was joined by a wiry, younger man. It didn't need a Mensa intellect to deduce that the bloodstains on his clothing belonged to someone else and had dripped there from the serrated cutting edge of the combined fighting knife and home-made knuckle duster he was clenching in his right hand.

"If it's money you want," Beardsley said calmly, "there's over fourteen hundred rupees in my wallet."

The Havildar gazed at him blankly but his companion appeared to understand English; sheathing his knife, he crossed the room and picked up the rumpled linen jacket Beardsley had draped over the back of the chair.

"Help yourself," Beardsley said drily. "The wallet's inside the breast pocket."

The Indian ran his hands over the jacket, found the bill-fold and took it out. Rifling through the contents, he tossed the personal snapshots and credit cards on to the floor, then stuffed the wad of rupee notes into a small drawstring bag attached to the belt around his waist. He smelt the wallet, decided it was made of pigskin and threw it away, his nose wrinkling in disgust that he had defiled himself by handling such an 'unclean' object. The plastic folder containing six hundred pounds in travellers cheques from Lloyds Bank, which he discovered in another pocket, joined the personal memorabilia on the floor. So did the passport, but only after he had compared the photograph on page three with the elderly, round-shouldered man standing before him with his arms raised.

"Have you quite finished?" Beardsley demanded, hoping the tremor in his voice sounded like anger rather than fear.

The Havildar spoke to the younger man in Hindustani, then waved the Springfield carbine at Beardsley, motioning him to lead the way downstairs. Moving out into the corridor, he saw Lal standing under guard at the head of the staircase, his head bowed, his wrists tied behind him, a rope around his neck as though he were an animal on a lead. The paunchy little guide was naked except for a pair of gaudy boxer shorts; as they drew nearer, Beardsley could see that the left side of his face was raw where one of the intruders had shaved him with the serrated edge of his knife.

"Are you all right, Lal?" he asked quietly.

The guide raised his head and turned to face him, tears welling in his brown eyes. "Oh, Colonel Beardsley, I am so very glad to see you. These fearful ruffians will not dare to harm me now."

Lal had been born some years after the British had left India but it seemed he had inherited an almost mystical faith in the power of the Raj of whom Beardsley had once fleetingly been a representative. His flowery English was likewise a relic of a bygone age and would have been hilarious in any other circumstance.

"Don't let these people see you're afraid of them," Beardsley said in a low voice. "With any luck, they won't have the whip-hand over us much longer."

Luck was the operative word. Anyone who spoke Urdu could understand Hindustani and although he was a little rusty, Beardsley had got the gist of what the Havildar had said to his companion. Both men were due for a big disappointment if they thought the British High Commission in Delhi would pay a king's ransom for him, but that was beside the point. From what he could gather, they were already holding several other hostages and kidnapping on that kind of scale involved a small army if what was happening in the Lebanon was anything to go by.

Beardsley felt a sharp stab of pain as the Havildar began to use the barrel of his carbine to urge him on down the stairs and out on to the street. Following on behind, Lal tripped over an uneven cobblestone in the road and was only saved from measuring his length in the dust by the halter round his neck which almost choked him.

In size and head of population, Patna was one of the largest villages in the State of Uttar Pradesh. Apart from the railway station on the branch line to Etawah, it had its own police post and a government-sponsored carpet factory. The latter was a rambling, partially derelict house situated in one of the alleyways off the main thoroughfare. A narrow wooden gate set in a mud wall opened into a courtyard where normally the carpets were left to dry off after they had been singed, combed, washed down and scrubbed with brooms. But no one was making any carpets that morning; instead, the factory had been commandeered and turned into a detention centre presided over by a woman whom Beardsley guessed was in her late twenties or early thirties.

"Sarana Kurmis," Lal gasped in awe.

"Who's she?"

"Only the leader of the largest and most ruthless band of dacoits in all India."

Dacoit: a Hindi word for one of a band of armed robbers. Beardsley gazed at the slender figure in jungle green fatigues with renewed interest and especially noted the dark, glinting eyes in an angular face dominated by high cheekbones. Dangerous, cruel, vicious were three adjectives which immediately sprang to mind and were given further credence by the venom in her voice when she spoke to the Havildar. Reacting to her sharp command, the man with the sawtooth knife removed the halter from Lal's neck and used the rope to tie Beardsley's wrists and elbows together behind his back.

"She was married at fourteen," Lal continued after their guards had moved out of earshot. "They say her husband was a drunkard who used to beat her regularly to obtain more money. He and his mother were dissatisfied with the bride price they had received from Sarana's family and they thought her parents would beggar themselves to save their only daughter from being maltreated."

"And did they?" Beardsley asked.

Lal nodded. "Oh yes. They went to a money lender and borrowed everything they could but it was all to no avail. The more they raised, the more Sarana's husband wanted. Eventually they ran out of money and when that happened, Sarana's husband decided to kill her and find himself another wife, preferably from a wealthier family with lakhs of rupees. Naturally, Sarana's death had to look like an accident, but that was easy to arrange; the cooking stoves used by our peasants are notoriously dangerous and unfortunate women are being burned to death every day. So it was planned that while his mother held Sarana fast, he would pour a huge jar of cooking oil over her and then set her on fire. Things did not work out the way they'd intended; Sarana proved too strong for her mother-in-law and her husband was too drunk to catch her again after she had broken free. That night, she returned to the house and killed them both in their sleep."

Sarana had left the village before their bodies were found and had then wandered the roads, staying one jump ahead of the police. She had slept with any man willing to pay the asking price and, more often than not, had subsequently battered them senseless before robbing them of everything they had. Eventually she had fallen in with a band of dacoits operating in the Banda District near Jhansi. The leader had taken her for his mistress and had continued to treat her as a harlot even after she had gunned down three policemen who'd arrived on the scene while they were robbing a sub-branch of the Bank of Baroda. That he should have become her sixth victim had therefore been almost inevitable. There had been many others during the course of the next ten years and according to the latest official figures, the authorities in Delhi were satisfied that to date, she had murdered some one hundred and twenty-eight men, women and children in cold blood. In the process, Sarana had become the undisputed leader of the largest and most vicious band of dacoits in the whole of central India.

"They are strong enough to take over a small town," Lal said in another whispered aside. "Furthermore, they can hold

11

on to it for as long as they like because none of the inhabitants will dare to raise the alarm. Everyone knows that although the police have arrested Sarana many times, no witness has ever lived long enough to testify against her."

"I can see that would be a positive disincentive," Beardsley said drily.

"These people are well organised, Colonel."

"So I've noticed."

They had overpowered the local police detachment and some members of the band were now strolling around the town in their uniforms. As long as the traffic moving in either direction was allowed to pass through Patna unhindered, no one would realise the village had been taken over by dacoits.

Beardsley looked round the courtyard. It was a lot fuller now than it had been when they'd arrived and it seemed to him that very few of the newcomers had their arms tied behind them.

"What have those people done to merit such preferential treatment?" he asked Lal, drawing the guide's attention to a particular group near the entrance.

"They are peasants."

"You mean they don't have any money?"

"Sarana likes to project herself as the champion of the down-trodden poor. I think some of their oppressors are about to be punished for their misdeeds and they are here to witness their just retribution."

From various little things he'd said during the past two days, Beardsley had formed the impression that Lal was a crypto communist at heart. Now, the evident satisfaction in his voice reinforced that view.

"Who are these so-called oppressors?"

"Landlords, money-lenders, tax-collectors and the like. You'll see soon enough."

Above the continual murmur in the courtyard, Beardsley suddenly heard a chorus of jeering voices and glanced over his shoulder towards the alleyway where the noise was coming from. Someone cried out as though in mortal agony and provoked a burst of raucous laughter. A few moments later, the gate was thrown back and a small, rather flabby-looking man stumbled into the courtyard, stark naked and bleeding from a dozen livid welts on his back and thighs where he

12

had been flayed with a rawhide whip. He was followed by at least a dozen heavily armed dacoits and eight other prisoners including a woman who was clutching the remnants of her sari together in an effort to retain some vestige of modesty. As Sarana rose to address the onlookers, Lal began to paraphrase her speech while simultaneously providing a running commentary of his own.

"The tubby fellow who has been whipped is the wealthiest landlord in Patna and she is asking the crowd who amongst them has suffered at his hands."

A stooped, foxy-looking man in a grubby dhoti stood up, eager to voice a list of grievances. Half listening to Lal as he droned on, Beardsley thought it was comparatively simple to find someone who was ready to denounce a neighbour. All you had to do was assemble a crowd and play on their collective greed and envy, working them up to such a pitch that it was only a question of time before they were baying for blood.

A second man got to his feet to relate how his youngest child had died of the fever because the landlord had bled him white and he'd no money left to buy the medicine his son had needed. After that, the accusations came thick and fast from every quarter, each witness vying to outdo his or her predecessor. The crowd started chanting their demands for vengeance carefully orchestrated by a number of strategically placed agitators in their midst. An old man screamed that he had been crippled by the landlord and received vociferous support when he implored Sarana to do the same to him. An equally noisy group urged her to impose the death penalty and suggested they should vote on it with a show of hands. The resultant deadlock was entirely predictable as was the way it was swiftly resolved.

Numb with horror, Beardsley watched the dacoits force the landlord to lie flat on his back and tried to close his ears to the victim's terrified scream as they placed a wooden anvil under each leg. The Havildar produced an angle iron picket from somewhere and using it for a sledgehammer, smashed first one kneecap, then the other. On both occasions, the bone shattered making a noise like a pistol shot.

Beardsley raised his eyes, looked up at the cloudless blue sky and prayed, silently reciting the Lord's Prayer he'd learned by rote as a child. Although sweat oozed from every pore and dripped from his chin, his body felt cold and clammy. Beside him, a grey-faced Lal trembled violently as though in the grip of a recurring bout of malaria. A crowd drawn from some of the most gentle people in the world had been whipped into such a frenzy that in their irrational rage, they were capable of tearing their perceived enemies limb from limb. As a young man, Beardsley had seen this blood lust before during the communal riots of '46 and '47 and knew what to expect. He did not want to look but the nerve-rending screams which punctuated the enthusiastic approval of the mob were an irresistible magnet.

He watched Sarana's men haul the landlord to his feet and hold him upright against a post, his feet just clear of the ground to ensure he remained conscious. With almost loving care, the Havildar slipped a rope around his neck and tied it loosely behind the post; then, using a piece of wood, he twisted the strands, windlassing them together to garotte him. He did it slowly, prolonging the moment of death to inflict the maximum suffering. When the landlord finally died, his demise was greeted with a sigh of disappointment from many of the spectators.

The show however was not yet over. A tall athletic man with a military bearing was singled out from the surviving prisoners to be indicted for corruption, bribery and extortion. His accusers lacked a certain spontaneity and sounded about as convincing as a bunch of amateur theatricals reading their lines for the very first time.

"He is a Police Inspector," Lal explained softly. "His name is Charan Singh and these people are telling Sarana he was always demanding baksheesh – that is alms, money . . ."

"And was he?"

"It's possible. These things happen in my country."

Whatever else he was, Inspector Charan Singh was either a very brave man or a proud and extremely foolish one. At first, he appeared to be cowed by the torrent of abuse from Sarana but he was merely waiting for her to come within range. As she stepped a pace nearer, he suddenly puffed out his cheeks and spitting like a cobra, he directed a stream of saliva into her face. Sarana reared back, her features contorted with fury; then she gave a blood-curdling scream and three of her followers jumped on Charan Singh, hacking and stabbing at his body with their knives. Presently, one of them held his severed head aloft, seeking the crowd's approval. But their mood had changed dramatically and there was an audible gasp of revulsion.

"I think they've had enough, Colonel." Lal gagged, failed to contain the bile rising in his throat and threw up. "I'm sorry," he spluttered, "but the sight of blood always did affect me and I can't help it."

"There's no need to apologise," Beardsley told him. "You wouldn't be human if you weren't sickened by what's happening here."

Lal was right about one thing, the villagers had had more than enough and were now afraid for themselves. Beardsley remembered how it had been during the Great Calcutta Slaughter of 1946, the high-pitched screaming of the crowd in the adjoining street coming nearer as his company of Rajputana Rifles moved towards the scene of the riot; then the sudden silence, the mob pattering away, the smell of their fear, and their victims lying dead in the road, hacked to pieces.

But Sarana and her followers did not share the villagers' revulsion. The show trial had a twofold purpose, to frighten the villagers into submission and implicate them in the crimes that had been committed ostensibly on their behalf. The slaughter wasn't about to stop because the latter objective had ceased to be obtainable. It did however proceed at a faster pace. The spectators were no longer required to give evidence; instead, the accused were indicted, tried and convicted by Sarana Kurmis. Sentenced to death, each victim was executed by a pistol shot in the head as they knelt before her. The woman died last and was murdered by Sarana herself. As she moved towards him with the Havildar in tow, Beardsley was convinced that he and Lal were next.

"This white face," she rasped, addressing Lal. "Who is he?"

"A sahib." The guide made a determined effort to control the quaver in his voice and started again. "His name is Colonel Sahib Beardsley."

"Is he rich?"

"He is a very important man, the British will pay you lakhs of rupees for him."

Beardsley gazed at Lal, a questioning look on his face as though waiting for the Indian to enlighten him. It was important to maintain the pretence that he didn't understand a word of Hindustani. Even supposing the High Commission in Delhi were prepared to pay the ransom, weeks could pass before negotiations got under way. If he was to escape, it was vital to lull his captors into a false sense of security so that they felt free to talk amongst themselves in his presence.

"These people will be leaving soon, Colonel," Lal said in a strained voice, "and you will be going with them." He cleared his throat, then looked away, apparently unable to face him. "They believe you are a very wealthy man," he added reluctantly.

"What sort of price have they put on my head?"

"Five lakhs."

Five lakhs – five hundred thousand rupees, say twenty-eight thousand pounds. Beardsley did the sums in his head and wondered if London would be willing to pay up. Twenty-eight thousand pounds was small beer but the government had said time and again that they wouldn't negotiate with terrorists and there was a principle at stake.

"Will you be delivering the ransom demand, Lal?" he asked.

"They will kill us both if I refuse, Colonel."

"I expect they would." Beardsley flexed his hands in a vain attempt to restore the circulation. The cords were biting deep into his wrists and he was convinced that his numbed fingers had swollen to twice their normal size. To add to his discomfort, a bluebottle settled on his eyebrow and dipped its proboscis into the sweat oozing from his forehead. "You should deliver the ransom demand to the British High Commission in Delhi," he continued. "Ask for Mr Goodman and don't let them fob you off with anyone else. Describe what has happened here today and make sure he realises these people mean business."

"You may rely on me, Colonel. When I was accompanying Sir Anthony and Lady Witherington on their grand tour of India last year, Sir Anthony said to me, 'I trust you, Lal, because I know your word is your bond.'"

The Indian guide had few rivals in the game of name-dropping and there were grounds for thinking that most of the titled people he claimed to know were figments of his imagination. Until a few hours ago, Beardsley had regarded Lal's obvious need to impress him as a mildly amusing trait but as of now, it was a positive irritant and he found it difficult to keep his temper in check.

"I'm sure Sir Anthony showed his appreciation," Beardsley said evenly, "and if I come out of this in one piece, you won't find me ungrateful either."

"One does not look for a reward, Colonel."

"I know that, but Her Majesty's Government will insist on giving you something far more tangible than just a medal in recognition of your services." He smiled encouragingly. "Now suppose you persuade Sarana that I'm definitely worth preserving?"

Lal did exactly that with growing confidence and a touch of arrogance. For a few bad moments, Beardsley feared the guide had gone over the top but then Sarana looked at him with a calculating gleam in her eyes and he fancied everything was going to be all right.

The Havildar seized his left arm and pushed him into one of the weaving rooms off the courtyard. The carpet factory was a rabbit warren of dark passages leading hither and thither so that by the time they emerged into a narrow street behind the building, Beardsley had lost all sense of direction. No one took the slightest notice of them as they walked through the bazaar. So far as the beggars, street hawkers, tailors, fortune-tellers and shop keepers were concerned, he didn't exist, and neither did the Havildar. There couldn't have been a man or woman amongst them who wasn't aware that Patna was in the hands of a band of dacoits, but survival it seemed lay in pretending that everything was normal.

The bustling alley led to an even busier square where, in addition to a parking lot for a dozen or so trucks, there was a fruit and vegetable market. Checking out the vehicles, the Havildar found one that was still loaded with baskets of water-melons. He called to a group of men squatting on their haunches outside a café, told the driver to come on over and ordered him to offload some of the baskets.

As soon as a space had been cleared midway between the tailboard and the cab, the Havildar climbed aboard, hauled Beardsley into the back and forced him to lie down on the floor. Working swiftly, he tied Beardsley's ankles together and secured them to his wrists so that he was arched like a drawn bow. Then he gagged him with a piece of rag and pulled a canvas sack over his head. Finally, the Havildar buried him from sight under a mound of water-melons.

In a dilapidated state and on its last legs, the truck was held together with bits of string and baling wire. The exhaust had been patched in so many places that little remained of the original system. The silencer was holed and the tailpipe had rotted away; soon after the driver moved off, the carbon monoxide fumes from the exhaust began to seep through the floorboards towards the rear of the truck.

CHAPTER II

HENDERSON LEFT the Ford Escort in the multi-storey car park below the General Hospital, then cut through the pedestrian underpass in Maid Marion Way and hurried on down Friar Lane towards the Market Square. As the proprietor and sole operative of the Gold Seal Inquiry Agency, close on eighty per cent of his income was derived from judgments handed down at the Nottingham Crown Court, while approximately seventeen per cent came from local solicitors whose clients were anxious to reduce the amount of maintenance they were obliged to pay their ex-wives. The remaining three to four per cent came from people who wanted to trace a missing relative and had looked him up in the Yellow Pages.

Alexandra Drummond belonged to the latter group, with the difference that she had been put in touch with him through a London-based firm of solicitors. Their appointment was for two fifteen; unfortunately, he had seriously underestimated the amount of time it would take him to serve a repossession order on a former colliery worker living in Beeston and he already several minutes late. The able Mrs Luckwell who came in four afternoons a week to deal with his correspondence would undoubtedly look after her, but that wasn't the point. It was he who'd fixed the time and his late arrival was unlikely to inspire Ms Drummond with confidence. Moving up another gear, Henderson half-ran past the Council House and turned into St Peter's Gate Walk.

The offices of the Gold Seal Inquiry Agency were two back-to-back rooms below a portrait studio at the bottom end of a small cul-de-sac. None of the buildings in St Peter's Gate Walk were particularly noteworthy but they had all been listed because they were part of old Nottingham and were said to have been associated with the lace trade at the turn of the century. In those days, they had been tied cottages for the workmen; eighty-seven years on, they were still the same inconvenient buildings despite renovation. The attraction for Henderson was the fact that the properties were rent-controlled and had a low rateable value.

Ms Drummond was an attractive, dark-haired young woman whom Henderson thought was aged twenty-eight to thirty which made her at least four years younger than himself. At five nine, she was also half a head shorter. She was smartly dressed in a well-cut navy blue suit over a white silk blouse and carried matching accessories which included a thin, executive-style briefcase. Guessing at her occupation, he thought she was either a high-powered company secretary or an accountant. In the space of a couple of minutes, he discovered she preferred to be called Miss as opposed to Ms Drummond, had a ready smile and a great deal of charm to go with it. She even had him believing she hadn't realised he was late for their appointment until he apologised.

"What have you done to your eye?" she asked after they had gone through to his office.

He hadn't done anything; the swelling was the handiwork of the former colliery worker who lived in Beeston. Annoyed at the prospect of losing his 1986 BMW 720, he had taken a swing at Henderson and had been a shade too fast for him. The punch had been aimed at his jaw; in trying to duck under the right hook, the blow had caught him above the left eye. The colliery worker should have left it at that and slammed the door in his face but he'd been overly ambitious and had come in close to give Henderson something more to remember him by. That had been his big mistake; still crouching low, Henderson had thumped him in the crotch. Thereafter, he'd had no difficulty in serving the prostrate miner with the repossession order.

"Would you believe I walked into a door?"

"If you say so." A smile hovered at the corners of her mouth.

"Such accidents do happen, Miss Drummond," Henderson said, poker-faced. From the top drawer of his desk, he took out a large notebook and opened it at a blank page. "I gather from your solicitors that you are anxious to trace a missing relative?"

"Actually, Colonel Beardsley isn't a relative." Her smile this time was definitely apologetic. "I can't think why Draycott and Draycott should have told you that. As a matter of fact, I'm not even sure he is missing; indeed, the British High Commission in Delhi are reasonably certain that he's dead."

"Now you've really lost me."

"Have you ever heard of the Finlayson Trust, Mr Henderson?"

"Can't say I have."

"It was set up in 1901 to perpetuate the memory of Lady Cynthia Finlayson, the wife of Sir George Finlayson, Governor of the United Province. The aim of the Trust is to further Anglo-Indian relations by providing a measure of financial assistance necessary to enable deserving youngsters from poor families to complete their high school education and perhaps go on to university. The selection committee is chaired by the Dean of Aligarh University in what is now Uttar Pradesh. As chairman of the financial committee, Colonel Beardsley was responsible for liaising with the Dean and supervising the disbursement of educational grants to the families of individual students. I'm the secretary and only full-time employee of the Trust. It's my job to satisfy the Charity Commissioners and the Inland Revenue that the Trust is a non-profit-making body and that its affairs are being properly conducted."

Alexandra Drummond hesitated as though uncertain how to continue.

"And?" he prompted her.

"Well, I'm not sure they are being conducted in accordance with our charter," she told him, frowning. "A few days ago, I opened a letter addressed to Colonel Rupert Beardsley from the Dean which led me to believe that there is a considerable discrepancy between the number of students we are supposed to be funding and those who are actually in receipt of a grant."

"You mean the Trust is being ripped off?"

"I think we're losing between twelve and fifteen thousand a year."

"That's peanuts, Miss Drummond."

"It isn't to us."

"No, what I meant is that no one in his right mind would risk three to five years' imprisonment for embezzling so little."

"I hope you're right. The fact is, Rupert Beardsley flew to Delhi on Thursday the twenty-eighth of May but instead of going straight to Aligarh, he joined a party of tourists on a package holiday to Jaipur, Fatehpur Sikri and the Taj Mahal. In Agra, he left the coach party, hired a guide and went on to Etawah. Along the way at a village called Patna, he was abducted by a gang of dacoits who sent a message to the British High Commission demanding a ransom of half a million rupees. This was on the eighth of June; ten days later, the badly decomposed body of a European was recovered from a well in Behmai some eighty-five miles from Patna. The corpse was identified by the laundry mark inside the shirt collar."

Alexandra Drummond placed the executive briefcase on her knees and unlocked it; delving inside, she brought out a slim, buff-coloured folder and gave it to Henderson.

"The folder contains a copy of the itinerary for the tour Rupert Beardsley joined. The company is Indus Tours and their representative at the Delhi office in Connaught Circus is a Mr Bernard Jervis. I've also included the name and address of the guide Rupert hired in Agra. Finally, there's a photograph of the Colonel together with a detailed report of his last physical examination."

"Where did you get that from, Miss Drummond?"

"Our records. Private medicine is about the only perk enjoyed by our trustees."

Henderson checked the contents of the folder. There was one further enclosure she had neglected to mention, a type-written letter from the Dean of Aligarh University on crested notepaper which was more grey than white and looked as though it had been recycled.

"This letter was the first intimation you had that someone was embezzling the Trust?" he asked.

"Yes. According to our files, far more students are in receipt of a grant than the Dean quotes in his letter."

"It takes at least two people to work a fraud like that," Henderson told her. "In your shoes, I'd ask the Dean for an explanation."

"Oh no, that would never do, Mr Henderson." She smiled wryly. "As I said before, the whole purpose of the Trust is to further Anglo-Indian relations. By asking the Dean for an explanation, we would be inferring that he was party to the fraud which would be the quickest way I know to destroy the special fellowship we have with the University. Besides, the Dean is absolutely above suspicion."

"So what exactly is it you want me to do?"

"I'd like to know why Rupert hired a guide and who he was going to see in Etawah. I'm also not entirely convinced that the body the police found in the well at Behmai was Rupert Beardsley."

Alexandra Drummond opened her briefcase again, took out a certified cheque for one thousand seven hundred pounds and gave it to Henderson.

"I believe you charge a hundred pounds a day for your exclusive services plus expenses. I'd like to hire you for as long as it takes to discover the answers to my questions. Hopefully, this is sufficient?"

Henderson glanced at the cheque and raised his eyebrows. "It's drawn against your own personal account," he said.

"I didn't think it would be right to charge the Trust with the cost of hiring a private Inquiry Agent, at least not yet awhile. Besides, it's my good name that's at stake."

"Seventeen hundred is still a lot of money."

"I can afford it, Mr Henderson." Her face lit up with a whimsical smile which was clearly meant to disarm him. "I don't think it would take you long to find that out for yourself," she added.

"The registered office of the Trust is in London?"

"Yes. Why do you ask?"

"I was just wondering why you looked for a private Inquiry Agent in Nottingham?"

"It's no great mystery. Colonel Beardsley came from this part of the world; he owns a large house in Southwell near the Minster."

Alexandra Drummond had a ready answer for every question he threw at her. It was as if she had anticipated the line he would take and had prepared herself accordingly. Undoubtedly, part of that preparation would have included an independent appraisal of his reputation which would have been easy enough to obtain. He was the only private detective in Nottingham who advertised his services in the Yellow Pages and her solicitors could have checked him out with any of the dozen or so legal firms in the city who'd engaged him at one time or another.

"How do I get in touch with you, Miss Drummond?" he asked.

"Through my solicitors, Draycott and Draycott. Their offices are in Chancery Lane and you'll find the address and telephone number in the folder I gave you."

Henderson looked up from his notebook. The page was still largely virginal and she hadn't given him the information he wanted. "Can I have your office number?"

"I'd rather you didn't phone me at the Trust. It's not that I mean to be deceitful but on the advice of my solicitors, I haven't told the Director that the fund is being milked by one of his fellow trustees. Mr Young thought we should wait until we had some positive information to show him."

"Mr Young is one of the solicitors at Draycott and Draycott?"

"Yes."

"Are you on the phone at home? I only ask in case I should need to get in touch with you during out-of-office hours."

"That's a little difficult. You see, I'm in the process of moving house." Her dark eyebrows met in a brief frown, then just as suddenly her face brightened visibly. "Still, in an emergency, you could always leave a message with Pamela."

"Who's Pamela?" Henderson asked dutifully.

"Pamela Wagnall; we were at Cheltenham together and have kept in touch. I'm staying with Pam and her husband while contracts are being exchanged on the flat I'm buying in Barnes. They live in Well Walk, midway between Hampstead Village and the Heath. Their phone number is 01-435 0056." She closed the briefcase and stood it on the floor next to her chair. "They're ex-directory so I'd rather you didn't phone me unless it's absolutely essential."

"Don't worry," said Henderson, "it'll have to be a dire emergency. And just to set your mind at rest, I can't remember the last time I was faced with one."

"Good." She nodded, indication that he'd said the right

thing; then in the next breath she asked him when he could start.

"That depends on the number of jabs I need – cholera, scrub-typhus, yellow fever . . ."

"None of them are mandatory. The Indian Immigration authorities won't even ask you for a vaccination certificate; I checked with my local travel agency."

"You don't mind if I clear my desk first, do you?" Henderson said with a gentle touch of irony.

"Touché." The laughter lines creased around her mouth and eyes, then picking up her briefcase, she got to her feet and shook hands. "I'm afraid I tend to be a bit pushy; of course, when you're the only girl as well as the youngest in a family of four, you can't afford to be a shy violet."

Shy – Alexandra Drummond? Henderson doubted if she even knew the meaning of the word.

"You'll need a visa," she continued unabashed, "and that can be a time-consuming business. Fortunately, we do have some influence with the Indian High Commission. Could you come up to London?"

"When?" Henderson suddenly realised he was still holding on to her hand and released it hastily.

"Tomorrow afternoon, if that's not too inconvenient," she said and opened the door to Sheila Luckwell's office.

"I think that can be arranged."

"Fine. I'll meet you outside India House in the Aldwych at four thirty."

Alexandra Drummond had him in the palm of her hand; she knew it, he knew it and so did Mrs Luckwell. He had been attracted to her at first sight but acknowledging she had established such a hold over him only gave rise to feelings of guilt. He shook hands with her again at the door, ignored the amused look Sheila Luckwell gave him and returned to his office.

He went through the folder a second time and rapidly came to the conclusion that Alexandra Drummond had told him next to nothing about Rupert Beardsley. There was, he knew, only one way to fill in the gaps; informing his secretary he was going to Southwell and would be away for the rest of the afternoon, he left to collect his Ford Escort from the multi-storey car park. On the way, he stopped off at Lloyds Bank to pay in the certified cheque, then visited Boots the Chemist to buy a pair of sunglasses to hide the swelling above his left eye.

*   *   *

Avery approached the house from the direction of Woodthorpe Road, turned right into Mapperley Hall Drive and went on down the steep hill, eventually stopping outside number 42 which belonged to ex-Detective Sergeant Henderson. The property was built on a shelf above the road and some thirty feet back from it. With the exception of the double garage on the left, the rest of the house was screened from view by a row of cypressus which over the years had become a tall, dense hedge. An estate agent's 'For Sale' notice was planted in the rockery bordering the driveway where it could be seen from the main road.

Alighting from the car, Avery made his way round to the back of the house. Although they had never met, he wasn't surprised that Henderson had decided to put the house on the market; the only thing that puzzled him was why he had waited so long. He could have understood Henderson moving out immediately after the event but almost four years had passed since Linda Morris, the woman police constable with whom he had been cohabiting, had been killed. In pursuit of a stolen car, she had run out of road on a tight bend and had wrapped the police Volvo round a lamp post. The yob who had been responsible for her death had been a seventeen-year-old tearaway with a choirboy's angelic face and a record of similar offences.

They should have thrown the book at him; instead, a young liberal-minded Inspector with a degree in Sociology had charged him with a simple Taking and Driving Away offence and an equally progressive magistrate had swallowed a bleeding hearts plea from the defence and had sentenced the accused to a hundred and sixty-eight hours' community service. 'Angel Face' had then proceeded to give Henderson a two-finger salute which was roughly the equivalent of poking a lion in the eye with a stick. Five months later the youth had been found unconscious in an alleyway with three cracked ribs, a broken nose, a fractured jaw and a large gap in his front teeth. Everyone had known who was responsible but, with the victim unwilling to identify his assailant and half the Force ready to give Henderson a cast-iron alibi, the liberal-minded Inspector hadn't been able to prove it. The Chief Constable however had demanded and got his resignation.

Avery pressed the doorbell until he succeeded in rousing Henderson's eleven-year-old Alsatian from his afternoon slumber, then popped two slices of malt cake through the letter box, almost losing his fingers in the process. The Alsatian had been a first class police dog in his day but he'd always had a sweet tooth and there wasn't anything he wouldn't do for a piece of malt cake. The first slice was just an appetiser to excite his saliva glands, the second contained a capsule of poison strong enough to put a horse to sleep.

He listened to the dog staggering about, and waited for him to collapse; then selecting a large stone from the rockery, he smashed the pane of rippled glass in the door and reached inside. The fact that the key wasn't in the lock didn't surprise him; as a former police officer, Henderson had done a stint on crime prevention and was the last person to make things easy for a thief. The ordinary house-breaker however wouldn't know that and he wanted the entry to look right.

No one could see him from Mapperley Hall Drive and the house was not overlooked at the back. Of the immediate neighbours, the married couple living at number 44 were both out at work and the gradient of the hill was such that only the rooftop of number 40 was visible. Backing off several paces, he ran at the door and raised his left leg to deliver a karate side kick, his foot slamming the keyhole with the force of a sledgehammer. The wood splintered with a loud crack like a pistol shot; when he kicked it again, the whole lock gave way and the door swung back on its hinges.

The Alsatian was lying on his right side, his eyes glazed, his tongue protruding. Avery pushed the door closed behind him, stepped over the dog and went upstairs. With four bedrooms, the house was far too large for two people and he assumed Henderson and the girl had bought it as a hedge against inflation. Both rooms at the front were sparsely furnished and looked as though they had never been occupied.

The master bedroom above the dining alcove was a shrine dedicated to the memory of Linda Morris. Her blouses, underwear, nightdresses and sweaters were neatly folded away in the drawers of the tallboy and matching dressing-table, her skirts, dresses and coats still hanging from the right-hand rail in the fitted cupboard. The only item of any value was the small diamond and sapphire engagement ring which he slipped into his jacket pocket before turning the place over. Everything went on to the double bed in a great untidy heap, then using a clasp knife, he slashed the dresses and undergarments the way an angry and frustrated petty thief might do after he'd discovered there was nothing in the house worth taking. He did a repeat performance on the small back bedroom Henderson was occupying across the landing, with the difference that he left the clothes intact after dumping them on the floor.

There were two phones in the house, one in the hall, the other in the kitchen on the dividing wall with the utility room. The bug he proposed to implant was the last word in microchip technology and consisted of a wire mike, power source and transmitter. The one he put in the kitchen he positioned on top of the bracket for the fluorescent tube and anchored it in place with sellotape where it wouldn't be seen by Henderson should he look up at the pinewood ceiling. Finding a suitable place in the hall for its mate was not as easy and in the end he was obliged to fix it on the back of a print of one of Peter Scott's watercolours. It wasn't the best hiding place in the world and he spent some minutes carefully examining the picture from every angle to make sure he'd re-hung it properly.

There was one finishing touch which remained to be done. Returning to the master bedroom, Avery chose a rose-coloured lipstick from the selection on the dressing-table and decorated the walls and mirror with obscenities. The shrill note of the telephone broke the oppressive silence as he was completing his art work. The caller allowed it to ring exactly eight times before he hung up, a pre-arranged signal which told Avery that Henderson had just left Southwell and was presumably on his way back to Nottingham. Completely unruffled, he added one more epithet, then went downstairs again and walked out of the house. No one else was around when he got into his car, but halfway down the hill he overtook an elderly man out walking his dog.

*   *   *

Henderson reached the T-junction at Oxton, decided to approach Nottingham from the north rather than take the back way home via Woodborough and turned right for the A614. Locating Beardsley's house in Southwell had not been quite as straightforward as he'd hoped. The Colonel wasn't listed in the telephone directory and his name wasn't on the electoral roll, a copy of which was held at the public library. The chief librarian was new to the area and had never heard of him, neither had his assistant. Fortunately, Beardsley was known to a Commissioner for Oaths whose offices were near the Saracen's Head Hotel. It transpired that the family home, known as 'Greenacres', was situated on the Newark Road and was owned by Beardsley's brother-in-law, Dudley Spencer, a sprightly and gregarious septuagenarian who, after talking to the Commissioner for Oaths, had invited Henderson round to the house.

Contrary to what Alexandra Drummond had led him to believe, Beardsley did not come from Southwell. The only son of a high-ranking officer in the Indian Civil Service, he had been born in Lucknow in 1924 and had returned to the UK at the age of eight to be educated at Orly House Prep School and then Radley College. In 1942, he had returned to India as a potential officer and had gone to Bangalore where, five months later, he had been commissioned into the Rajputana Rifles.

Beardsley had had what in army circles was described as a good war, winning a Military Cross in the Arakan followed by an immediate award of the Distinguished Service Order some nine months later at the battle of Imphal while still only a junior captain. Although he'd stayed on after the war, the granting of independence in 1947 had meant that there was no longer a place for Beardsley in the Indian Army.

29

Soldiering was however the one job he'd been trained for and wanted to do. On returning to the UK, he had been granted a regular commission in the Sherwood Foresters and posted to the Regimental Depot where eventually he had met his future wife at an official cocktail party. According to Dudley Spencer, his post-war army career had been somewhat humdrum and although Beardsley had been promoted to Lieutenant Colonel ahead of his contemporaries, he had never commanded his regiment.

At the age of fifty, he had retired from the Army and joined the board of the Finlayson Trust. He had also gone to work for the Foreign and Commonwealth Office as a Queen's Messenger, which was a fancy name for a diplomatic courier. The Southwell connection really dated from 1981 when Beardsley's wife had returned to 'Greenacres'. The marriage hadn't been going through a bad patch, Dudley Spencer maintained, but knowing her husband would have to retire in the not too distant future, Nancy had decided to return to the town where she had grown up. When the time finally came for Rupert to give up his job, they proposed to sell the flat in Stanhope Square but until then, he'd continued to live in London while spending every free weekend in Southwell.

Their plans had never come to fruition because Nancy Beardsley had died in 1983 after a short illness. Nancy's share of 'Greenacres' and the income she'd enjoyed from a trust had reverted to the family, but it seemed Beardsley hadn't been short of a bob or two and no one could have given him a more glowing character reference than his brother-in-law.

Henderson turned off the main road into Mapperley Hall Drive and went on up the hill. Approaching the roundabout near the top, he tripped the offside indicator and pulled across the road to run into the driveway of number 42. He left the car on the front, let himself into the house and immediately called the office, using the phone in the hall. Although Mrs Luckwell would have long since departed, she would have left a message on the answering machine had a prospective client tried to make an appointment in his absence. No one had, but Sheila had decided he should at least be inoculated against cholera and had made an appointment for him at nine sharp in the morning. She had also made a provisional booking on a British Airways flight to Delhi in a little under forty-eight hours' time.

Henderson replaced the phone and walked on through the hall into the kitchen. The moment he saw Prince lying on the floor of the utility room, he knew the Alsatian was dead and was filled with a murderous and implacable hatred for whoever was responsible. Prince had been Linda's dog and the last remaining link with the past and a very special relationship that had been on the brink of becoming more permanent in the conventional sense when it had been brutally terminated. What Henderson found upstairs only served to fuel his anger.

He returned to the hall, picked up the phone again and dialled 999.

A cool, well-modulated voice said, "Emergency – which service do you require?"

"Police." He spat it out, the venom in his voice making it sound like a four-letter expletive. Then the operator patched him through and he was asked for his name and address. "Jack Henderson," he said, "42 Mapperley Hall Drive, subscriber's number Nottingham 029195. I want to report a break-in."

"Yes, sir." The police officer was annoyingly calm. "Has anything been stolen?" he asked.

"A large slice out of my life," Henderson told him.

Four miles away across town, the spools were turning on a Grundig recorder capturing his every word.

CHAPTER III

THE POLICE constable manning the desk at Hyson Green was new to the area and didn't know Henderson from Adam. He was however used to dealing with name-dropping civilians who presumed upon a casual acquaintance with a particular officer in order to get what they hoped would be preferential treatment. The mere fact that Henderson knew Detective Sergeant Preston was the crime prevention officer didn't impress him one little bit; what did make the constable think twice was the way the station officer greeted Henderson by his first name and asked if there was anything he could do for him. Surreptitiously lifting the phone, the constable rang the CID room to inform Preston an old friend had come to see him.

Detective Sergeant Danny Preston was a plump, affable man who liked his whisky and smoked far too many cigarettes. Now aged forty-five, he had been a detective sergeant when Henderson had joined the Force as a probationary constable and had long ago reached his ceiling. For as long as he could remember, Danny Preston had been a sort of elder counsellor and his advice was still sought after by at least one superintendent Henderson knew of. Crime prevention could have been a sinecure for a tired man – the occasional lecture, a word of advice on how to protect your property in one easy lesson; all of it very practical stuff and worthwhile too. It was also a good public relations exercise but Preston had made something more out of the job than the terms of reference had laid down. He was in fact a walking encyclopaedia of information and knew the names and track records of every prostitute on the game in Hyson Green, who was pushing what drug and where, and the location of every shebang or illegal drinking den in the area. And just to round things off, he had more informants among the ethnic minorities than the rest of the CID put together.

"Who gave you that shiner, Jack?" Preston asked as soon as they were settled in his smoke-laden office.

"I walked into a door," Henderson told him, giving the stock answer to what was rapidly becoming a stock question.

"Is that why you're rubbing your arm?"

"I've just been innoculated against cholera. If a certain young woman has her way, I'll be flying out to Delhi tomorrow afternoon."

"Some people have all the luck."

"Not always."

"Quite." Preston lit a cigarette and drew on it hungrily. "I hear your place got turned over yesterday evening," he said.

"You may also have heard that my 999 call didn't exactly provoke an electric response from your people. It must have been all of half an hour before anyone showed up on my doorstep and even then they sent along a boy who looked as though he'd only just started to shave."

"What was stolen?"

"Linda's engagement ring, a few trinkets – the whole lot couldn't have been worth more than two hundred and fifty."

"Well, there you are then," Preston said philosophically. "Breaking and Entering is such a growth area, we can't afford to do more than take an inventory of the stolen property. Did they mess the place up?"

"It was a solo job and the son of a bitch decorated the walls with a few well-chosen epigrams."

"You're lucky he didn't shit on the floor; that's what most of these tearaways do when they end up empty-handed."

"I don't think the guy who did it was an amateur. He killed the dog."

"Bastard," Preston said without heat.

"The poison was in a slice of malt bread," Henderson continued. "I found some crumbs in his saliva where he'd drooled on the floor. Now I ask you, Danny, how many people knew that Prince had a weakness for malt bread?"

"The neighbours?"

"Maybe. This guy also knew a thing or two about karate. He kicked the door in with the sole of his left foot. Judging by the marks he left, I reckon he takes a size eight which would make him on the chunky side, say a hundred and fifty odd pounds and around five seven."

"He could be tall and skinny."

"Not with a broad fitting shoe; beanpoles don't usually have wide feet." Henderson paused, then said, "He probably arrived by car."

"Why?"

"Because the house is up for sale and quite a few people have been to see it. Usually they're accompanied by a rep from the estate agents but one or two prospective buyers have come on their own and merely walked round the house, viewing it from the outside. The point is that the thief probably thinks my neighbours are used to seeing a car parked outside number 42, but that doesn't mean they're unobservant. Door to door enquiries may give us a description of the car and its driver."

"I think CID can find a police constable to do that." Preston mashed his cigarette in an ashtray already brimming over with stubs. "Anything else?" he asked.

"Forensic might care to have a look at this." Henderson dipped into his jacket pocket and brought out a plastic bag containing a lipstick. "None of the prints on it are mine, Danny. If the intruder's got any previous form, we should be able to identify him."

He saw the way Preston was eyeing the lipstick and knew what the Detective Sergeant was thinking. To have kept Linda's things all this time was inward-looking and unhealthy. Well, he had news for Danny; he'd finally let her go, the intruder had seen to that. Last night he'd carried all her clothes out of the house and stuffed them into the dustbin.

"One last thing. I took Prince to the vet this morning and arranged for the senior partner to do a post mortem. I told him to send the results on to you."

"How long are you going to be in India?"

"I would hope no more than a week, but you never can tell."

Preston opened the bottom drawer of his desk and took out a bound notebook with semi-stiff covers. "I think we'd better put your house on the unoccupied list," he said. "You don't want to come home and find the place has been emptied of furniture in your absence."

*   *   *

Avery returned to the large detached house in West Bridgford, parked the car on the garage front and let himself into the hall. His wife, Deidre, was employed in the accounts department of Jeavons in the Victoria Centre, and their two daughters attended Nottingham High School. There was therefore no good reason why any members of his family should be there at eleven o'clock in the morning, but he played it safe just in case and called out to let them know he was home. Although it would not have bothered him too much had anyone answered, he preferred to listen to the recordings in complete privacy.

The fourth bedroom was only a shade larger than a walk-in cupboard and no one had objected when Avery had appropriated it as his study. A dropleaf table, which he utilised as a desk, took up the whole of one wall leaving just enough space in the rest of the room for two three-drawer filing cabinets and a swivel chair. The synthesised receiver manufactured by Racal Communications Limited weighed a fraction over forty-six pounds and was too heavy to be positioned anywhere else but in the centre of the table. Designed primarily for electronic warfare operations in the field, it was capable of monitoring transmissions in the HF to Ultra High Frequency range, and was programmed to activate the Grundig tape-recorder on the floor whenever there was a transmission from the house in Mapperley Hall Drive.

Avery saw no point in locking the door to his study. Deidre and the girls knew about the surveillance equipment but they never mentioned it to anyone else because they were aware that his job depended on their silence. Getting down on all fours, he crawled under the table to check the Grundig and saw by the figures in the window that there had been another transmission from the house. Rewinding the tape, he then depressed the play button and listened intently. The phone

35

call lasted all of four minutes, told him no more than he already knew and ended with a definite clunk as Henderson put the phone down.

Avery backed out and sat down at the table to write up the latest intercept in his notebook. Although there was a phone within reach, he was not disposed to use it; the man who'd briefed him had been very coy when he'd asked if the surveillance operation had been authorised by the Home Office. Illegal wire taps were apt to go sour on the perpetrators and if he didn't watch his back, no one else would, least of all the people in London. Phone calls could be traced and he wasn't about to make things easy for anyone who was of a mind to sell him short in an emergency.

A naturally cautious man, he wiped the tape clean, then left the house and drove south on the road to Loughborough. The public call box he chose to use was a good eight miles beyond the outskirts of Nottingham. The London area code told him the subscriber he'd been instructed to call was located somewhere in the Bayswater postal district. Since he didn't have a name and address for the number, he wasn't surprised when a synthesised voice asked him to wait for the tone signal before leaving a message.

"This is your friendly bird dog," Avery said tersely. "At approximately 1830 hours yesterday evening, Henderson made a 999 call to report that his house had been broken into. It was a busy evening crimewise and it was some time before a police mobile was able to respond to the emergency call. For technical reasons the conversation between subject and the police constable was only captured intermittently. Henderson told the officer that after letting himself into the house, he used the phone in the hall to call his office downtown to see if his secretary had left any message for him. He discovered the break-in when he walked into the kitchen. The constable went through the motions and made a list of the items which allegedly had been stolen. Henderson has been around long enough to know there was no way the police would waste a moment longer on this case than they had to, but you could tell he didn't like it . . ."

Avery saw that he had less than half a minute to go and fed the coin box with a handful of loose change from his trouser pocket.

"After the police officer had left, he made several unsuccessful attempts to get through to a London number before he finally raised a woman called Judith who turned out to be his married sister. Henderson told her that he was going to India on business and wondered if she could give him a bed for tonight, the fourteenth of July. I couldn't hear what Judith said to him but after a brief pause, he wanted to know if she was sure Tim wouldn't mind. Then he told her he would be coming up to London by car and to expect him about seven thirty. This morning Henderson rang his bank and asked them to have seven hundred pounds in travellers cheques ready for collection at eleven a.m. . . ."

Avery glanced at his notebook. The private detective had called his office some time later to leave a message for his secretary on the answering machine, but London didn't want a verbatim report of what he'd told Mrs Luckwell to do in his absence. There was, he decided, only one item they would be interested to hear.

"One last thing," Avery continued. "Henderson told his secretary that if she needed to get in touch with him, he would be staying the night with his sister. Her name is Mrs Judith Newman and her telephone number is 01-954 4021. I reckon you people can get the full address out of British Telecom."

Avery hung up and left the call box. It was another chilly summer day with the temperature barely touching sixty but the sweat was running down his face as though they were having a heatwave.

*   *   *

Henderson arrived by taxi a good fifteen minutes late for his appointment to find Alexandra Drummond patiently waiting for him outside India House. Whereas he was in a muck sweat, she looked very cool and elegant in a polka dot blouse with short sleeves and a pale blue slimline skirt.

"I'm sorry I'm late," he said. "I should have known better than to come up to London by car. I had to leave the damned thing in the underground garage in Hyde Park."

"There's no need to apologise, Mr Henderson," she told him smilingly. "I didn't get here on time either. As a matter of fact, I only beat you to it by a short head."

He doubted if that was true but it was nice of her to say so.

"The Visa Department is round the corner."

"Oh, right."

He fell into step beside Alexandra, as he had now come to think of her. She was wearing a pair of high-heeled sandals which made her about the same height and he was conscious of the envious glances other men were casting in his direction as they made their way round to the side entrance. Opening the door, he ushered her into a dark hallway, then followed the directional arrow which pointed them to a narrow staircase. He didn't mean to stare at her bare legs but it was difficult to ignore them when they were right in front of his eyes. Shapely calves, neat ankles and he could tell at a glance that she had never crammed her feet into a pair of badly fitting shoes for the sake of fashion. A well-heeled young woman in more ways than one; expensive clothes and the kind of perfume which came from a small bottle costing an equally small fortune.

"I think you'd better hang on to this," Alexandra said and handed over a cloakroom ticket which the attendant on the landing had just given her. "It's all highly organised," she added tongue in cheek.

The Visa Office was crowded with rows of expectant applicants gazing hopefully at a large visual display unit suspended from the ceiling. Every so often, one of the officials behind the counter which fronted the whole of the inside wall would press a buzzer to change the number displayed on the screen. It was currently showing A61; Henderson's cloakroom ticket was B97.

"We're going to be here for ever," he said, thinking aloud.

Alexandra steered him to one of the windows on the far side of the room, then produced a visa application form from her handbag.

"I'm afraid you have to complete one of these. Perhaps you could use the window ledge to write on?"

Surname, forenames, date and place of birth, occupation and passport number; he printed the answers to the questions in block capitals. Against purpose of visit, he wrote tourist holiday, saw from a footnote that the visa was going to cost him twelve pounds and reached for his wallet.

"That won't be necessary, Mr Henderson."

"You mean they're going to stamp my passport for free?"

"No, I'm going to pay; it will cut down the paperwork."

"How come?"

"You won't have to charge it up to expenses."

Alexandra took charge of his passport and visa application, walked over to the deserted Enquiries desk at the counter and pressed a buzzer to summon assistance. Some moments later, a thin-faced woman with glossy black hair pulled back into a bun emerged from what Henderson assumed was the staff rest room.

Another buzzer sounded and the number A63 appeared on the screen as a young couple left the counter to join the queue waiting to pay the visa fee at the Bank of India desk. A man in the second row of bench seats compared his ticket with the number up on the VDU, then leapt to his feet and strode purposefully towards the vacant space at the counter. The cycle was finally completed by a perplexed-looking Japanese whom one of the bank clerks directed to the next window where yet another official was waiting to receive his passport, visa application and, more importantly, the bank's receipt for twelve pounds.

Henderson turned to look at the Enquiry desk again, saw that the woman with the bun hairstyle had vanished and assumed Alexandra had failed to short-circuit the system. He could not have been more wrong; before the next 'A' number appeared, the official re-surfaced and Alexandra beckoned him to join her outside on the landing.

"Your visa," Alexandra said and returned his passport. "It's valid for three months but you can't go into the prohibited zones."

"Where are they?"

"Officially, it's just Assam but I doubt if you would be very welcome in the Punjab. There's a rather nasty civil war in the making up there, has been ever since the Sikh extremists resorted to terrorism in furtherance of their political aspirations for a separate State."

"Well, that travel restriction shouldn't affect me," Henderson said and followed her down the staircase.

"Quite." She turned to face him again on the pavement

outside India House. "When are you planning to leave for Delhi?" she asked.

"On the British Airways flight tomorrow afternoon. I'm staying the night with my sister in Stanmore."

"But first you've got to collect your car from Hyde Park."

"Yes."

"Well, if I were you, I'd walk up to Holborn and take the Central Line to Marble Arch. It's a lot cheaper than going by taxi and probably quicker too."

"Thanks for the tip. Are you by any chance going my way?"

"Only as far as Kingsway. The Finlayson Trust is in Bell Yard next to the Royal Courts of Justice."

He didn't blame Alexandra Drummond for wanting to distance herself from the hired help. There was, after all, nothing in their contract which said she was obliged to socialise with him, but all the same, he couldn't help feeling there was more to it than a desire to keep their relationship on a proper business-like footing. From the moment they'd first met, she had erected a series of protective barriers. The only way he could get in touch with Alexandra was through her solicitor at Draycott and Draycott or leave a message with the Wagnalls. He didn't know where she lived or the address of the flat she was buying in Barnes.

"I'm afraid this is where we part company." Alexandra put on a face which was intended to convey just how much she personally regretted it.

"Right." Henderson shook her outstretched hand. "If all goes well, I should be able to give you a preliminary verbal report by a week tomorrow."

"I'm impressed, Mr Henderson, but don't rush things. I've never confused speed with efficiency. I really want to be sure we know exactly why Rupert joined Indus Tours in the first place and what prompted him to set off for Etawah. Should you find yourself running short of money, just cable Mr Young at Draycott and Draycott and he'll arrange drawing facilities for you with the Bank of India."

"That's very thoughtful of you, Miss Drummond, but I hope I shan't need it."

"I believe in being prepared for every eventuality," Alexandra said.

Henderson thanked her again, said goodbye for the second time and moved off towards the Underground station. The Finlayson Trust was located in Bell Yard; Alexandra wouldn't lie about a thing like that because the information was verifiable, but he instinctively knew she wasn't going back to the office. He continued on up Holborn Kingsway for another hundred yards or so until he reached the junction with Portugal Street and then turned about.

He walked quickly and was approaching the Royal Courts of Justice in Fleet Street when he spotted Alexandra Drummond on the opposite side of the road near the entranceway to Middle Temple. As he watched, she raised her right arm, flagged down a passing cab and spoke briefly to the driver. A few moments later she was heading west towards Charing Cross and Trafalgar Square.

* * *

Judith Newman was busy scraping the new potatoes which she intended to serve with the lamb chops when the doorbell rang. Convinced her brother had arrived earlier than expected, she dried her hands on the kitchen towel, then went through the hall to open the door to him, only to be confronted by a stocky, cheerful-looking engineer from British Telecom.

"Mrs Newman?" he enquired politely and showed her his identity card. "I understand your phone is out of order?"

"I don't think it is."

The engineer reached inside his shirt pocket and produced a fault card. "Subscriber's name, address and telephone number," he said, reading from it, "Major T. L. D. Newman, 17 Montgomery Close, Stanmore 4021." He looked up, an engaging smile on his mouth. "I hope we got that part right?"

"Yes, but I still don't think . . ."

"The exchange supervisor reported the fault after a caller had asked one of her operators for assistance in obtaining your number."

"What caller?"

He glanced at the card again. "It doesn't say. Mind you, that isn't the sort of info they tell us anyway. However, if there's nothing wrong with your phone, could I ask you

41

to sign this docket so that we can strike the job off the work sheet?"

"I think I'd better check to make sure it is working," Judith told him.

"Good idea. If it's not in the hall, I suggest you close the door first. You can't be too careful these days and I shan't be offended."

Judith took him at his word even though the phone was in the alcove under the staircase. Lifting the receiver, she discovered the line was dead and wondered how long it had been like that. She hadn't spoken to anyone today, not even her husband, Tim, but it had certainly been in working order last night when Jack had called her from Nottingham.

The man from British Telecom wasn't a bit surprised. "These things happen," he said philosophically. "Could be the micro-switch has gone bust though usually you get some prior warning of this – a lot of crackling on the line which eventually clears itself. Whatever the problem, it won't take us long to rectify it." He jerked a thumb over his shoulder at the yellow van parked by the kerbside. "To save time, my mate will check the line back to the junction point just in case it's an external fault."

"We've got an extension in the sitting room."

"That's okay, I'll take a look at it." He gave her another gleaming smile, then said, "You know our motto – we aim to please."

He was everything British Telecom could ask for – polite, cheerful, helpful and efficient. He so impressed Judith Newman that she insisted on tipping him despite his protests that it really wasn't necessary. It was the first time the service engineer had been rewarded by a housewife whose home he had just bugged.

Chapter IV

THE SUN was shining and the weather forecast on the eight o'clock news had promised that for once that summer it would be a fine day with temperatures in the south of England reaching seventy-three Fahrenheit, but the atmosphere inside number 17 Montgomery Close was decidedly chilly. The cold front had been occasioned by the congealing eggs and bacon in front of the empty place at the head of the breakfast table and Henderson thought it was unlikely to disperse with his sister, Judith, in her present mood.

"Would it help if I said I was sorry?" he asked lightly.

Judith stared at him over the rim of her coffee cup, then carefully set it down in the saucer. "It might if you knew why you owed Tim an apology, but you don't, do you? You think he's making a mountain out of a molehill."

"I can't see why he had to get so uptight. All I did was ask him if he'd known Rupert Beardsley."

"How old is Tim?"

"Thirty-seven going on thirty-eight."

"And Beardsley was sixty-three when he died – does that make them contemporaries, Jack?"

"No, but Tim could have run into him at some time or other in his career."

"You said Beardsley had retired in 1974 at the age of fifty. Tim was then barely three years out of Sandhurst, so you tell me what the chances are of a subaltern in the Royal Corps of Signals even being on nodding terms with a Lieutenant Colonel in the Sherwood Foresters?"

"I don't know the Army like you do."

"You're not a fool, Jack," Judith said angrily. "You were aware of the age difference between them and were perfectly capable of drawing your own conclusions. But no, you had to keep fishing for information – 'How can a civilian like me discover the exact date Beardsley retired?' and so on. Before he knew what was happening, you'd persuaded Tim to call for Beardsley's personal file from the Army's record office in Hayes."

"Tim's a grown man, Judith; he didn't have to say yes."

"You made it practically impossible for him to say no. The way you feigned amazement when he tried to point out that obtaining Beardsley's file wasn't as easy as you seemed to think was tantamount to accusing him of being mean-spirited. Tim may be in the Military Secretary's Department but that doesn't mean he has the God-given right to call for any file that takes his fancy. There's a section which does nothing else but record the movement of personal documents and he'll be in hot water should anyone ask him why he wants Beardsley's. I don't have to remind you how much he stands to lose, do I?"

Henderson shook his head. His brother-in-law was regarded as a high-flier by the Army Board and he'd appeared in the June list for promotion to Lieutenant-Colonel at the age of thirty-eight. They had started grooming Tim for stardom at an early age, sending him to read History at Bristol University where he'd met Judith in his third year. If he put a foot wrong now at this stage of his career, everything he and Judith had worked so hard for would go by default, and the red tabs which surely would be his one day would become part of the great perhaps.

"You use people," Judith continued. "You knew last night that Tim regretted making the offer as soon as the words were out of his mouth, but you wouldn't let him off the hook. You had to remind him again this morning."

And ruined his breakfast in the process, Henderson thought, glancing at the mute testimony on the plate at the head of the table.

"All right, Judith," he said quietly. "What do you want me to do?"

"I think you already know the answer to that question."

Judith was the younger by sixteen months but she had always acted like an elder sister ever since their mother had run off with a travelling salesman when he'd just turned fourteen. Henderson supposed it had something to do with the fact that from being a schoolgirl, she had become overnight the woman of the house with two pretty helpless males to look after. University had been her fairy godmother and he'd often wondered if she had taken up with Tim Newman because the army could offer her a better and more exciting life. The third year student and the fresher; no two ways about it, his sister had certainly gone after Tim Newman and had held on to him after he'd gone back to the Army with a first class degree under his belt. And what had Tim acquired in return? An attractive, intelligent young woman who'd become a very supportive wife and a damned good mother to the boy and girl she'd borne him.

"Do you have Tim's office number?"

"Yes, but there's no point in ringing before nine thirty; he's in a meeting."

"You're incredible, you know that?"

"Have I made things difficult for you, Jack? I mean over Beardsley."

"I shouldn't think so. I was just curious to know why a man with such a brilliant war record didn't make it to the top."

"A chestful of medals isn't necessarily a passport to success. You need a good brain, the right jobs at the right time, good connections and a fair slice of luck. I'm not sure which comes first." Judith reached for the coffee pot and without bothering to ask him first, topped up his cup. "What time do you have to be at Heathrow?"

The abrupt change of subject was pure Judith. People who didn't know his sister were left floundering, unable to see the connecting thread between the previous topic of conversation and the new one, but he knew the way her mind worked. As with any other talking point, she simply felt they'd said all there was to be said about Rupert Beardsley and it was time to move on to other things.

"I'm supposed to check in by 1500, one hour ahead of the estimated time of departure."

"Oh, good, that gives us practically the whole day together."

With both children away at boarding school, Judith was virtually a free agent which meant that unless he was quick off the mark, she would organise every spare minute for him.

"What would you like to do, Jack?"

"I want to have a look at Stanhope Square."

"Stanhope Square?" Her eyebrows came together in a puzzled frown. "Where's that?"

"South Kensington. Beardsley used to live there. I'd like to know a little more about him and I'm hoping some of his former neighbours can help me."

"Must you? We don't see one another very much these days." The disappointed note in her voice was obviously genuine.

"There's nothing I'd like to do more than spend the day with you, but this is business."

"You're not going up to town by car, are you, Jack?"

"No, I thought I'd leave it at the Airways Garage opposite Heathrow and catch a Piccadilly Line train from the Terminal."

"I suppose that would be the most sensible thing to do." Her face suddenly brightened. "I know, why don't you stay the night with us on your way back to Nottingham?"

He tried to point out that he couldn't say when he would be returning from Delhi but Judith refused to listen to him. In the end, he found it a lot easier to fall in with her plans than dig his heels in. She could not have been more delighted; neither could Tim Newman when Henderson telephoned his office to let him know he could forget about Rupert Beardsley.

*   *   *

The Victorian town houses in Stanhope Square were arranged in a hollow square around a small park heavily planted with evergreen shrubs and enclosed by iron railings. Apart from the padlocked gate, several prominent notice-boards made it very clear that the park was for residents only. Like all the other houses, number 18 had been converted into luxury flats; the one Beardsley had occupied was on the first floor directly above that of a sprightly eighty-year-old and her rather timid and much younger companion.

As well as being the oldest resident, she had lived in Stanhope Square longer than anyone else and could remember the people who had owned the flat before the Beardsleys. It didn't take Henderson long to realise that she had a soft spot for the Colonel and was somewhat biased in his favour.

In her opinion, Beardsley had been a gallant and charming gentleman and no one had been more sorry to learn of his untimely death. But what had shocked her most was the speed with which his relatives had cleared out the flat and put it on the market. She assumed the flat had been acquired by the Shiraj Development Corporation who owned most of the other properties in the Square, but only Mr Charlesworth, the liaison officer between the tenants' association and the parent company, could confirm that.

In a less affluent neighbourhood, the liaison officer would have been the equivalent of a caretaker or janitor. Rent free accommodation was one of the perks of the job and Henderson thought this could well have been the major attraction for the present incumbent. Charlesworth was a thin weasel-faced man in his forties whose obsequious manner vanished the moment the companion who'd escorted Henderson to the basement flat across the park left them alone together.

"You were a friend of the Colonel's?" he asked.

"I've met his brother-in-law."

"That's not what the old girl told me on the phone before she sent you over here. I was given to understand you'd known the family for donkey's years."

"I can't think how she got that impression."

"Let me ask you another question, Mr Henderson. What's your connection with the Beardsleys?"

"I'm a private Inquiry Agent . . ."

"Then I don't have anything to say to you," Charlesworth told him bluntly.

"The Colonel's brother-in-law isn't happy about the report he received from the British High Commission in Delhi. I've been hired to find out what really happened to him."

"I bet."

"I received my instructions from Draycott and Draycott. If you don't believe me, I suggest you ring their offices in Chancery Lane and ask to speak to Mr Young."

"You got their number?"

"Try looking them up in the telephone directory, then you won't have to take anything I say on trust."

"I don't think we need to go to all that trouble, do we?" Charlesworth went through his pockets, found a crumpled packet of cigarettes and lit one. "What exactly is it you want from me?"

"Some confidential information about the people who live in Stanhope Square, this housing association the lady in number 18 mentioned, and the property company you represent."

"That could cost me my job."

"No one's going to hear a word from me." Henderson took out his wallet, extracted a ten pound note and placed it on the desk. After a suitable pause, he added another tenner.

"Well, I don't know," Charlesworth said doubtfully.

"Take it or leave it. I'm not the Bank of England."

"I'm not complaining, Mr Henderson." The caretaker pocketed the money swiftly, then put on a winning smile to show he meant it. "Who do you want me to start with?" he asked cheerfully.

"Beardsley."

The smile rapidly faded. "There's not a lot I can tell you about the Colonel," Charlesworth admitted reluctantly. "You see, he wasn't one of our tenants so I didn't have much to do with him."

"Do you mind explaining that?"

"There's not a lot to it. Most of Stanhope Square is owned by the Shiraj Development Corporation who moved into the property market when they gobbled up a company called Axemouth Holdings in 1971. The only titles they haven't been able to acquire since then are the four apartments belonging to the Finlayson Trust. I don't suppose the corporation would be too worried about those flats if they were concentrated under one roof, but they're not and that's what bothers them. It doesn't make my job any too easy either."

There was a widespread feeling amongst the residents that the privileged few whose apartments belonged to the Finlayson Trust were getting a far better deal than they were. As the liaison officer between their association and the Shiraj Development Corporation, Charlesworth was the man who caught all the brickbats.

"Who are these lucky people?" Henderson asked him.

"An Arab gentleman called Hamid al Kalifah, a Mr Henry Lapointe and the Carlton-Smythes. Don't ask me what they do for a living. My only contact with them is the newsletter

I leave in their mail boxes whenever the residents association wants to change the rules governing the use of community amenities such as the park.''

"Has anyone moved into the flat Beardsley used to occupy?''

"Not yet.''

The front room of Charlesworth's basement flat had been converted into an office. Displayed on the wall behind the executive-style desk was a list of the tenants arranged in sequence beginning with the occupants of 1A. A third column headed 'Remarks' showed who was away and the dates they were due to return from holiday or wherever. There were twenty houses in Stanhope Square subdivided into a total of eighty apartments, all but four of which were accounted for. The reason for the discrepancy was self-evident.

"Who looks after the flats belonging to the Finlayson Trust?''

"They do," Charlesworth said. "If one of their apartments is broken into, a burglar alarm is triggered in the local police station.''

The aim of the Finlayson Trust was to further Anglo-Indian relations by providing financial support to enable deserving students from poorer families to complete their high school education and go on to university. According to Alexandra Drummond, she was the only full-time salaried official, yet it seemed the Trust was prepared to denude its resources on maintaining four expensive apartments and equipping them with a high-tech security system.

"How long has Mr Lapointe been living in the Square?'' Henderson asked.

"About fifteen months. He should be moving on soon; the people with the Finlayson Trust rarely stay longer than a year and a half. Perhaps that's why they keep themselves pretty much to themselves. The Colonel was an exception though; he was here before the Shiraj Development Corporation took over the rest of the Square.''

Grace-and-favour apartments for the seemingly well-off? Charity begins at home goes the proverb, but somehow Henderson doubted if this sentiment was uppermost in Sir George Finlayson's mind when he'd established the Trust in memory of his wife.

"Care for a drink?''

Henderson glanced at his wristwatch and saw that it was past one o'clock. "Thanks all the same," he said, "but some other time. Right now, I've got a plane to catch."

A number of things didn't add up, but a certified cheque for seventeen hundred pounds had done wonders for his bank account and he hadn't been hired to examine the financial affairs of the Finlayson Trust.

*   *   *

The Moguls had given India the Taj Mahal, the Red Fort, the Jama Masjid mosque and a string of palaces; the British had built the biggest railway network in the world and had commissioned Lutyens to create New Delhi, the capital and administrative heartland of the subcontinent. Of all the majestic buildings on the Raj Path, none impressed Lawrence Goodman more than the Secretariat North Block which was now the offices of the Ministry of the Interior. And of all the Indian officials he'd encountered during his six years with the British High Commission no one had impressed him more than Manik Bhose.

Manik Bhose was the youngest of three sons born to a wealthy merchant in Bombay. Of his brothers, one was a two-star General and currently the Commandant of the Army's staff college at Wellington, while the middle one was the Operations Manager of Air India. After reading Jurisprudence at Bombay University, Manik Bhose had spent a year at the Central Law School in London but, although called to the Bar, he had never practised in Chambers. Instead, he had joined the Civil Service and had won his spurs in the Justice Department. There was no doubt in Goodman's mind that Manik, whom he regarded as a close friend, was destined to be a future head of the Civil Service. Intelligent, cool under pressure and decisive, he was also a cultured and entertaining companion.

The one cross he had to bear in life was Madhu, his twenty-nine-year-old wife and glamorous movie queen. The star of at least a dozen major box office successes, she preferred to remain in her luxury villa on the coast ten miles north of Bombay in order to be near the studio. A vain, thoroughly spoilt and superficial young woman, she occasionally made a fleeting pilgrimage to Delhi between films to be with her husband. When Goodman had phoned Manik Bhose at noon and made an appointment to see him that afternoon, he'd learned that Madhu was on her way back to Bombay, leaving her husband deflated and unhappy, the way she always did. Several hours later, he still looked down in the mouth.

"It's good to see you again, Lawrence," he said manfully. "To what do I owe the pleasure?"

"I've had a cable from London about the late Colonel Rupert Beardsley. It appears his brother-in-law isn't happy with the explanation he received from the Foreign and Commonwealth Office. Specifically, he wants to be assured that we didn't bury the wrong man in the English cemetery."

"I don't see how we could have made a mistake, Lawrence. The body was identified by the dental charts London provided."

"Quite."

"The pathologist who carried out the post-mortem is one of the best in his field. He wouldn't make such a fundamental error."

"I agree. However, it seems a couple of fifty-pound traveller's cheques belonging to Colonel Beardsley were presented and cashed after his death. The banks concerned are the Amalgamated Farmers Trust and the Uttar Pradesh Federal Reserve, both located in Agra."

The background hum from the air-conditioning unit ceased abruptly, the sure sign of a power failure which might last for a few minutes or continue for hours. The temperature in the room began to rise almost immediately.

"Are you thinking what I'm thinking, Lawrence?"

Goodman wondered if Manik was referring to the power cut or Beardsley, then decided he meant the latter. "That Beardsley is still alive?" he asked and then shook his head. "One can't ignore the forensic evidence."

"So?"

"You tell me."

"I would have thought it was perfectly obvious," Bhose said irritably. "What we have is a simple case of fraudulent conversion perpetrated by two crooked bank clerks and the guide hired by the Colonel. What was his name?"

"Lal."

"Yes, that's the man. Do you have the serial numbers of the cheques?"

Goodman unzipped his briefcase, took out a cablegram and gave it to Bhose. "This is a photocopy of the telex I received from London. You'll find the details you want in the second paragraph."

"Good. I don't pretend to know how he got his hands on the cheques but no doubt the police will find that out when they question him."

"You're going to have Lal arrested?"

"A crime has been committed. A hundred pounds may not seem much to you, Lawrence, but even if it's split three ways, it's still a fortune to someone like him. Besides, there may be other cheques in the pipeline."

"Will Mr Henderson be allowed to see him while he's in police custody?" Goodman asked.

"Who's Mr Henderson?"

The information was there in the first paragraph of the telex he had just given him but evidently Manik had been too wrapped up in his own affairs to take it in.

"He's a private Inquiry Agent. Beardsley's brother-in-law wants to know why the Colonel left the coach party he was with to go to Etawah and Henderson's been hired to find out. I imagine Lal is one of the few people who might be able to tell him."

"Bad luck."

"The Foreign Office has asked the High Commission to give him every assistance." Goodman took out a handkerchief and mopped up the beads of perspiration on his forehead. "This is the time of the year we call the silly season back home when there is a dearth of news. With every editor hungry for a good story to fill his front page, I'd hate to see the Beardsley affair become a cause célèbre."

"I hope you're not trying to twist my arm, Lawrence?" Bhose said lightly.

"Heaven forbid. But as one old friend to another, I need all the help I can get."

"One can hardly ignore such a heartfelt plea." Bhose looked at the photocopy of the telex again. "Unfortunately, your cable from London doesn't say when we may expect to see this Mr Henderson."

"The Foreign Office didn't think it advisable to ask him. But don't worry, he'll make his presence known to me soon enough. He will certainly call on the local manager of Indus Tours here in New Delhi and Mr Jervis will steer him in my direction. Jervis will do this without any prodding from me because he is aware that I'm the official Lal talked to after he was released by the dacoits."

"What if Henderson goes straight to Agra without bothering to see you first?"

"All the better," Goodman said blandly. "Sooner or later, he'll run into a brick wall with the police and then he's bound to seek assistance from one of us. Private detectives are a similar breed to press reporters; that's why I shall be helpful but not obsequious. They're suspicious if you appear too eager to please, vindictive when they think you're being deliberately obstructive."

"I'm sure everything will go according to plan." Bhose allowed himself a faint smile. "However, I think I will take out a little insurance on the side and warn our Immigration people to keep an eye out for Mr Henderson. I wouldn't want him to slip in and out of the country without our knowing it."

"Thank you, Manik."

Goodman stood up, eager to leave the sweltering office now that their business had been successfully concluded. Then, as they shook hands, the power was restored and the cool draught from the air-conditioner made him reluctant to venture out into the furnace that was Delhi at the height of summer.

*   *   *

Preston raised the plastic beaker to his lips and sipped tentatively. The tea he'd obtained from the station's vending machine looked anaemic but at least it didn't taste like lukewarm dishwater.

One way and another, he'd had a fairly hectic afternoon. Some people would say that lunch with the Round Table was a real doddle, but the young businessmen of Nottingham expected to be informed and entertained by their guest of honour and he'd never been able to give a talk off the cuff. But the biggest bind was having to refuse all the drinks his hosts had tried to press on him. The Chief Constable had never been known to pass up an opportunity to further good relations with the public and had detailed him to give a careers talk to the students of Bestwood Comprehensive that same afternoon and he could hardly have turned up at the school smelling like a brewery. Throw in a visit to a Sikh jeweller and the proprietor of a boutique on the Mansfield Road, both of whom wanted his advice on how to make their premises secure, and no one could say he hadn't earned his pay on this shift.

Preston lit a cigarette. There were times when he envied Jack Henderson, and this was one of them. Here he was stuck in a rut while his former colleague was on the way to Delhi, all expenses paid. At this very moment, Henderson was probably relaxing in the club section of a 747, a stiff drink within reach and a pretty stewardess ready to dance attendance on him. One thing was certain, he didn't have to contend with a telephone demanding his attention while he was having a quiet drag. Lifting the receiver, Preston grunted into the mouthpiece and found he had the Detective Chief Inspector from the Sherwood Street Headquarters on the line.

"This break-in at 42 Mapperley Hall Drive," the DCI said tersely. "I've had a police cadet making door-to-door inquiries. He's come up with one witness, a retired schoolmistress who lives across the road from your mate, Henderson. She was dead-heading the roses in her front garden the day before yesterday and remembers seeing the car parked outside the place. A dark blue saloon, make unknown, but it was definitely a 'B' registration because she remembered thinking at the time that it was only two years old. She thinks the numbers were 831 or it might have been 318 or even 183, but she's absolutely positive the area code was VVZ . . ."

"Yeah?"

"Hasn't the penny dropped?" the DCI asked.

"Not so far."

"You're slipping, Danny; there's no such area code as VVZ."

Preston was willing to bet the DCI hadn't known that either before the computer at the vehicle licensing bureau in Swansea had rejected the search enquiry, but he let it pass.

"Did she give the police cadet a description of the driver?"

"She didn't see him drive away, only heard him leave. As far as I'm concerned, Sergeant, that's the end of the inquiry. Okay?"

"Yes, sir. Thanks for trying."

"That's all right," the DCI said. "Just don't come to me for any more favours."

Preston laughed, promised he wouldn't, and slowly put the phone down. In his own mind, he was sure the retired schoolmistress had seen a car with a VVZ area code and that meant the intruder had gone to a great deal of trouble to ensure the vehicle couldn't be traced. Preston knew a place in Arnold where you could get a licence plate made up with no questions asked. When Henderson returned from his jaunt, he thought it might be worth their while if the two of them had a quiet word with the owner.

Chapter V

Henderson had never experienced anything quite like it. By a quarter to eleven, the temperature had risen to a hundred and three Fahrenheit and the relatively cool atmosphere which had greeted him when he'd walked out of Indira Gandhi airport in the early hours of the morning was now a distant memory. From the airport, the cab driver had taken him straight to the Taj Mahal, a luxury hotel on the outskirts of Delhi where he'd been lucky enough to obtain a room with private bath on the eighth floor. After unpacking his suitcase, he'd shaved, freshened up under the shower and then breakfasted in his room before hiring another cab to take him downtown to the Indus Tours office in Connaught Circus.

Bernard Jervis, the local manager of Indus Tours, was a short stocky man in his late thirties whose light brown hair appeared to be receding from his forehead with almost indecent haste. The walrus moustache which decorated his upper lip was the one growth area. He was wearing knee-length khaki stockings and KD shorts with a matching Clydella shirt and looked for all the world like a District Commissioner left over from the days of the Raj. Photographs of the first charabanc tour organised by the company in 1927 and the electric fan on his desk which circulated the warm air in the office were ancient enough to sustain the illusion.

"I've been expecting you," Jervis said as they shook hands. "Had a cable from Draycott and Draycott to say you'd been retained by the family to enquire into the circumstances of the Colonel's death and would I give you all the assistance I could."

Up till now, Henderson had been under the impression that he was working for Alexandra Drummond but he didn't bother to put Jervis right. "That was very efficient of the solicitors," he said.

Jervis nodded. "So how can I help?"

"By answering the jackpot question. Why did Colonel Beardsley leave the coach party he was with at Agra?"

"Lawrence Goodman asked me the same thing and I couldn't tell him either."

"Who's Goodman?"

"One of the First Secretaries at the British High Commission. He was the man Lal was told to see by Colonel Beardsley when he learned the dacoits were going to hold him for ransom."

Goodman wasn't mentioned in the brief Alexandra Drummond had given him but conceivably the Foreign Office hadn't told her the name of the official in Delhi who'd identified the body. Beardsley's connection with the Finlayson Trust had been on a purely voluntary and part-time basis; first and foremost, he was a Queen's Messenger and had passed through Delhi on countless occasions, according to Dudley Spencer, his brother-in-law. It was therefore likely that he had met Goodman on one of his official visits.

"I hear the body was identified by the laundry mark on the shirt collar?"

"I think you'll find there was more to it than that," Jervis told him.

"I'm sure there was. What's your opinion of Lal?"

"He's one of the best guides we have – honest, reliable, knows his subject and gets on well with the tourists. He's our longest serving employee and has been with us for every tourist season from March through to December since 1971." Jervis smiled. "I'd also describe him as pro-British and a bit of a snob."

"If he works for Indus Tours, how was Colonel Beardsley able to hire him?"

"Lal had four days off; what he does in his free time is his concern. If the dacoits hadn't grabbed him, he would have been back on duty at the right time."

The guide, it seemed, was a paragon of virtue. Beardsley had evidently trusted him and the Indian hadn't betrayed that confidence even after he knew the Colonel was dead. Henderson reminded himself there was always the possibility that what Lal didn't know he couldn't tell. Then too, he was unlikely to get much change out of Goodman if Beardsley had gone to Etawah on Foreign Office business, but he could only give it a shot.

"I'd like to meet your guide," he told Jervis. "Can you arrange it if I go down to Agra?"

"I don't see why not." The tour manager got up, walked over to the filing cabinet, removed a buff-coloured folder from the top drawer and returned to his desk. "When do you want to see him?"

"Tomorrow?"

"I'll just have a look at our tour programme." Jervis opened the folder, found the page he wanted and scanned it rapidly. "Lal is due to meet a coach party at Fatehpur Sikri in the morning which means he should be back around two. It'll then take him approximately an hour to get them settled into their hotel. You could contact him between half three and six before he takes the group on to see the Taj Mahal by moonlight."

"Fine. How do I get there?"

"The Taj Express, a special, air-conditioned luxury train, does the round trip each day but it's usually fully booked. Failing that, most trains to Bombay and Calcutta stop at Agra. A word of warning – Lal's on a tight schedule and he'll want to nip back home between sight-seeing visits to change his clothes. I'm not saying you will miss him but it might be safer to plan on staying overnight."

"Where do you suggest?" Henderson asked.

"The Taj View. If you like, I can get one of my assistants to make a reservation for you by telex."

"I'd be very grateful if you would."

Jervis tried the office intercom, found it wasn't working and went next door to tell the clerk in person. When he returned several minutes later, he was accompanied by a matronly looking woman in a dark green sari.

"This is Mrs Patel," he said. "I've asked her to make us a pot of tea while we're waiting for an answer from the Taj View Hotel."

Mrs Patel gave Henderson a welcoming smile, asked if this was the first time he'd been to India and expressed a hope that it would prove to be a memorable visit. Then leaving a tray containing a milk jug, a bowl of sugar and two cups and saucers on the desk, she practically glided out of the room.

"A very efficient lady," Jervis said. "I'm lucky to have her. She came into the office one morning and asked me for a job – just like that. Must have been two and a half years ago, shortly after her husband was knocked down and killed on his way to work. I'd hate to think what state our filing system would be in if it weren't for Mrs Patel. You want a particular file, she can put her hand on it just like that," he added and snapped his fingers.

"A kind of human electronic retrieval system?"

"Better. Unlike your microchip gadgetry, a power failure doesn't affect her."

"Could she tell me where and when Colonel Beardsley made his booking with Indus Tours and whether he'd ever travelled with you before?"

"I guarantee Mrs Patel will have all the answers you want inside a minute."

Jervis was one of life's supreme optimists. The pot of tea arrived and Henderson sat there drinking it, the sweat oozing from every pore while Mrs Patel rummaged through the filing cabinets in the outer office. Finding the latest invoice wasn't the problem, checking the records to see if he'd used Indus Tours before was a much more time-consuming business and it took her all of twenty minutes to put the information together.

There was no record to show that Beardsley had been a long-standing client of Indus Tours. Indeed, his one and only booking for a package holiday with the company had been made a mere four days before the remainder of the tour party had been scheduled to arrive in Delhi by KLM from London via Amsterdam. Furthermore, his booking had been made locally and paid for in cash.

"Could I have a look at the itinerary for this particular tour?" Henderson asked.

"'Memories of the Raj'?" Jervis opened the top drawer of his desk and took out a cyclostyled programme. "Day One," he said, reading from the broadsheet, "check into hotel a.m., rest period until two p.m., then visit the Red Fort and Jama Masjid, the magnificent mosque built by the Emperor Shah Jehan, etc, etc. Here, see for yourself."

Another day was set aside in Delhi to visit, amongst other places of interest, the Victory Tower dating back to 1200 AD and the India Gate designed by Lutyens, before going on by coach to Jaipur. Three days later, just as Alexandra Drummond had indicated in her brief, the tourists had journeyed to Agra via the deserted but wholly intact city of Fatehpur Sikri. And at Agra, Rupert Beardsley had deserted his travelling companions with the intention of going to Etawah by car.

"What excuse did the Colonel give for not returning to Delhi with the others?" Henderson asked.

"None. He gave the British escort in charge of the party a handwritten letter absolving Indus Tours of all responsibility. Keith Royles was a little dubious about it, so he telephoned the office to get my okay. I didn't see any reason to stand in Beardsley's way; hell, all the Colonel was passing up was the return coach trip to Delhi."

"Keith Royles was the British escort?"

"Yes, he returned to England a fortnight ago; he had an urgent telegram from home. Fortunately, head office in London managed to get hold of this lecturer on Anthropology at Brunel University who's been on our books for years and he agreed to fill in during the long vac."

Henderson read the itinerary again, looking for a pattern which might explain Beardsley's behaviour. It seemed to him that he had expected to meet someone in Delhi and they had failed to show up, but that a few days later, Beardsley had received a message advising him of an alternative rendezvous in Agra and he had booked himself on the 'Memories of the Raj' tour. Why he should have chosen to do this was far from clear; it could be that he'd simply wanted to kill time and Indus Tours had offered him an interesting way of doing so or, alternatively, the package holiday had provided a useful cover for him. In any event, the contact had evidently not turned up and there had been yet another message, this time directing him to Etawah. It was a pretty fragile theory; whether it would stand up to any kind of examination depended on what Lal and the First Secretary at the British High Commission had to say.

"What are my chances of seeing Goodman today?" Henderson asked.

"You can but try." Jervis picked up the phone on his desk and placed it within Henderson's reach, then looked up the number in the directory. "You want to dial 601371 and ask for him by name."

After explaining who he was and what he wanted to see him about, Goodman could not have been more helpful. Office hours in the hot season were from eight till one and again in the evening from four to six. Mornings were always his busiest time but he could squeeze Henderson in during the last half hour before lunch. On the other hand, his diary was a complete blank that evening and there would be no need to rush things if they met at four. Henderson said how much he appreciated his helpfulness, confirmed that four o'clock would suit him fine and put the phone down. Moments later, Mrs Patel entered the room again to say that she had managed to book a room with private bath for him at the Taj View, Agra. Everything, it seemed, was going very smoothly.

*   *   *

With his Mongolian features and wrestler's torso, Lal thought the Sub-Inspector was the most intimidating man he'd had the misfortune to meet since his encounter with the dacoit in Patna who'd scraped the left side of his face with a sawtooth knife. He was also the first ranking officer Lal had seen in the nine hours which had passed since the police had descended on number 29 Telegraph Lines to arrest him at three o'clock in the morning like some common criminal. The fact that his family didn't know which police station they had taken him to merely increased his apprehension.

"This is an outrage," Lal told him in a high-pitched voice. "You have no right to detain me. I demand to see my lawyer."

He could see the Sub-Inspector hadn't understood a word he'd been saying but he continued to speak in English because it made him feel superior. It was also a lot safer which, in turn, made him dangerously bold.

"You are a very foolish man and I am telling you there will be serious trouble when Mr Chatterjee gets here. In case you don't know, Mr Chatterjee is a close personal friend of Mr Justice Ansari, the High Court judge."

"Hindi," the Sub-Inspector said tersely. "You will speak to me in Hindi."

"I shall do nothing of the kind."

The Sub-Inspector got up and walked round his desk. Enclosing Lal's jaw in the palm of his right hand, he pressed the fleshy cheeks inwards with his thumb and middle finger. "I said you will speak to me in Hindi," he grunted. "Thikhai?"

Lal nodded, his mouth oval-shaped like a fish gasping for oxygen. "Very good," he mumbled, then gulped. "I mean – thikhai."

"Good." The Sub-Inspector released his tight grip on Lal's jaw and gave him a none too friendly slap across his face. "Name, address?" he demanded.

"V. P. Lal, 29 Telegraph Lines, Agra Cantonment, Agra."

"You work for the Post Office?"

"My father does; we are living with him temporarily."

Temporarily was now eleven years and the house he'd set his heart on overlooking the maidan, which the bride price had not been large enough to secure, was as far away as ever.

"Occupation?"

"Official guide." Lal cleared his throat nervously. "What am I supposed to have done?" he asked.

"Stolen the equivalent of eighteen hundred rupees from the sahib who hired you."

"The English Colonel? What idiocy."

The Sub-Inspector slapped his face, then gave him a back-hander with sufficient force to make his nose bleed. "You cashed two of his traveller's cheques here in Agra, one with the Amalgamated Farmers' Trust, the other at the Uttar Pradesh Federal Reserve."

"Nonsense. Show me the man who says I did."

"Hold your tongue, imbecile, and listen to me." A meaty hand grabbed Lal by his shirt front and shook him like a rag doll. "I will give you a pencil and a sheet of paper and you will write me a full confession naming names."

"I am not doing anything until I see my lawyer, Mr Chatterjee."

The Sub-Inspector punched him in the stomach, then roared for the Havildar to come into his office with the duty constable. No further instructions were necessary; twisting both arms behind his back and forcing them upwards until the wrists were nestling between his shoulder blades, they frogmarched him out of the room, along the corridor and into an airless cell that stank of urine. To help Lal on his way, the Sub-Inspector kicked him up the backside, his rounded toecap finding the coccyx at the base of the spine with unerring accuracy. Gasping in agony, Lal went down on all fours and vomited over the wooden board he was supposed to sleep on.

"Make yourself comfortable," the Sub-Inspector told him. "You'll be waiting a long time for Chatterjee."

Lal could well believe it. His father would assume that the police had taken him to the cantonment station and that was where he would send the lawyer. But less than an hour after he had been arrested, they had sent him on to this hell hole of a police post in the festering slums across the railroad tracks from Agra Fort. Like a wounded animal, he crawled into a corner, lay down on his left side and curled himself up in a tight ball.

*   *   *

The British High Commission was located on Shanti Path Avenue in the Chanakyapuri diplomatic enclave, with the Norwegian Embassy on one side and the Australian on the other. Set well back from the tree-lined road, it faced the embassies of China and the German Democratic Republic. The building itself looked as though it had been transplanted from the Thames Valley stockbroker belt and given a colonial facelift. Goodman's office was at the rear, overlooking a large walled garden that was mostly lawn and which several water-sprinklers managed to keep a verdant green in the dry season. With two large clumps of flame-red bougainvillaea in flower most of the year round, the gardeners didn't need to plan anything else.

People who were asked to describe Lawrence Goodman always began with his nose. Badly mis-shapen as a result of a traffic accident, it made an immediate and lasting impression. Indeed, it was the one physical attribute which years afterwards remained in the minds of those whose acquaintance with him had been limited to a fleeting encounter. His pleasant, cheerful manner, dry sense of humour and helpfulness were usually rapidly forgotten.

"What can I tell you about Colonel Beardsley?" he asked as soon as Henderson was settled in a chair.

"Could we start with Lal and why he was given specific instructions to get in touch with you personally?"

"That's easy. Rupert was one of the Queen's Messengers assigned to the Far East and frequently visited the High Commission to deliver Foreign Office Confidential briefings. He often stayed the night with my wife and I in our house on the diplomatic cabbage patch. When he was kidnapped, he wanted to make sure we heard about it in the shortest possible time. It was therefore only logical that he should tell Lal to convey the ransom demand straight to me."

"Did the Foreign Office know he was on the board of the Finlayson Trust?"

"Oh yes, he was quite open about it and since there was no possible conflict of interest, the Service saw no reason to object."

"Was he a secretive man?" Henderson asked.

"Who – Rupert?" Goodman chuckled, seemingly amused by the thought. "There wasn't a devious streak in him; in fact, I doubt he knew the meaning of the word."

"He didn't tell his brother-in-law or anyone at the Trust that he was planning to go to Jaipur and Agra."

"Really? You do surprise me. Rupert certainly told me he had a few days' leave coming to him and had decided to visit some of his old haunts."

"Do you have any idea why he sugared off to Etawah?"

"Not personally. But according to Lal, he'd learned that a Jemadar Rav, one of the old Viceroy Commissioned Officers who'd been with him in Burma, was desperately ill in hospital. Naturally, the Indian authorities checked all the hospitals in the city but they were unable to trace the Jemadar. Although the police questioned Lal at length, he was unable to throw any light on the man's identity. In the end, they took the view that Rupert had told him a little white lie to satisfy his curiosity."

Henderson wondered if there was more to it than that; Beardsley had commanded Indian troops during the war and was said by his brother-in-law to be fluent in Urdu. That being the case, Henderson asked himself why such a man should want to hire a local guide, and couldn't think of one convincing answer.

"The body they buried in the English cemetery here in Delhi – are we sure it was Beardsley's? I understand from Mr Young that the corpse was badly decomposed and could only be identified by the laundry mark on the shirt collar."

"Who's Mr Young?" Goodman inquired politely.

"The solicitor at Draycott and Draycott who briefed me on behalf of the surviving relatives."

Henderson could lie convincingly when it was necessary. He did so now, not so much from a desire to protect Alexandra Drummond but rather because disclosing her involvement would only complicate matters.

"I'm afraid you've been misinformed," Goodman said, still affable. "The laundry mark was only one tiny piece of corroborating evidence; Rupert was, in fact, identified by the dental chart which the Foreign Office obtained from his dentist."

Jervis had told him the same thing but no one, not even Alexandra Drummond, had said how he'd died. He wondered why everyone was being so reticent about the post-mortem and decided to do a little digging on his own account.

"The solicitors think Beardsley was murdered," he said bluntly.

"No one else does. Rupert may have died from carbon monoxide poisoning but there's no evidence to show the kidnappers deliberately connected a flexible tube to the exhaust pipe and clamped the nozzle over his nose and mouth. On the contrary, from particles found on his clothing, there is reason to believe Rupert left Patna in the back of a truck buried under a pile of vegetables. When you've been out here as long as I have, you'll know that a large number of the vehicles on the road would never pass an MOT test in the UK. It's likely the exhaust system had more holes in it than a colander and the fumes seeped through the floorboards in the back of the truck."

"Do you people use the Finlayson Trust to channel aid to deserving causes?"

"Good heavens no; where on earth did you get that idea?"

"Beardsley was supposed to go to Aligarh," Henderson said. "The Trust had arranged for him to see the Dean of the

University. Some of the board members think he ducked the appointment because he had more important matters to attend to on behalf of the Foreign Office."

Goodman had an answer for that one too and his explanation sounded equally plausible. Even supposing they wanted to, there was no way the Foreign Office could use the Trust without the board's consent and their legal advisers would never countenance the idea. Once it became an adjunct of a government department, the fund would lose its charitable status and would be taxed accordingly. Then too, Her Majesty's Opposition would give the Minister responsible for overseas aid a rough ride if they suspected the taxpayers' money was being distributed by a quasi official organisation. Even so, there was still one small point that bothered Henderson.

"So why did you inform the Trust of Beardsley's death?" he asked.

Goodman hesitated for a moment, then said, "I suppose you could say it was simply a matter of courtesy. We were aware of Rupert's connection with them and it seemed only right to let his fellow board members know what had happened to him after the next-of-kin had been informed."

Henderson was inclined to believe him. For one thing, he had been much more open with him than had Alexandra Drummond. Amongst her other omissions, she had failed to mention that Beardsley had been a Queen's Messenger and it was difficult to believe she hadn't known that. The old adage that whoever pays the piper calls the tune was the only reason he decided to keep plugging away.

"What happened to the taxi driver Beardsley hired in Agra?"

"Tara Singh?"

"If that's his name." Henderson smiled. "What did Lal have to say about him?"

"Not a lot. The last time he saw him, Tara Singh had got the car up on blocks and was attempting to replace the rear axle. He told Lal not to bother about getting him a bed at the Excelsior Hotel as he would be working through the night. Lal was confident that Singh was not present in the courtyard of the carpet factory when Sarana Kurmis and her gang murdered nine villagers."

Other than his name, Goodman knew next to nothing about

the driver. From the moment Lal had made contact, his one concern had been to secure Beardsley's release and to this end the British High Commission had been authorised to pay the ransom demanded by the kidnappers.

"You can forget all the hard-nose talk about not dealing with terrorists," Goodman continued, "that's just for public consumption. In any case, the dacoits are just a bunch of gangsters, not a political movement. All of us here knew we had to pay up if we wanted to see Rupert alive again."

"The Indian Government had no objection to you dealing with Sarana Kurmis?"

"None whatever. Hell, they're prepared to do a deal with the woman themselves and would give her a free pardon tomorrow provided she and her followers would kindly agree to lay down their arms and go back to wherever it was they came from. As it happened, we never entered into serious negotiation with Sarana; the men she assigned to guard Rupert botched things up and he was probably dead before Lal contacted us. At any rate, his body was found before we could get a message back to her."

Once the corpse had been identified beyond all reasonable doubt, the British High Commission had ceased to keep a watching brief on the investigation and had left matters to the Indian authorities. With that, their interest in Tara Singh had waned and they'd no longer been concerned to know of his whereabouts.

"If you need it, I might be able to get his address from the Ministry of the Interior."

"That would be helpful."

"So where can I reach you?" Goodman asked and looked suitably impressed when Henderson told him.

*   *   *

There were six of them, proud-looking men whose ages ranged from nineteen to thirty-four. Their leader, Baldev Singh, had been in Amritsar the day the Army had stormed the Golden Temple on the orders of Indira Gandhi, the she-devil in Delhi who had been determined to crush once and for all the Sikh demand for a separate nation. His father, uncle and two older brothers had been cut down in the slaughter which had followed the cease-fire. The official Board of Inquiry may have absolved the Army of blame but Baldev Singh knew that his family had been executed in cold blood after the surrender and had vowed to avenge their deaths.

He had been overjoyed when Indira Gandhi had been assassinated by members of her own personal bodyguard. Baldev Singh had been equally gratified when the former Commander-in-Chief of the Army's Central Command and the man responsible for mounting the operation at Amritsar had been gunned down while driving through the rush-hour traffic in Poona. But tomorrow, he and his followers would strike a blow that would make all India shudder.

The sandtable model of the ambush site which he'd constructed in the fire-gutted and abandoned house was crude but effective. Using four lengths of timber to retain the bucket loads of fine earth his henchmen had carried in from the surrounding fields, Baldev Singh had fashioned a panoramic view of the landscape. A collection of small stones represented the village of Mudki, the red juice of betel nut traced the path of the country road, and gouge marks in the dirt the dried-up nullahs that would become raging streams when the monsoon broke. The truck they'd stolen that afternoon was represented by an empty packet of Red and White cigarettes, while the bullock cart they'd borrowed for the occasion was a box of matches.

Briefing his men in the flickering light of a hurricane lamp, he showed them their individual fire positions which they would take up in the morning and explained exactly how the ambush would be sprung. Then he set them to work, stripping and cleaning their Chinese-made Kalashnikov AK 47s.

CHAPTER VI

THE AMBUSH site Baldev Singh had chosen was exactly twelve miles south-west of Faridkot and some twenty-four miles as the crow flies from the Indo-Pakistani border. The first bus to Faridkot departed from Mudki at five; by the time it reached their position an hour and ten minutes later, it would have stopped at four outlying villages and would have a full load of passengers on board. When the driver rounded the curve up ahead, he would see a truck canted over at an angle on the right-hand side of the road, its offside front wheel in the ditch, the body partially blocking the carriageway. As he reduced speed to negotiate the obstacle, he would find the road blocked by a bullock cart lying on its side. For the sake of realism, they had slaughtered the oxen, cutting the animals' throats with their Kirpan, a curved ceremonial sword. The bloodstained, apparently lifeless body by the roadside provided the final authentic touch.

Singh believed the bus driver would assume the bullock cart had been on the wrong side of the road when the oncoming truck had appeared round the first loop of the elongated 'S' bend and as a result, there had been a fatal accident. Reacting to the situation as he saw it, the bus driver would stamp on the brakes then, as his vehicle skidded to a halt, the corpse by the verge would come to life and open fire at point blank range. Two gunmen up on the rise overlooking the road would immediately rake the nearside of the bus with their Kalashnikovs.

The ambush party had been in position for almost two hours and his men were becoming restless and impatient. Although they hadn't started talking amongst themselves yet, there was a lot of unnecessary movement and far too much noise for his liking. Everything he had told them last night about the necessity for total silence had clearly been forgotten, but that was only to be expected from men who lacked the self-discipline of the trained soldier. The waiting however could not last much longer; the blood-red orange of a sun was some way above the horizon now and the freshness of the early morning had already been replaced by a foretaste of the naked heat to come.

Baldev Singh froze, his head tilted to one side as he strained his ears to catch the distant sound of a vehicle. The possibility that he could be mistaken and was simply imagining it never entered his mind. In a quiet but authoritative voice he told his men to get ready, then moved back to where the other two gunmen were lying in wait beyond the overturned bullock cart.

The bus came on, the throbbing note of its engine becoming perceptibly louder. Baldev Singh thought it was travelling quite fast and wondered if the driver would be able to pull up in time after swerving to avoid the truck. He told himself that nothing would go wrong and checked the Kalashnikov again to make sure the selector switch was on auto. He heard the brakes come on with a loud squeal and in that same instant, the dead man ignored all the orders he'd been given and opened fire while the bus was still rolling. Two, perhaps three seconds later, the gunmen positioned on the high ground joined in.

Consumed with rage at their sheer stupidity, Baldev Singh sprinted forward and arrived on the scene in time to see the bus plough into the bullock cart, reducing it to matchwood before careering across the road to come to a violent halt with the front wheels in the ditch opposite the embankment on the right. The idiot who'd sprung the ambush too soon was nowhere to be seen and the two gunmen on the high ground had also ceased firing. As the front wheels dropped into the ditch, the dead bus driver was thrown forward by the sudden impact and collapsed over the steering wheel. The whole weight of his body from the waist up fell on the air horn ring and the resultant strident blast shattered the unnatural silence which had followed the initial burst of firing. The surviving passengers panicked and screamed hysterically as they fought with one another to leave the bus by the emergency exit at the rear.

Singh reached the emergency exit, aimed at the young woman in the white sari who was frozen in the doorway and fired a short burst, hitting her in the stomach and chest. Four men and a young boy had already escaped and were legging it as fast as they could towards the nearest village. Whooping with unholy joy at the prospect of a chase, he went after them with all the loose-limbed style of a top class athlete. He caught up with the boy first and killed him with a single shot to the head which blew his skull apart, then dropped a skinny man who was holding his dhoti above his knees so that he could run faster. Had the others split up, one of them at least would have survived but in their collective fear they stayed together and paid the inevitable price.

Though out of breath and sweating profusely, Baldev Singh made his way back to the bus in an exultant mood. The single decker had been riddled from end to end and there was no sign of movement among the passengers inside, but that didn't necessarily mean all of them were dead. Adjusting the sling so that he could carry the Kalashnikov bandolier-fashion across his back, he pulled the dead woman clear of the emergency exit, then drew his ceremonial sword and climbed aboard.

There were bodies piled two deep throughout the entire length of the centre gangway, others were jammed under the seats where they had sought cover from the murderous hail of fire. A few had died upright in their seats despite the bone-shattering impact of a super-velocity round travelling at two thousand three hundred and thirty feet per second. He moved slowly forward towards the driver up front, stabbing the corpses with his sword as he went. One of them, a scrawny man with matchstick legs, came to life with a loud squeal as the blade sank into a lean buttock.

"Get up," Baldev Singh told him. "Do as I say and I won't hurt you."

The Hindu didn't believe him but there were grounds for thinking he wanted to very much. Using the backrest of the nearest seat for support, he dragged himself upright and turned about to face his assailant, the conflicting emotions of fear and hope reflected in his eyes.

"Shabash." Baldev Singh bared his teeth in what was supposed to be a reassuring smile, then plunged his sword into the Hindu's abdomen to a depth of four inches and ripped the blade upwards towards the breastbone, effectively disembowelling his victim.

The girl was lying under the seat directly behind the driver, her left leg pinioned under one of the corpses blocking the gangway. In an effort to hide herself completely, she had drawn the other limb up to her stomach; unfortunately, her foot was still exposed and it was the gold bangles around her ankle which attracted Singh's attention. When she flinched at his touch as he fingered them, he tightened his grip and hauled her out into the open.

At the most, she was barely fourteen years old but she had a well-developed figure for her age and the bangles indicated that as a married woman, she was not inexperienced. Considering the hail of fire which had been directed at the driver, it was nothing less than a miracle that not only was she still alive but unharmed. He raised her chin with the flat of his bloodstained sword, told her softly she was his to enjoy, then led her out of the bus.

The way the others looked at her was an unmistakable sign that he was not the only one who had been sexually aroused by the massacre, but they would have to wait their turn. Furthermore, it was vital to distance themselves from the scene of the ambush before the alarm was raised. Imposing his will on them, Baldev Singh ordered the driver to back their truck out of the ditch and turn it around to face the way they'd come. There was still no sign of the fool who'd opened fire too soon but there was a shattered AK 47 under the bus and a bundle of rags which could be a body. For a moment, Baldev Singh toyed with the idea of setting fire to the single decker but, on reflection, he decided somebody in the village down the road was bound to see the column of black smoke rising into the sky.

As always, the vultures were the first on the scene. They arrived singly, wheeling and soaring above the bus before settling down on the high ground above as if to ponder their next move. The alarm was eventually raised by the driver of the first bus from Faridkot and the police appeared a good hour after the last victim had died. By that time, Baldev Singh and his followers were approaching Kot Kapura, thirty-two miles to the south-east. By then, the Hindu child wife had already been raped by every man in the back of the truck.

*　　　*　　　*

Henderson alighted on to the crowded platform and was immediately engulfed by swarms of would-be porters wanting to carry his suitcase. A blind man thrust a tin mug at him, a legless cripple squatting on a large skate board raised a claw-like hand begging for alms, as did a harridan whose mouth was stained a deep red by the juice of betel nut. Ignoring the outstretched hands plucking at his shirtsleeves, he edged his way past the station master's office into the booking hall.

He had no idea where he was; unable to get a seat on the air-conditioned Taj Express, he'd caught the down mail-train to Calcutta which had stopped at two other stations in Agra, one on the outskirts, the other in an unidentified ramshackle suburb. He wouldn't have got off at this stop either had it not been for the Indian gentleman sharing his first class compartment who'd informed him the train would be crossing the Jumnah River when it left the city station.

The glare hit him as soon as he walked out into the yard. So did the smell of cowpats mixed with chaff which were used as solid fuel after they had been baked in the sun. Half a dozen street hawkers were selling water-melons, over-ripe bananas, cakes, tea, chilled fizzy drinks and curried vegetables in chapati, so that, for a moment, Henderson thought he'd wandered into the market place. There were no taxis in the yard, only a couple of tongas, the drivers of which were both fast asleep. Rousing the one whose horse seemed least likely to drop dead between the shafts, Henderson told him he wanted to go to the Taj View Hotel.

It wasn't the most comfortable ride he'd ever had; the tonga's hard suspension left a lot to be desired, the seat cushion was stuffed with horsehair and the driver had the uncanny knack of finding every pothole in the road. Turning left outside the yard, they went down a narrow, unnamed street, avoided a cow which was standing motionless in the middle of the road, then turned left again into an even busier and narrower alleyway and bumped over the railroad tracks at the unmanned level-crossing at the far end of the lane. Thereafter, they seemed to go round and round in circles before joining the main road opposite a fort.

"Agra Fort," the driver told him before he could ask, then pointed to a huge archway the far side of the moat. "Delhi Gate."

The brownstone fort was built on a hillock and dominated

the river. The lower ramparts, which were the first line of defence forward of the moat, were a good twenty feet high while those in the rear were close on sixty. There were bastions every hundred yards or so which in bygone days had enabled the garrison to enfilade the moat with cannon fire.

"Very impressive," Henderson said in what was a considerable understatement.

They turned right, clip-clopped through a park that had been laid out in Queen Victoria's time and whose statue had been replaced by one of Nehru in a saintly pose. The heat was still oppressive but at least there were now fewer flies dipping their suckers into the rivers of sweat on Henderson's face. Five minutes later, the driver halted the tonga outside what at first sight appeared to be the entrance to a palace.

"This is the Taj Hotel?"

"Yes. Taj," the driver said and nodded his head emphatically.

Henderson didn't see how it could be; the staff weren't in evidence, there were two coaches parked under the trees and a small boy wanted to sell him a wad of picture postcards the moment he stepped down from the tonga. He paid the driver five rupees, then gave the boy the same amount to look after his suitcase and promised to double it if his luggage was still there when he returned.

He strolled through the entrance and on past the souvenir shops into the garden. No photograph of the Taj Mahal Henderson had ever seen had really captured its grandeur. The glare from the white marble tomb the Emperor Shah Jehan had built in memory of his wife was almost painful on the eyes; when the sun caught the gold crescent on top of the dome, the reflected light could be seen from Tundla Junction twenty miles away across the plain.

He tagged on to a group of tourists, followed them past the ornamental ponds and climbed the steps leading to the monument. Then he walked round the outside to stand between the farthest minarets, gazing out across the wide sweep of the river at the burning ghats on the opposite sandbank where the dead were cremated. Away to his left, heatwaves danced and shimmered above the steel girders of the railway bridge, creating the illusion that the whole structure was oscillating.

Down by the water's edge, a group of women were laundering a pile of clothes, pounding them relentlessly against a rock. Not twenty yards from them, a pair of water buffaloes were cooling off in the river. Alexandra Drummond however was not paying him to admire the view.

The tonga had vanished by the time he returned but his suitcase was still there guarded by the youthful entrepreneur. There was also a taxi driver touting for hire whose command of English led Henderson to believe he actually knew where the Taj View Hotel was.

His faith wasn't misplaced; a little over fifteen minutes later, Henderson was unpacking his clothes in the hotel room Mrs Patel had reserved for him. Things began to go awry again when the tour party arrived and he learned that Lal had failed to meet them at Fatehpur Sikri. The harassed tutor from Brunel University who was the official escort didn't know what had happened to him or where he lived. Fortunately for Henderson, Alexandra Drummond had included Lal's address in the folder she had given him.

*   *   *

In the days of the Raj, there had been three quite separate Agras – the cantonment where the Army and British administrators lived, the Anglo-Indian enclave, and the city itself which was inhabited entirely by the indigenous population. The Anglo-Indians who ran the railways, the postal and telegraph services and filled the lower echelons of the civil service were strategically placed midway between the cantonment and the city where they acted as a buffer separating the two communities. Although the city remained divided after Independence, it was on socio-economic rather than racial grounds. It was also a fact that the cantonment and former Anglo-Indian enclave had gradually become one entity, though the better houses near Laurie's Hotel and the Club were still occupied by the Army and top civil servants.

Under the Raj, number 29 Telegraph Lines had been classified as a Type 4 bungalow which meant that it had been considered suitable for deputy heads of sections. Set back from the road, the bungalow was fronted by a U-shaped drive and a scorched lawn. The wide veranda on all four sides was simply a means of keeping the interior passably cool during the hot season and had not been intended as a status symbol by the architect who'd designed the building in the early 1920s. Currently, the bungalow was occupied by Mr Lal senior, deputy head of stores control, maintenance division (Agra), a grizzled sixty-one-year-old civil servant who'd been with the Inland Telegraph since leaving High School.

Henderson had taken the precaution of borrowing one of the bi-lingual desk clerks from the Taj View Hotel, but he needn't have bothered. English had always been the lingua franca for middle management and Lal senior was particularly fluent.

"Actually, it was your son I wanted to see," Henderson said as the Indian led him into a cool dark room at the rear of the bungalow.

"Which one?"

"The guide."

"Ah, my first born." His face clouded. "The police arrested him at three o'clock yesterday morning; they said he had stolen a lot of money from his employer."

"That's odd; the manager of Indus Tours told me that your son was the best and most reliable guide they had."

"The money he stole belonged to an English gentleman."

"Beardsley?"

"I didn't ask. My eldest son is always wanting to make a lot of money quickly and for a long time now I have been expecting something like this to happen. His wife is constantly reading magazines and nags him because she cannot live in a palace like a film star."

The old man had two other sons. The youngest had just qualified as a doctor and was doing his internship in Delhi, while the middle one was a magistrate. It seemed only the first born had been a disappointment to him.

"Does your son have a lawyer?" Henderson asked.

"Oh yes – Mr V. K. Chatterjee – he is very good."

"Do you know where the police are holding him?"

"They told me they were taking my son to the cantonment station."

Lal had been reluctant to disturb Chatterjee in the middle of the night so he'd waited until almost nine and had then gone to the lawyer's office on Mahatma Gandhi Way. By the time Chatterjee had arrived at the police station, the shift had changed and the duty Havildar had denied all knowledge of the prisoner. To prove his point, he'd allowed the lawyer to check every cell.

"And he still hasn't found your son?"

"I have every confidence in Mr V. K. Chatterjee. He will leave no stone unturned in his pursuit of justice."

It didn't seem to Henderson that he'd turned over too many in the last thirty-six hours. "I'm sure you're right," he said tactfully. "But I used to be a police officer and I know how to keep a suspect under wraps."

"Under wraps? What is that?"

"It's an old trick," Henderson explained. "You move a prisoner around in order to keep him apart from his lawyer for as long as possible. By the time the counsellor does catch up with his client, you hope the suspect has made a damaging admission. A so-called voluntary statement wouldn't be any good because it wouldn't conform with the Judge's Rules; what you are hoping to get from the suspect is a pointer to the whereabouts of some piece of hard evidence which will stand up in court."

The old man gazed at him thoughtfully. The only sound in the room came from the large rotating fan in the ceiling which created a rather ineffective breeze.

"I would like to meet your Mr Chatterjee," Henderson said after a lengthy silence. "I may be able to help him."

"How?"

"By bringing pressure to bear in the right quarter. The Englishman whose money your son is alleged to have stolen worked for the British High Commission, and I am a friend of his family. Between us, I'm sure we can persuade the police to be a little more co-operative."

It was a somewhat extravagant claim. There was no telling how Goodman would react to a request for help and just how much influence he had with the Ministry of the Interior was open to question too. He had offered to obtain the address of Tara Singh, the driver Beardsley had hired in Agra, but had failed to deliver. The old man, however, looked suitably impressed.

"When would you like to see Mr Chatterjee?"

"As soon as possible," Henderson told him.

"Perhaps we could see him at four o'clock? He should be back at his office by then."

"Where does he live?"

"On The Mall of course," Lal said as if surprised that he should ask.

"Why don't we call on him?"

"What, now?"

"Yes. Is there any reason why we shouldn't?"

Lal could think of several and reeled them off. This was the hot season and Mr Chatterjee would be resting. Apart from that consideration, he did not receive anyone at his house other than family and friends and then only by express invitation. Finally, of course, he was a very busy man and they would have to make an appointment with his clerk.

"That won't be necessary," Henderson said firmly. "Mr Chatterjee will have to forgo his afternoon nap for once because your son is entitled to see the lawyer of his choice anytime he wants."

Lal sighed. His whole demeanour suggested he couldn't understand why Henderson was so intent on making life difficult for all concerned. However, he wasn't disposed to make an issue of it and even agreed to accompany him to Chatterjee's residence, though with marked reluctance.

They walked out of the bungalow into a blast furnace that rocked Henderson back on his heels. He could feel the latent heat of the sun-baked earth through the soles of his suede chukka boots and the prickly-heat rash on his neck started itching again as the sweat got to it. The taxi driver and part-time interpreter who'd been waiting on the veranda followed them out to the car. Although all four windows had been left open, the interior was like an oven, the air stale and enervating.

The Mall where Chatterjee lived was two miles away; it seemed very much longer.

*　　　*　　　*

The statistics made grim reading. Of the forty-eight victims who had been killed in the ambush, seven were children under the age of twelve, a figure which included a four-month-old baby girl. A preliminary medical examination revealed that amongst the women who had been gunned down, two had been pregnant, a fact which would lead some newspaper editors to up the total body count to fifty.

In addition to a Chinese-manufactured AK 47 assault rifle, one hundred and eighty-two spent cases were recovered from the scene of the ambush. All were 7.62 mm calibre and were from the same lot and batch number of MP 1943 ammunition. Ignoring the rounds found in the vicinity of the boy and the four men who had been shot some distance from the bus, the police came to the conclusion that six men had been involved in the ambush. A nitrate test confirmed that the corpse which had been found under the single decker had been one of the gunmen. Although there was no means of identification on the corpse, there was no mistaking that he was a Sikh.

There was no way the authorities could suppress the news, nor did they wish to. Bad as the incident had been, they were conscious that any attempt to censor the radio would only give birth to even worse rumours with predictable consequences. The only point at issue was whether or not they should disclose the fact that one of the assassins had been a Sikh. If the ambush had taken place in Uttar Pradesh, it might have been possible to attribute the massacre to Sarana Kurmis, but this was the Punjab and no one would believe a gang of dacoits had committed the atrocity.

In the end, it was decided to delay the release of an official announcement until 1300 hours in order to give the police and Army time to put their forces on full alert. The incident was therefore the lead story on the one o'clock news broadcast by All India Radio.

Chapter VII

Mr Chatterjee was a small man with a hawk's face, dark glittering eyes and a sharp tongue. He resented anyone disturbing his afternoon nap and he didn't welcome unexpected visitors, especially the likes of Mr Lal senior whom he considered socially inferior. Determined to be unpleasant, he kept them waiting on the doorstep while he changed into a pair of slacks and a fresh shirt. Even then, he wasn't disposed to invite them inside.

"Now, what's the problem?" he asked in Hindi.

Mr Lal told him, then translated for Henderson's benefit in unison with the desk clerk who'd been paid fifty rupees for his services as an interpreter.

"We will continue in English," Chatterjee said and glared at Henderson. "Though why your affairs should concern this gentleman is beyond me."

"Mr Goodman has expressed an interest in the case."

"Who's he?"

"One of the principal Secretaries at the British High Commission," said Henderson. "I'm here to keep a watching brief."

Chatterjee made the connection as he was meant to. "You and Mr Lal had better come in," he said. "The other two can wait in the servants' quarters round the back."

Henderson followed the lawyer into the study at the front of the house and groped his way to a chair. The curtains were drawn to keep the room tolerably cool and it was some moments before his eyes became accustomed to the gloom. Moving to the window, Chatterjee switched on the air-conditioner and opened the curtains a fraction to let in a shaft of light.

"Exactly what is your interest in my client, Mr Henderson?" he asked.

"There are some questions I want to put to him about Colonel Beardsley."

"To do with the crime he's alleged to have committed?"

"In a way."

"This may come as a surprise to you but the Raj no longer exists, which means you have no legal jurisdiction in this country."

"Jurisdiction isn't an issue, Mr Chatterjee. We'd like to know what Colonel Beardsley said to your client when he hired him to go to Etawah. So would your Minister of the Interior."

"Why should he be concerned?"

"It's a matter of State Security," Henderson lied. "So I hope you know where the police are holding Mr Lal's son."

"I will do shortly."

"There's a buzz going round Delhi that certain police officers are determined to keep him in solitary confinement until this whole thing blows over."

"The Commissioner of Police is a close personal friend," Chatterjee said loftily. "He was out when I telephoned his office yesterday morning but I left word for him to get in touch on his return."

"Not exactly a lightning response, is it?"

"What?"

"Who knows how much longer you'll have to wait." Henderson shrugged his shoulders. "Of course, if you're sure Lal is all right there's nothing to worry about."

Chatterjee frowned at his wristwatch. The police had arrested his client in the early hours of Thursday morning; thirty-six hours later, he still had no idea where they were holding him. Henderson thought it didn't say a lot for his friendship with the Commissioner.

"No one is above the law," Chatterjee announced pompously, having given the matter some considerable thought.

"You're absolutely right," Henderson assured him.

The lawyer picked up the phone, rang police headquarters and asked for the Commissioner. On learning that he still hadn't returned, Chatterjee demanded to be put through to his deputy but had to be content with the Divisional Officer in charge of the Criminal Investigation Department. Understanding the thrust of their conversation wasn't all that difficult even though it was conducted in Hindi. From being merely truculent, the Indian became increasingly angry before he ended up delivering what sounded like an ultimatum.

"Damned impudent fellow."

"I bet he told you he'd never even heard of your client," Henderson said sagely.

"He will wish he'd never heard of V. K. Chatterjee before I've done with him. Fortunately, the Quarter Sessions are being held in Agra this month."

Chatterjee rang the Government Rest House where the judge was staying, apologised profusely for disturbing him and then practically got down on his knees to request an audience. His gratitude on being granted one knew no bounds.

"Do you mind if I come with you?" Henderson asked.

It was the last thing the lawyer wanted but he had been led to believe that the Minister of the Interior had expressed an interest in the case and he wasn't anxious to have the people in Delhi breathing down his neck. Lal senior, who'd given every sign of being ill at ease in Chatterjee's company, muttered something about his son being in good hands, then added it was time he was getting back to the office.

The Government Rest House was barely a ten-minute journey door to door. Chatterjee however had an over-protective attitude towards his 1981 Oldsmobile and in his anxiety not to scratch the paintwork, it took him an age to back the car out of the garage. And even when they had The Mall to themselves, he was still content to dawdle along at twenty miles an hour.

The judge was even slower. By the time Chatterjee reappeared clutching the writ he'd asked for, the interior of the Oldsmobile was like an oven and Henderson's shirt was patched with sweat.

The Criminal Investigation Department was co-located with the Mobile Response Force in the police lines on the outskirts of the city. The Divisional Officer in charge of the detective squad was no fool; knowing what was in the wind, he had made arrangements to be called out on a job before they arrived. He had also been wise enough to leave a message with his administrative assistant who informed them that the mix-up over Mr Lal had now been sorted out and, as a result, he had been returned to the cantonment station.

It wasn't the only pre-emptive measure the police had taken. With Lal waiting to greet them with the news that the station officer had told him he was free to go, the writ was rendered superfluous. Chatterjee was not exactly overjoyed and left Henderson to introduce himself.

"Why have they released you?" the lawyer demanded. "Did you make a statement?"

"I told the officer in charge what little I knew," Lal admitted reluctantly.

"In other words you agreed to sign what amounted to a confession?"

"No, definitely not. I told the Inspector that the Amalgamated Farmers' Trust was not a very efficient bank and they weren't used to dealing with traveller's cheques. I said the teller had probably kept the cheque in his cash drawer because he didn't know what to do with it and that's why it didn't show up until after Colonel Beardsley was dead. I didn't say anything about the Uttar Pradesh Federal Reserve. How could I, when I've never had anything to do with them?"

"And so the police realised they have made a grave mistake and decided to let you go?"

"Yes."

"Then we shall sue them for false arrest," Chatterjee said triumphantly.

"There's nothing I'd like better," Lal told him, "but I'd have to think about it first."

Henderson thought the guide's nose was swollen and although some attempt had been made to clean him up, his clothes still looked the worse for wear. The police had obviously scared Lal shitless and he wasn't going to sue them no matter what Chatterjee said. The lawyer knew it too and made his anger clear by the way he got into his Oldsmobile, slammed the door and then gunned the V8 engine into life. The tyres squealed in protest and left a cloud of dust in their wake as he shot out of the police compound.

"Mr Chatterjee is a very busy man," Lal said gravely, "always on the go. I feel honoured he consented to represent me."

"Indeed." Henderson gave the interpreter fifty rupees for his trouble and another ten for the fare back to the Taj View Hotel, then ushered the portly guide into the taxi which had followed them from Chatterjee's house in The Mall to the Government Rest House and on to the police compound. "I'll give you a lift home," he said, climbing in after him.

"That's exceedingly kind of you."

"Not at all; there's a couple of things I'd like to ask you about Colonel Beardsley, starting with the reason why he wanted to go to Etawah."

"The Colonel represented the Finlayson Trust, a charitable organisation founded by Sir George Finlayson, Governor of the Bombay Presidency . . ."

There was no stopping Lal. Whether Henderson liked it or not, he was going to get an expanded and snobbish version of the entry in *Who's Who*, much of it the product of the Indian's fertile imagination.

"The Colonel found a message waiting for him at his hotel in Jaipur," he continued. "The Trust had learned that the grandson of one of Sir George Finlayson's former retainers was lying seriously ill in hospital in Etawah. The grandson had been a Jemadar in the Punjab Regiment and the Trust asked the Colonel to visit him in order to find out if there was anything he needed."

"So why did he hire you?"

"Colonel Beardsley could neither speak nor understand Hindi, so he needed an interpreter. He knew I could speak English jolly well and he said I was a most agreeable fellow. We became great friends."

"Did he tell you he'd been to India before?"

Lal nodded. "During the war with the Sherwood Foresters, a very famous English regiment from Nottinghamshire whose Colonel-in-Chief is now Her Royal Highness the Princess Royal, Mrs Mark Phillips, Dame Grand Cross of the Royal Victorian Order. Since 1968, they have been amalgamated with the Worcestershire Regiment, another fine regiment whose officers are definitely county people . . ."

Beardsley had obviously recognised Lal for what he was and had played on his innate snobbery by feeding him the kind of pap that appeared in the society columns. It seemed to Henderson that Beardsley had found a neat way of satisfying the Indian's almost insatiable curiosity while giving nothing away about himself.

"Tell me about Tara Singh, the driver you hired," he said, interrupting Lal. "Is he an old friend too?"

"The first time I met Tara Singh was the day we all left for Etawah. And I didn't hire him; Colonel Beardsley did, he said the hotel had recommended him."

And the last time Lal had seen him was later the same day when Tara Singh had been trying to repair the back axle of their car. "Do you know where he lives?" Henderson asked.

"There is a small Sikh community on the Jhansi Road. He didn't tell me the number of his house."

"But you'd recognise him again?"

"Indeed I would."

"Good, I'd like you to help me find him."

"When?"

"Right away, if you can."

"I'll need to change first."

"Of course." Henderson reached for his wallet. "Naturally, you'll be paid for your services."

"That won't be necessary."

"I insist."

"Just my usual fee as a guide then," Lal said and left him to guess how much that might be.

*　　　*　　　*

The naked body of the child wife whom Baldev Singh and his followers had kidnapped was found by the roadside beyond the village of Nathana Dun some one hundred and ten miles from the scene of the ambush. No attempt had been made to conceal the victim and a miniature ceremonial sword had been inserted in her rectum to let the world know who had been responsible for the atrocity. The body was found at 1415 hours, an hour and a quarter after details of the massacre near Faridkot had been broadcast by All India Radio in their one o'clock newscast. However, ugly rumours had already begun to spread like wildfire by word of mouth long before the discovery of the latest outrage.

The rumours had erupted throughout the Punjab and Uttar Pradesh spawned by a combination of idle speculation, hatred and professional agitators which the newscast had unwittingly provoked. Hindu temples were said to have been razed to the ground, a priest in Aligarh had been beheaded and at least a dozen women had been drenched with petrol and set on fire. Each story was embroidered in the telling so that few people were prepared to believe that the death toll had only increased by one when the media eventually reported the rape and murder of the child wife.

The backlash was felt in Delhi first where a mob went on the rampage in the Dayabasti District of the city. Shops, homes and business premises were systematically wrecked and looted, cars were overturned and put to the torch, individual Sikhs were attacked with iron bars, wooden staves, knives, hammers, billhooks and left for dead. An old man seeking refuge in a police post near the Jama Masjid mosque was torn limb from limb in front of the Havildar and two constables on duty who were powerless to intervene.

Well within an hour of the riot starting, the Army was out in force on the streets.

*   *   *

Agra seemed unnaturally quiet. When Henderson had stepped off the train that morning the city had pulsated with life, but now it was as if the population had migrated to another town. The few people who were out and about looked and acted as if they would have preferred to be elsewhere. Then the driver said something in Hindi and Lal answered him in a similar worried sounding voice.

"What's the matter?" Henderson asked.

"The driver is saying he doesn't like the look of things. He is thinking something is wrong."

"Like what?"

"He is not knowing." Lal leaned forward and pointed to the radio under the dashboard. "His wireless is not working."

The more agitated Lal became, the more it showed in his quaint usage of English. Glancing to his left, Henderson saw a truckload of steel-helmeted police parked in a small, otherwise deserted square.

"Looks as though our driver isn't the only one who thinks there could be trouble."

"Not any more," Lal told him with evident relief. "The unpleasantness is over."

There were none of the usual signs to show that it had even started. No half bricks, no broken bottles, just pats of cow dung in the alleys instead of the debris a rioting mob always left behind.

"Any idea where we are?" Henderson asked.

"Not far from the Jhansi Road." Lal spoke to the driver in Hindi again to make sure he was right, then gave Henderson a confident smile. "We turn left at the end of the bazaar and join the main trunk road to Jhansi via a side street."

One lane looked very much like another and Henderson doubted if he could find his way back to this part of the city without a guide. There was nothing to distinguish this bazaar from the one he'd seen near Agra Fort – same open-fronted shops selling the same brassware, candles, rugs, mats, cooking pots, sweetmeats, the same uneven sidewalk beside an open drain. The whole area reminded him of one vast maze and it wasn't until they reached the Jhansi Road that he saw any semblance of order.

The trunk road ran arrow straight and was just wide enough to accommodate single line traffic flowing in either direction. The Sikh quarter consisted of a dozen or so crumbling villas on the outskirts which were set close together as though each one was seeking the protection of its neighbour. Like some of the dwelling places in the city, the flat-roofed houses looked as if they had been constructed by the occupants themselves using whatever building materials happened to be at hand. In most cases it was difficult to tell whether the owners had run out of home-made bricks before they had been able to finish the job or if successive monsoons had simply undermined the foundations. The only common feature was a mud-walled outer courtyard which was in an even more dilapidated condition than the building it fronted.

"We've arrived," Lal said, pointing out the obvious after their taxi driver had pulled off the road and stopped.

"But you don't know which house belongs to Tara Singh?"

"Regrettably, no."

"Then I suppose we'd better get out of the car and knock on a few doors," said Henderson.

The street was deserted and ominously quiet, like the rest of the city they'd motored through. Henderson tried the nearest house, found the door which opened into the courtyard was locked and bolted, and moved on to the neighbouring villa.

"I am thinking we should avoid this place," Lal said.

The wrought-iron gate which hung askew on its hinges with the drawbar hopelessly out of line with the recess in the door post was not an obstacle, but the dog most certainly was. The mongrel was about the same size as a whippet and had a pointed, vicious-looking muzzle. The right foreleg was missing and there was a large festering sore on the same rib cage. When he saw them at the gate, his tail remained between his legs but there was nothing submissive about the way his lips drew back to reveal needle-sharp fangs. He was easily the most rabid animal Henderson had ever seen.

"You're right," he said. "Better safe than sorry."

They tried two other houses without success, then found one where the wall enclosing the courtyard had all but collapsed. The occupants did their best to give the impression they weren't at home but Lal kept pounding on the door until they finally capitulated and opened it. The man who confronted them was holding an axe in his right hand and looked as though he'd seen a ghost. His eyes darted nervously about the open courtyard and from the tense manner in which he answered Lal's questions it was obvious that his one aim in life was to slam the door in their faces in double quick time. The only thing which prevented him from doing so there and then was the fact that Henderson's foot was in the way.

"So what's he got to say for himself?" Henderson asked.

"He is expecting much trouble," Lal said in a worried voice. "Sikh terrorists in the Punjab ambushed a bus this morning and killed all the passengers. At least fifty men, women and children were murdered. It was on All India Radio."

"Well, now we know why the police are out in strength on the streets. Tell him everything is okay and there's nothing to worry about, then ask him if he knows where we can find Tara Singh."

Lal did just that but the Sikh didn't look at all reassured. His tense expression remained unaltered and his negative head-shakes told Henderson he had never heard of the taxi driver long before the guide translated his reply.

"He is telling me that no one with that name is living in Agra."

"I gathered as much. Question is, do you think he's stating a fact or merely guessing?"

Lal shrugged his shoulders. "Who knows? There are so many Sikhs and he might not want to confess he hasn't met all of them."

Asking a Sikh if he knew someone called Tara Singh was a bit like asking a Mr Smith in England if he was acquainted with his namesake Bill.

"On the other hand, he could be right, Mr Henderson. If Tara Singh lives in this part of Agra, I would expect him to know most of his neighbours."

Henderson got as far as suggesting they might have better luck next door, then suddenly froze. The baying sound in the distance was unmistakable; he had heard it before on a Saturday afternoon at the City football ground when a section of the crowd had been hell-bent on making trouble. The Sikh tried to close the door but when he couldn't do so because Henderson's foot was still in the way, he promptly kicked him on the shin. When that failed to have the desired effect, he lashed out with the axe and came within an inch of decapitating Henderson.

As if possessing a sixth sense, Lal ran towards the road. Unfortunately, the taxi driver was even quicker; cranking the engine of the Tata into life, he took off like a rocket before the guide could stop him. By the time Henderson arrived on the scene, all he could see was a cloud of dust the car had left in its wake.

The mob emerged from a side street approximately fifty yards to their left and began to attack the nearest Sikh-occupied house. Someone hurled a petrol bomb at the building, the first of many which exploded on impact with a hollow whoof. A break-away group gathered round a black sedan parked by the roadside, tipped the vehicle over and set it alight before moving on to the next target. A stone landed near Henderson, an inaccurate ranging shot which preceded an equally inaccurate bombardment.

"Come with me," Lal yelled to him from a safe distance. "Do not stop to argue with them, Mr Henderson, they will not listen to you."

A bottle sailed through the air and struck the ground a few yards in front of Henderson. Filled with soda water, it fragmented like a hand grenade but with appreciably less kinetic energy. Instinctively he threw up a hand to shield his eyes from the splinters and felt a sharp blow on the elbow. Moments later when he lowered his arm, a ribbon of blood trickled down towards his wrist from a nick caused by a jagged piece of glass. Heeding Lal's advice, he retreated before the advancing mob, keeping just far enough ahead of the leading elements to be a good stone's throw out of range.

The first house to come under attack was already well ablaze and the flames were beginning to lick the neighbouring property. There was no sign of the Fire Brigade, which Henderson thought was understandable, but he couldn't think what had happened to the police, especially the truckload from the Mobile Response Force he'd seen less than a mile from the Jhansi Road. Out of the corner of his eye, he spotted a figure kneeling behind the parapet on the flat roof of the building immediately to his right, then heard a loud report as the man discharged his ancient fowling piece at the mob.

The buckshot consisted of nails, ball-bearings and shards of metal, and the spread was such that the beaten zone covered the entire width of the street. He saw only one man go down but at least a dozen others were injured to varying degrees. Far from deterring the mob, the casualties they'd taken merely increased their blood lust.

Henderson glanced over his shoulder. He and Lal had retreated about as far as they could go; any farther and they would find themselves in the open countryside. Common sense told him that if the violence should spread to the rural areas, no village constable could hope to maintain law and order on his own. The mob had already demonstrated that they regarded any outsider as their enemy and he had no reason to believe people's attitudes would be any different in the countryside. Their best and safest course of action was to circle back into the city where at least the police were in evidence. Running after Lal, he caught up with the Indian fifty yards beyond the last house and dragged him into the fields of maize bordering the road.

"Where are you taking me, Mr Henderson?"

"Back the way we came."

"But it's not safe to go back."

"Don't worry," Henderson told him, "we'll be making a wide detour. That way we should avoid any unpleasantness."

He ran on, Lal stumbling beside him nursing a stitch and gasping for breath. Several houses were on fire now and it looked as though the drifting smoke would screen them from the mob on the Jhansi Road. The illusion was short lived; up ahead, a woman suddenly appeared out of the smoke and ran across their front. The elderly man who followed on a few yards in rear was obviously doing his best to keep up with her but he had a deformed leg to contend with and his best years were behind him. So too were his pursuers, but not for long; within a few strides the nearest one had caught up with him and was using his wooden stave to good effect, clubbing the Sikh about the head and shoulders until he went down. A second Hindu joined in to finish the old man off, leaving his three companions to go after the woman.

Henderson changed direction to intercept them. An inner voice told him not to be so bloody stupid but he couldn't close his eyes to what was happening around him. He came on, waving his arms and yelling like a Dervish in the hope that his antics would distract them long enough to give the woman a chance to make good her escape. It didn't work; one of her pursuers, who was armed with a length of steel piping, stopped dead, turned to face him and took a swipe at his head. Henderson ducked under the swing, kicked his adversary on the shin, wrenched the tube from his grasp and jabbed the Indian in the stomach with it, laying him out cold.

The woman had reached the stage of physical exhaustion where she could run no farther and was endeavouring to keep the low stone wall surrounding an artesian well between herself and a short, bandy-legged man armed with a sickle. Every time he feinted to go one way, she darted the other, but the stalemate wouldn't last much longer. The second man had made a wide encircling movement and it was only a question of seconds before she was trapped like a fly in a spider's web.

Henderson glanced over his shoulder; the odds were still four to three if he included the two Hindus who were still battering the old man as he lay unconscious on the ground. The woman however had no means of defending herself other than with her bare hands and was therefore unlikely to be much of a help. Lal too was unarmed but was doing the best he could from a safe distance by stoning the men who were attacking the prostrate Sikh. Unfortunately, his intervention was not exactly decisive and, worse still, his aim was usually way off target.

The odds needed to be reduced in the shortest possible time. Wielding the steel pipe with both hands, Henderson went for the man with the sickle and broke his right arm just below the elbow, then caught him with a back swing to shatter the other arm in case he was tempted to pick up the sickle again the moment his back was turned. The man screamed, sank down on to his knees crooning to himself in pain. Above his anguished cries he heard Lal shouting and whirled about to find himself confronting the men who'd bludgeoned the elderly Sikh.

One man to his right and slightly to the rear, two more facing him intent on breaking his skull with their staves, the woman somewhere between him and the low stone wall and Lal grubbing around in the dirt to ammunition up with stones. Henderson registered the positions of friends and foes alike as he twisted, ducked and turned while using the steel pipe to parry each blow aimed at his head.

The paratroops arrived from nowhere, tough, well-disciplined soldiers from the Airborne Forces training centre on the Fatehpur Sikri Road. The corporal in charge of the detachment barked an order, then fired a shot above their heads to remove any lingering doubts. Henderson didn't think the order applied to him and failed to raise his hands. By the time it dawned on him that there were no privileged exceptions, one of the paratroopers standing behind him had started to deliver a butt stroke with his rifle. The blow caught Henderson in the small of his back. The last thing he remembered before he blacked out was an agonising stab of pain in the region of his left kidney.

Chapter VIII

The military hospital on Krishna Menon Avenue dated back to the latter part of World War Two when elements of the US Army Air Corps 14th Air Force had been stationed in Agra. Some months before VJ Day, the bungalow-type complex had been taken over by the Royal Army Medical Corps at a time when there were no British units in the garrison and battle casualties were being treated elsewhere. With few patients to look after other than those in the Indian Army Wing, the Commanding Officer had instituted a programme of self help to give the hospital a face-lift while simultaneously providing gainful employment for his soldiers. The gainful employment had involved sowing every parcel of ground with grass seed and lining the dusty paths with stones which had then been assiduously whitewashed. Forty-two years later, the lawns were still mainly brown but the white-washed stones gleamed like newly capped teeth.

"Part of our heritage from the British Raj," Henderson's doctor had assured him in fluent English. "One must keep up the old traditions."

The Indian Army had given him the best of medical treatment; he was no longer passing blood in his urine and the X-rays showed that no permanent damage had been done to his kidney. But ten days in hospital was a very long time when the only person he was able to converse with was the senior resident physician. The hours dragged, especially now that he was fit enough to leave, yet all the good doctor would say was 'soon' whenever he asked about a date for his discharge.

Henderson listened to the footsteps on the veranda and glanced at his wristwatch, the one item of his personal effects which had so far been returned to him. 11:30; too late for a mid morning cup of tea, too early for lunch and visiting hours were in the evenings. Henderson went back to the week-old

93

copy of *The Times* which the doctor had given him, but not for long. The footsteps stopped outside his room; looking up from the newspaper, he saw Lawrence Goodman standing in the doorway.

"Surprised?"

Henderson nodded, then got up and perched himself on the edge of the bed. "You're the last person I expected to see. What are you doing in Agra?"

"Wet-nursing a visiting trade delegation from the UK." Goodman moved towards the only chair in the room which Henderson had just vacated and sat down. "They're on a jaunt to Akbar's Tomb this morning so I thought I'd drop by to see how you're coming on."

"I'm fine. I'd feel better still if they would only tell me when I am going to be discharged."

"I hear you were required to give evidence before a Board of Inquiry?"

"Is that what they call it? All I know is that some Major in the Paras turned up here with an interpreter and took a statement from me. He wanted to know how I came to be caught up in the riot. I told him it wasn't from choice and that we just happened to be in the Sikh quarter when it all started."

"Who's we?" Goodman asked casually.

"Lal, the taxi driver and me. We were looking for Tara Singh, the man Beardsley hired."

"Yes, I'm sorry I failed to obtain his address for you. I don't suppose you had better luck, did you?"

"No one we asked had ever heard of him."

"Maybe Tara isn't his given name and is simply a family one?"

"The only man who would know the answer to that is dead," said Henderson.

"Quite. The one thing you can be reasonably certain about is that no one calling himself Tara Singh came from this neck of the woods."

"Do you mind telling me why?"

"Because the Indian authorities carried out what amounted to a population census the day after the Army had restored law and order. Every Sikh domiciled in the area was required to register and had to be vouched for by two independent referees.

94

Delhi wanted to be absolutely sure they knew precisely how many people had been killed in the riot."

Henderson listened to him with only half an ear. According to Lal, it was Beardsley who'd hired their driver, but that couldn't be right. If the ad hoc census had been conducted with anything like the efficiency Goodman had implied, the authorities would have come up with a Tara Singh or someone with a very similar name. That had to mean the Sikh had been sent to Agra to pick Beardsley up from his hotel.

"Maybe the taxi driver lives in Etawah?"

"What?"

"Nothing, I was just thinking aloud." Henderson paused, then said, "Are the authorities satisfied that Beardsley was kidnapped by dacoits?"

"Their leader, Sarana Kurmis, was identified by dozens of witnesses. She made sure everyone in Patna knew who they were dealing with. There's nothing like a spot of intimidation to make people toe the line."

"Are there any Sikhs among her henchmen?"

"I doubt it; she's butchered every member of the race who's been unlucky enough to cross her path. Her latest victim was Charan Singh, the officer in charge of the police detachment in Patna." Goodman took out a silk handkerchief and wiped the sweat from his forehead. "You're not pro Sikh by any chance, are you?" he asked suddenly. "I mean, do you sympathise with their political aspirations?"

"What prompted that question?"

"The way you go looking for them."

"We seem to be losing our sense of proportion; I am trying to locate one lousy cab driver."

"The Army says you were fighting alongside them when they were attacked by a mob."

"For Christ sake," Henderson said irritably. "I was simply protecting one Sikh lady from being chopped into little pieces by four Hindus. What is everybody getting so damned touchy about?"

"The majority of Sikhs are domiciled in the Punjab and the extremists among them would like to establish a separate, independent nation. To achieve this aim, they are prepared to use force and therefore you have the makings of a nasty civil war going on up there. Ten days ago, a group of terrorists ambushed a country bus and slaughtered fifty men, women and children, all of them Hindus. As a result, Hindu mobs went on the rampage in Delhi, Lucknow, Kanpur and Agra seeking vengeance, which was just what the terrorists wanted. You know why?"

"To undermine the government?"

"You're close," Goodman said, "but not quite close enough. The Sikhs are a warrior race; ever since the days of the Raj they have always formed a disproportionately large element in the Indian Army. So far, the Sikh Regiments have remained loyal to the government; the extremists hope that by provoking the Hindus to retaliate, the tit-for-tat killings will eventually reach such a scale that these units will become disaffected. If that should happen, the politicians really will be in trouble. The people in Delhi know they're sitting on a powder keg so it's understandable if they're suspicious of any European who appears to be over friendly towards the Sikhs."

Henderson mulled it over; the message was clear enough but he wanted to hear it spelt out. "Are you trying to warn me off?" he asked.

"I suppose I must be," Goodman said and smiled engagingly. "Actually, what I'm really urging you to do is exercise a little caution. If you want to continue looking for your missing taxi driver it's okay by me so long as you don't get yourself arrested. The police spent a considerable amount of time and energy looking for Tara Singh after Colonel Beardsley disappeared, but to no avail. He had simply vanished into thin air along with all of Rupert's belongings."

"Are you saying he stole them?"

"The police are convinced he did. We never recovered any of Rupert's possessions and he could have got a good price for them in Delhi or any place else you care to mention."

"Do you believe that?"

"I think it's the most likely explanation. Your Tara Singh had a lot going for him. The odds against tracing a missing person, especially someone who wants to disappear, are phenomenal; the population census can never be more than a guesstimate when so many births, marriages and deaths go unrecorded and where professional letter-writers in every village of any consequence will provide you with a set of identity papers for a small consideration. Of course, if Lal had been able to remember the registration number of the taxi it might have made all the difference, but he couldn't even say what colour it was with any certainty."

"What about the spare parts dealer in Patna who sold him the replacement back axle?"

"Back-street traders out here don't bother themselves with such mundane things as bills, invoices and receipts. It's likely Rupert paid through the nose for that spare part and Tara Singh split the profit down the middle with the dealer."

Henderson weighed the percentages. If by a million to one shot he succeeded where the police had failed and ran Tara Singh to ground, what good would it do his client? He would never know whether the answers to his questions were truthful, flights of fancy or simply a pack of lies. Beardsley hadn't been murdered; his death had been an accident, the result of sheer incompetence on the part of the kidnappers. It was the one fact he'd learned during the past twelve days which he was certain of. Beardsley himself was still an enigma and there were a number of conflicting things he'd been told about the man by Alexandra Drummond and Goodman to indicate that both parties had been economical with the truth when talking about him. And if Lal's hearsay evidence was to be believed, the Colonel had been less than frank about himself.

He wondered how far Goodman would go to defend the dead man's reputation. "The Trust have made certain innuendoes about Rupert Beardsley," he said. "Apparently the Board has anted up more funds in the way of student grants than can be accounted for."

"They should call in their auditors."

"They already have and the figures show that the fund is being milked of fifteen thousand a year. I can't vouch for the accuracy of the audit, but the way the grants are disbursed it's evident that Colonel Beardsley was the only man who was in a position to organise the embezzlement, which is pretty upsetting for his surviving relative."

"Did the Board make that allegation in writing?"

"More or less," Henderson said.

"Then you should advise the family to consult a solicitor. I know you can't bring an action on behalf of the deceased but the Board have libelled Rupert by inference and they should be made to eat their words."

"You don't think he was capable of embezzlement?" Henderson said innocently.

"Of course he wasn't. Rupert was the most painfully honest man I've ever met. He wouldn't dream of inflating a claim for expenses by so much as a penny, never mind swindling a charity out of fifteen thousand a year."

"No hidden vices?"

"Absolutely none."

"Any financial problems?"

"He inherited his wife's money."

"How about alcohol?" Henderson persisted. "Was he a boozer?"

"He may have liked a drink but he didn't have a problem."

It obviously took a lot to ruffle Goodman but there was a sharp edge to his voice now which was new to Henderson.

"I know a dozen men who'd vouch for Rupert," he continued angrily, "and I'd be the first one into the witness box."

The declaration was a shade over the top and he had a feeling that Goodman wouldn't have been anything like so forthcoming if there had been the slightest chance he would be called on to testify. His posthumous testimony was not entirely valueless however.

"Thanks," said Henderson.

"For what?"

"You've just erased a big question mark against Beardsley. Soon as I'm discharged, I'll phone the client's solicitors and tell them I'm calling it a day."

"You're going home?"

"There's no point wasting any more time out here."

Goodman did not voice his relief, nor did he show it, but the impression remained long after they'd said goodbye that he was secretly pleased. It was also a fact that an hour later, the hospital authorities told Henderson they proposed to discharge him forthwith if that was convenient.

*   *   *

Lal did not like the escort who had replaced Keith Royles. The lecturer from Brunel University might be an expert in the field of anthropology but he was no gentleman. He was totally unreasonable, had an unpleasant manner and treated him like dirt. There was really no call for the Englishman to come the high hat when all he had done was suggest one minor amendment to the tour programme.

"I don't understand your objections," Lal said obstinately. "I should have thought our travelling companions would have welcomed my suggestion with open arms. They had had a long and tiring morning, not all the electric fans on the bus were working properly, and you must have observed how weary some of the older members of the party had become after walking round the deserted palace at Fatehpur Sikri. This is a luxury hotel and all the rooms are air-conditioned; they won't thank you if we drag them off to see the Taj Mahal at sunset when the temperature will still be eighty degrees in the shade."

Lal paused, hoping for some kind of reaction which would tell him that his argument had not fallen on deaf ears, but the university lecturer merely gazed at him contemptuously.

"Let us show them the Taj Mahal by moonlight instead," he said, pressing on. "Now that really is a sight worth seeing. We could leave the hotel after they have had dinner – say at nine p.m. when it will be much cooler."

"What's in it for you, Mr Lal?" the lecturer said curtly.

"Nothing. I simply wish to see my friend, Mr Henderson, who is in hospital."

"We'll leave for the Taj Mahal at five."

"Then I regret that you'll have to manage without me."

"What?"

"I just told you, I'm going to see my friend."

Lal turned his back on the university lecturer and walked out of the hotel. It occurred to him that he was also walking out of a job.

*   *   *

Only the name of the street where the Telegraph Office was located had been changed since the departure of the British, otherwise the building itself was still the same sun-bleached miniature version of a Covent Garden warehouse. Having bribed the cab driver to wait for him, Henderson walked into the gloomy hall, tagged on to the queue which had formed opposite the one window that was open and patiently waited his turn to book a phone call to the UK.

Agra was five hours ahead of Greenwich Mean Time and it was now almost ten a.m. in London. It was therefore pointless ringing the Wagnalls in Hampstead on the offchance of catching Alexandra Drummond before she left for the office. Delving into his pocket notebook, he looked up Draycott and Draycott. The clerk who made a note of the number he wanted triumphantly announced that there was at least a fifteen-minute delay on all calls to London and instructed him to sit down on the wooden bench to the right of the entrance until he was paged to the phone. A half hour later, the same clerk called out his name and pointed to the middle booth of three.

The switchboard operator at Draycott and Draycott who took the incoming call was polite, cheerful and eager to appear helpful. Unfortunately, she put him through to one of the secretaries and he spent several frustrating minutes explaining who he was and why he wanted to speak to Mr Young before the solicitor finally came on the line.

"Good morning, Mr Henderson," Young said. "I trust you are fully recovered?"

"You got my letter then?"

"It arrived the day before yesterday."

The airmail letter had taken a week to get there which made Henderson wonder if the military censors had opened and read it first.

"There was a small paragraph about the ambush in *The Times*," Young continued, "but we'd no idea the communal disturbances had spread to Agra."

"We?"

"Well, naturally I told Miss Drummond that you were in hospital. She was very concerned and wanted to send a telegram urging you to come home as soon as you were fit to travel."

"I don't need much encouragement." Henderson paused, then told Young what little he'd learned from the manager of Indus Tours, the British High Commission and Lal. It didn't add up to much and he said so, loud and clear. "I could go to Etawah but frankly I think it would be a waste of time and money. Even if I succeeded in tracing the Sikh taxi driver, I don't believe he can tell me anything I don't already know. Colonel Beardsley was certainly being secretive about something but as far as milking the Trust Fund goes, I'm sure he's as pure as the driven snow."

"I fancy Miss Drummond will be relieved to hear it."

"So I'm coming home."

"When do you expect to be back in London, Mr Henderson?"

"Tomorrow, if I'm lucky. It really depends on how soon I can get a seat on a plane."

"Quite. Is there anything else I can tell Miss Drummond?"

"No, I think that's about it for now."

Henderson said goodbye, replaced the phone and backed out of the airless booth; as he turned about, he almost bumped into Lal.

"Ah, Mr Henderson." The guide beamed with pleasure and pumped his hand enthusiastically. "They told me I would find you here."

"Who's they?"

"The military authorities at the hospital. I could not let you go without saying goodbye and thanking you from the bottom of my heart. I shall always be in your debt."

"Why? I haven't done anything."

"How like an Englishman to be so modest." Lal released his hand and wagged a disapproving finger. "But I cannot allow you to leave my country without partaking of my hospitality. If it had not been for your intervention, the police would have charged me with stealing those wretched traveller's cheques."

"I think you'll find that is due to Mr Chatterjee, not me."

"Then to cap it all, you make me the hero of the hour. My picture has been in all the newspapers and no end of reporters have interviewed me wanting to know why I saved the Sikh woman at the risk of my own life . . ."

Henderson smiled and edged towards the counter to pay for the call.

"I told them I was only following your fine example, but they wouldn't listen to me. I feel very bad about it."

"You shouldn't," Henderson told him. "I couldn't have managed without you."

In the aftermath of the riot, the politicians had wanted a folk hero people in both communities could look up to and Lal had filled the bill. 'Hindu man saves Sikh woman from mob' made the kind of headline any PR man would give a month's pay for.

"I thought you were angry with me, Mr Henderson."

"What on earth gave you that idea?"

"The hospital authorities. Every time I asked after your health, they said you refused to see me. I wouldn't have known you'd been discharged if one of the sweepers hadn't told me when I went there this afternoon. I had to bribe the orderly room Babu to find out where you'd gone."

Henderson pocketed the change from a hundred rupees. "Well, I'm glad you found me. I wouldn't want to have left with you thinking all was not well between us."

"I am so relieved we are still friends," Lal said and screwed up his eyes as though delighted by the news. "May one ask if you are going via Etawah on your way back to the UK?"

"No, it would be a wasted journey."

Any number of people had made that clear to him. In fact, his imminent departure from India was being greeted by the authorities with something approaching a collective sigh of relief. The Indian Army had certainly done their bit to speed him on his way; whether or not the Brigadier commanding Agra garrison had feared his career would go down the sink if he decided to sue the Indian government for damages, he did not know, but whatever the reason, the Army could hardly have done more for him. Free medical treatment, and no question of him having to pay for the room he'd never occupied at the Taj View; there had been no limit to their kindness, they'd even collected his baggage from the hotel to save him the trouble.

"Your task is finished then?" Lal said.

"Yes. Colonel Beardsley was evidently a very popular man; everyone seemed to like him and I think that will be of some comfort to his family."

"Mr Royles did not get on with him. He said Colonel Beardsley was a liar, but of course I knew he was wrong. In my opinion it was simply a case of mistaken identity."

Keith Royles, the Indus Tours escort who'd left the company and returned to England after receiving an urgent telegram from home. Some people were simply incompatible and perhaps he and Beardsley had taken an instant dislike to one another. But it seemed there was more to it than that.

"Mistaken identity?" Henderson repeated.

"Mr Royles used to do the North West Frontier – Lahore, Peshawar and Rawalpindi. He told me that was where he'd seen the Colonel before but for some reason Colonel Beardsley had denied it most vehemently."

"When was this?"

"Two years ago."

Beardsley was an enigma. First, he had hired Lal as an interpreter when he was already fluent in Hindi; then he hadn't wanted anyone to know he had been in Pakistan. The question was – why?

Henderson glanced at his wristwatch; he had less than half an hour to catch the 1640 to Delhi but his curiosity had been aroused and there were other trains. "Is there some place we can go for a quiet chat?" he asked.

"The Telegraph Club," Lal said. "I am an honorary member and the barman is a great friend of mine."

CHAPTER IX

HENDERSON PASSED through Customs, made his way to the bank of pay-phones in the concourse of Terminal 4 and rang the Airways parking lot. The girl who took the call directed him to the pick-up point beyond the cab rank where he was collected by a minibus which arrived less than fifteen minutes later. It was the only part of his return journey from India that hadn't been a foul-up.

The farewell drink with Lal had developed into a dinner en famille at 29 Telegraph Road which had lasted until the small hours and had resulted in him missing the last train to Delhi. Lal had insisted he stay the night and had roused him in plenty of time to catch the Up Mail departing at 0700 hours but the taxi his hosts had ordered had arrived late and had then broken down on the way to the station. The run of bad luck had continued in Delhi; the best any airline could do was offer him a standby seat and unusually heavy bookings had led to an enforced twenty-four-hour stopover.

Henderson wrote a cheque for the parking fee, dumped his suitcase in the back of the Ford Escort and drove out of the compound. At the first intersection on the dual carriageway, he made a U-turn and headed into London. Before finally leaving Delhi, he'd called his sister, Judith, to warn her not to expect him much before six p.m. which gave him roughly nine hours to locate Royles. Although Lal's story concerning the row Beardsley was supposed to have had with the courier was probably a gross exaggeration, he reckoned it was worth looking into. Leaving the Escort in the underground garage at Hyde Park, Henderson took a cab to the head office of Indus Tours in Regent Street.

The Personnel Manager was a Mr Wynford Evans, a small, earnest-looking man with a lilting Welsh accent whose judicious manner suggested he was a frustrated would-be lawyer.

First impressions were often misleading, but in this instance they were reinforced for Henderson by the way he proceeded to cross-examine him.

"You say Mr Jervis advised you to see me?"

Henderson nodded. "The local office didn't have a forwarding address but Jervis said you would have one because Royles would have got in touch about his severance pay, National Insurance contributions and so on."

"Mr Jervis should also have told you that it is not company policy to disclose the home address of former employees to unauthorised persons." Evans allowed himself a brief smile. "Of course, if you were a police officer it would be a different matter."

"What I have to discuss with Mr Royles could eventually involve the police."

"Really?" Evans pursed his lips while he wrestled with the problem, then suddenly announced his decision. Brevity was not one of his strong suits. "Well, I'm afraid that until the police make their interests known, I'm not prepared to bend the rules. It would be unethical."

"Perhaps I should explain the background to this inquiry," Henderson said patiently. "Have you ever heard of a charitable organisation called The Finlayson Trust?"

"No, I can't say I have."

"Neither had I three weeks ago. The fund was established to promote Anglo-Indian relations with grants in aid for educational purposes. My client has discovered that Colonel Beardsley, who was one of the trustees, was siphoning off fifteen thousand a year. We're both sure he was using the money to buy gold illicitly and smuggling it out of India in the diplomatic bag."

"I don't see what this has to do with Keith Royles," Evans observed.

"Beardsley was frightened of being blackmailed so he used him as a middle man to buy the gold from the dealers. I imagine he paid Royles a commission."

"Can you prove this?"

"I think so." Henderson used his imagination to embroider his story. "There was a tiff. I can't say what caused it; maybe Royles was dissatisfied with the commission he was receiving or perhaps it suddenly dawned on him that he was working for a crook, but whatever the reason, Beardsley took off for Etawah in a huff. You may have heard that he wanted to visit a former comrade in arms who was seriously ill in hospital but the Indian authorities have been unable to trace the mysterious Jemadar Rav. Personally, I think he was hoping to find himself a new middle man.''

In an effort to prise some information out of Evans, he had effectively libelled a dead man. The only justification for the smear was the fact that the Welshman looked as if he was now ready to believe him.

"Beardsley was in India three or four times a year on behalf of the Trust,'' Henderson continued remorselessly. "He may only have travelled with Indus Tours on one occasion but he always made a point of seeing Royles before he left.''

"What do you intend to do about Keith?'' Evans grimaced as though just pronouncing the name left a nasty taste in his mouth.

"Have a quiet chat with him. If he's prepared to make a statement to the effect that he was acting on behalf of Beardsley, the Trust will instruct their solicitors to file a claim on the Colonel's estate.'' Henderson could see that Evans was wavering and pressed on. "We don't want to drag the police in if it can be avoided – I imagine you feel the same?''

Evans got to his feet and walked over to a three-drawer filing cabinet in the far corner of the office. Opening the centre drawer, he took out a slim green folder and returned to the desk. It didn't take him long to come up with the information Henderson wanted.

"The last address we have for Mr Royles is 23 Belmont Court, Grove Street, Vauxhall, SE11.'' He looked up from the folder. "Have you got a car, Mr Henderson?''

"Not with me.''

"Then your best bet is to take the Bakerloo line from Piccadilly Circus, then catch a suburban train from Waterloo. I understand Grove Street is only a few minutes' walk from Vauxhall station.''

"Thanks for the tip,'' said Henderson.

*   *   *

Grove Street was roughly halfway between Vauxhall and Queens Road, Battersea. Anyone who took a mere five minutes to get there from the station had to be a serious contender for an Olympic gold medal. One of four apartment blocks on a housing estate, Belmont Court was easy enough to find given the right directions. These Henderson eventually got from a copy of the *London Street Finder* purchased from a newsagent just short of Grove Street.

Number 23 Belmont Court was on the fifth floor midway between the external staircase at either end of the building. The front door was secured with a padlock and hasp and the side window had been boarded up. From the splintered woodwork around the keyhole, it was evident that someone had used a sledgehammer to break into the flat.

Henderson side-stepped to his right and rang the bell next door. The woman who answered it only opened the door as far as the security chain would allow. She was in her sixties, had blue-rinsed grey hair, a thin rather pinched face and a nervous manner. She seemed a little less apprehensive when he produced a laminated card bearing the logo of the Gold Seal Inquiry Agency above a head and shoulders photograph of himself.

"Are you from the Council?" she asked.

"No, I'm making inquiries about one of your neighbours – a Mr Keith Royles."

"Oh, you're a policeman . . .?"

"Well, I suppose I'm a detective of sorts," Henderson said.

"And you want to know about the ruckus next door?"

"What else?"

"You'd better come in then." She slipped the chain, opened the door and flattened herself against the wall so that he could step past her into the narrow hallway. "We'll use the sitting room at the back, it's the end door on your right."

The sitting room was no more than twelve by nine. Two over-stuffed armchairs, a footstool and a twenty-six-inch television made it seem even smaller. The windowledge was crowded with bric-à-brac and ornaments from a variety of seaside resorts. So too was the shelf above the radiator.

"Souvenirs – my late husband collected them. He liked to

107

have a memento of where we'd been on holiday. Didn't hold with going to Spain and places like that."

"Really?"

"My name's Vi Matthews. What did you say yours was?"

"Henderson, Jack Henderson."

"Never wanted to go abroad," Vi continued. "Said he wanted to see his own country first. We started at Walton-on-the-Naze in Essex; didn't get any farther than Polperro in Cornwall . . ."

"About the rumpus at number 23," Henderson reminded her. "You want to tell me what happened, Vi?"

"I didn't see a lot, did I? Soon as I heard them skinheads charging down the landing I knew there was going to be trouble so I locked and bolted my front door."

"When was this?"

"Yesterday evening around five thirty. They weren't fooling around, those skinheads – tyre levers, hammers – you name it, they had it. I was really scared I can tell you." Vi broke off to tell Henderson to make himself comfortable, then found a packet of cigarettes in the handbag by her chair and lit one. "Anyway, next thing I heard was a bloody great bang as they smashed the door in and shortly after that Charlie began screaming . . ."

"Who's Charlie?"

"Didn't that young copper who was here last night tell you anything?"

"I like to get the facts first hand," Henderson told her.

"Charlie is Charlie Freeman; he's a chef, works in some restaurant up the West End. Had a day off yesterday, didn't he?"

Henderson smiled. Vi had the Eastender's habit of turning practically every statement into a question as though the listener was already aware of the facts and was therefore in a position to confirm them.

"I don't know," he said gently, "you're supposed to be telling me."

"Well he did, and that was his bad luck because they did him over good and proper, broke his arms, cracked his ribs with their boots and left his face looking like a raw hamburger – or so that young constable told me – but of course you'd know all about that."

"Yes. Any idea why they attacked Charlie?"

"I think they were really after that other fella . . ."

"Royles?"

"That's him. Some people round here think Charlie is a queer but he's the one who's a bit gay if you ask me."

If she was right and Royles was a homosexual, it might explain Beardsley's antipathy towards him, the sort of man who believed all queers deserved a good horse-whipping.

"Charlie's a bit of a fitness fanatic," Vi continued. "Something of an amateur boxer too, but he was crying like a baby when they'd finished with him."

The assault had occurred in broad daylight and at a time when most of the neighbours would have been at home. But it seemed no one had lifted a finger to help Freeman until it was all over.

"Didn't anyone think of ringing 999?" Henderson asked.

"The police? You've got to be joking. The only time we see you lot round here is when you're turning over somebody's flat. There are a couple of nasty street gangs on this estate but you coppers don't want to know, do you? I don't go out nights any more, I've been mugged that often."

A climate of fear pervaded the whole estate. Henderson felt it as he walked through the housing complex. Every street light had been broken, no wall had escaped the attention of the graffiti artists with their aerosol spray cans and judging by the number of wrecks he'd seen, any vehicle which was left unattended for any length of time was automatically vandalised. Nearing Belmont Court, he had to step off the pavement to avoid three skinheads and even the ten to twelve-year-olds, who were kicking a football around on what passed for a playing field, had looked menacing.

"I never could understand why Charlie was so friendly with that fella Royles, always offering to put him up between trips abroad. That boy was worth two of him."

It transpired that Violet Matthews had known Charlie for the best part of four years and clearly had a soft spot for him. He was, Henderson gathered, the only person on the estate who had volunteered to do her shopping when for several weeks she had been too frightened to leave the flat after the last time she had been mugged.

"Do you have any idea where Mr Royles might have got to, Vi?"

"Search me. All I know is he arrived home a good twenty minutes after they had carted Charlie off to Lambeth Hospital. He took one look at what them skinheads had done to the flat and stayed just long enough to pack his bags and get the place boarded up."

Henderson decided he had stretched his luck about as far as it would go. Vi had told him all she knew about Royles and if he asked her any more questions she would begin to wonder why the police were more interested in him than the victim of the assault.

"You've been a great help, Vi," he told her and started moving towards the door. "I wish I could say the same for your neighbours."

The football match was still in progress when he left Belmont Court but there was no sign of the skinheads he'd encountered earlier on. All the same, Henderson remained on edge until he reached the comparative safety of the Wandsworth Road.

*   *   *

The police constable drew a chair up to the bedside and sat down. Yesterday evening he had been on patrol in Wandsworth Road and had responded to the 999 call from Belmont Court. By the time he had arrived at number 23, the assailants had been long gone and Freeman had been on his way to hospital. The fact that the ambulance men had beaten him to it had been an early indication of the kind of help he could expect to receive from the neighbours. There were a large number of black and Asian families living on the estate; given their antipathy towards the police, he had known he could expect little assistance from them, but the hostility he had encountered from the white residents had surprised him.

None of the neighbours on the fifth floor of Belmont Court had seen the men who'd attacked Freeman and it had rapidly become evident that the police would never have known about the incident had the ambulance men not reported it. He wondered if Freeman would prove equally uncooperative. Although in uniform, the constable produced his warrant card and introduced himself. In the usual formal language, he then informed Freeman that he was making inquiries about an incident at Belmont Court which had occurred the previous evening.

"I don't see how I can help you," Freeman said and grimaced in pain. "It all happened so bloody fast, I didn't get a good look at their faces."

"And of course they were wearing nylon stocking masks."

"How did you guess?"

"Suppose we start at the beginning with your full name, home address, date and place of birth?" The police constable opened his notebook at the page he wanted, then said, "According to the hospital authorities, you are Charles Albert Freeman, born in Houndsditch on 17th February, 1964 and currently residing at 23 Belmont Court. Are those details correct?"

"Yeah."

"All right, Mr Freeman, now tell me in your own words exactly what happened."

"There's not a lot I can tell you. I was sitting at home watching TV when I heard this bloody great bang. Next thing I know, three maybe four blokes are kicking the shit out of me."

"Why?"

"You must have heard it from the neighbours – they're always bad-mouthing somebody."

"The woman next door says these men beat you up because they don't like gays."

"She's got it all wrong; they were after my lodger, Keith Royles. He's gay."

"But you're not?"

"Course not." Freeman grunted and caught his breath. The police constable studied his notebook. Freeman was never going to admit that he was a homo and pressing him on the subject would only be a waste of time and effort. "So why did they take it out on you instead of Royles?" he asked.

"As a warning to Keith. They were counting on him to do a bunk as soon as he learned what had happened to me."

"You could be right."

"You were still on the premises when Keith came home, weren't you?" Freeman asked.

"Yes."

"I bet he was shit scared?"

"He certainly had the wind up. Stayed just long enough to pack a bag and wouldn't even tell me where he was going."

"That's Keith," Freeman said with morose satisfaction.

"What I want from you, Charlie, is a description of your assailants. And don't give me any rubbish about nylon stockings obscuring their faces because I'm not going to believe it."

"I don't give a fuck what you believe." Freeman paused to give himself time to think, then said, "I'll tell you this, they were all bigger than me. Two were about my age, say twenty-two to twenty-four but the one who put the boot in was a bit older and had gingerish hair."

Freeman had been on the receiving end of a really good stomping; one eye had been closed to a slit and his face was grossly swollen and bruised, but he wasn't going to lift a finger to help the police. It was a typical example of the kind of ghetto loyalty which existed within any inner city.

"You mentioned a fourth man," the police constable said patiently.

"Yeah, he was there as a look-out."

"Same height, same build, same colour as the other three?"

"No, he was a fucking Paki," Freeman said with a flash of hatred that caused him to groan in agony.

*   *   *

Henderson surrendered the return half of his ticket at the gate on platform 4, turned left outside the barrier and walked through the concourse towards the footbridge at the far end of Waterloo Station which led to the Shell Centre. Opposite the subway exit to York Road, he stopped by the bank of pay-phones and looked for one which still operated on a coin box. Feeding twenty-five pence into the slot, he punched out the area code and subscriber's number for Draycott and Draycott. When the girl on the switchboard answered, he asked her to connect him with Mr Young.

"It's me again," he said. "Jack Henderson. I'm back in England."

"I trust you had a pleasant journey?"

"I slept most of the way."

"Good," Young said automatically and immediately changed the subject. "I passed your message to Miss Drummond after you telephoned on Tuesday and she seemed happy enough at the outcome of your investigation. I assume you will be submitting a written report and itemised account of your expenses in due course?"

"I could let you have an interim statement."

"But I understood you'd completed your inquiries?" Young said puzzled.

"I may have been a little premature in saying that. There have been certain developments in the last forty-eight hours which I think Miss Drummond should know about."

"I see."

A faint rustle in the background told Henderson that the solicitor was looking for a blank sheet of paper.

"If you'd care to give me the details," Young continued, "I'll see she gets the information as soon as possible."

"No, I want our client to hear it from me in person." He opened his copy of Nicholson's *Street Finder* at the appropriate page, then said, "You tell Miss Drummond to meet me in Lincoln's Inn Fields at the top of Serle Street at one fifteen."

"But she may have a prior engagement."

"Then she'd be well advised to break it because if there's still no sign of her at two o'clock, I'll be knocking on the door of the Finlayson Trust."

"I don't think that would be very wise . . ."

"Never mind the legal opinion," Henderson said tersely, "just deliver the message."

CHAPTER X

EVEN AT a distance when it was impossible to distinguish her features, there was no mistaking Alexandra Drummond. Some women slouched, others splayed their feet outwards or walked pigeon-toed, but she strode up Serle Street as though she owned it. The swagger owed something to the stylish outfit she was wearing, a pair of well-cut khaki-coloured slacks and matching blouson jacket which had been left unbuttoned to reveal a cotton sweater. As she started across the road, Henderson got up from the park bench and went forward to greet her.

"Good afternoon, Miss Drummond," he said politely, "and thank you for giving up part of your lunch hour to meet me."

"It's my pleasure, or at least I hope it is." An engaging smile appeared. "Anyway, you wouldn't have got in touch with Mr Young if it wasn't important," she said and slowly walked on in the direction of High Holborn.

Henderson fell into step beside her. "Did you know Beardsley was a Queen's Messenger?" he asked.

"Yes, it was hardly a State Secret."

"What about the four apartments the Finlayson Trust owns in Stanhope Square? Are they a State Secret?"

"I don't know who you've been talking to," Alexandra said calmly, "but your information is out of date. Those flats were sold to the Foreign Office sixteen years ago around the time when the Shiraj Development moved into the property market."

Alexandra must have been roughly twelve years old then but Henderson didn't bother to ask her how she knew; no doubt she'd have a plausible explanation for that too. But there was another aspect that puzzled him.

"A man called Charlesworth who's the liaison officer for

the Development Corporation believes the apartments still belong to the Trust."

"It probably suits the Foreign Office to foster that impression. After all, they don't want the IRA targeting any of the properties."

"Why didn't you tell me all this before now?"

"Because it never crossed my mind to do so. For one thing, why would Rupert's occupation be of any interest to you?"

"He was frequently in India on Foreign Office business," said Henderson. "If he was on the take, he might have claimed the cost of his air fare from the Trust when Her Majesty's Government had already paid for it."

"I'm sure he would never have stooped to that. Rupert always told us when he was going to India on official duty and asked if there was anything we'd like him to do while he was out there."

"And that makes him an honest man in your book?"

"If I'd not had doubts, I wouldn't have come to you, would I, Mr Henderson?"

"I guess not. I had a long talk with Lal after I'd telephoned Mr Young. He said that Keith Royles, the tour representative in charge of Beardsley's group, had told him the Colonel was a bloody liar. It seems Royles had seen him before when he was escorting tourists round the North West Frontier, but when he tackled him about it, Beardsley vehemently denied he'd ever been in Pakistan."

"Could it have been a case of mistaken identity?"

"Apparently Royles was absolutely convinced it wasn't. It's conceivable Beardsley denied being in Rawalpindi because he sensed Royles was a homosexual and was determined to have nothing to do with him."

"That would be Rupert all right." Alexandra frowned, then said, "Rawalpindi is where they are supposed to have run across one another before?"

"More or less. It seems Royles was dining at the Imperial Hotel and Beardsley was across the room from him at a corner table. There was a Pakistani with him, a plump middle-aged man and quite short; he looked very prosperous and departed in a chauffeur-driven Cadillac."

"Did Lal give you his name?"

"I'm not sure Royles knew who he was; at any rate, he never told Lal."

"I see."

Alexandra walked on, apparently deep in thought. Henderson had a feeling that she had never been entirely straight with him starting right from the day she had walked into his office, something he would never have tolerated from any other client. He couldn't begin to explain why Alexandra Drummond should be the exception. There was no special relationship, nor had she ever given him any cause to think there could be one; he only knew that he was prepared to go out of his way to please her. There had been other attractive women in his life but there was an aura about her which he had never experienced with Linda when she was alive. The fact that he could bring himself to compare the two women without feeling a tinge of guilt surprised him.

"Royles got a telegram," Henderson continued. "I reckon it was from his boyfriend and it probably said something like 'Come home, all is forgiven'. Anyway, he left India shortly after Beardsley disappeared. He's no longer with Indus Tours but they were able to give me his address. I went there to have a quiet chat with him but a bunch of skinheads had beaten me to it. Royles wasn't at home when they called so they put his boyfriend in hospital which was their way of telling him that he wasn't exactly welcome on the housing estate. He got the message all right and took off like a scalded cat."

"Can you find him again?"

"I could try, if you want me to."

"If it's a question of money . . . ?"

"It isn't. Your retainer is still good; time spent in hospital doesn't count."

"Oh, I can't have that, you wouldn't have been injured if you hadn't been looking for that Sikh taxi driver."

"It's all right; I'm insured against loss of earnings." Henderson glanced sideways at her. "Does the Trust operate in Pakistan?" he asked.

"No, our work is confined to what used to be known as the United Provinces."

"Would the Foreign Office have used Beardsley on some sort of hush-hush job in Pakistan?"

"Rupert – a spy?" Alexandra laughed. "He was probably the last man on earth they'd dream of using. As a real life caricature of the ex-Indian Army Colonel, Rupert was far too conspicuous for any undercover work."

The passport photograph of Beardsley bore that out and made him look slightly ridiculous. However, Lal had said nothing to his detriment and, more importantly, neither had Goodman. It left Henderson with a gut feeling that Alexandra had gone over the top in dismissing the possibility and he wondered at her motive.

"How will you trace Royles?" she asked.

"I think he's only got one string to his bow; since he's no longer with Indus Tours, chances are he's gone to some other travel agency. Whoever they are, they'll have contacted his former employer to find out what sort of man they're hiring."

From Evans, he would also try to obtain the name and address of any next-of-kin Royles may have nominated. If the courier was running scared, he would be looking for a safe bolthole and a relative might well provide one.

"You will let me know how the inquiry is progressing from time to time?"

"Naturally. Do I continue to get in touch with you through Mr Young?"

"That would be best," Alexandra said.

"And when his office is closed?" Henderson persisted.

"I'm still camping out with the Wagnalls; the exchange of contracts on the new flat is taking longer than I expected." She glanced at her wristwatch and frowned. The gesture was a shade too obvious and he guessed what was happening next. "I ought to be getting back to the office," she said, "the finance committee is meeting at two forty-five."

It was a transparently thin excuse but Henderson wanted to believe it and he found himself hanging on to her outstretched hand longer than was necessary as they parted company. He watched her walk away until she was no longer in sight, then made his way across town to the head office of Indus Tours in Regent Street.

Evans wasn't best pleased to see him again but the frigid atmosphere rapidly thawed after he told the Welshman about the incident at Belmont Court. Given his eagerness to protect the tour company from any unfavourable publicity, Henderson experienced little difficulty in obtaining a sight of the company file on Royles.

The top enclosure was a letter to the Discount Travel Agency in Tottenham Court Road confirming that Royles had been a model employee whom the company had been sorry to lose. Borrowing the phone with Evans' permission, Henderson called the travel agency and spoke to the manager who confirmed that Royles was a member of his sales staff. The manager also told him that he hadn't turned up for work that morning.

Free life insurance was one of the perks enjoyed by employees of Indus Tours. In the event of his death, Royles had nominated his paternal aunt, Patricia Royles of Look-Out Cottage, Warfleet Creek, Dartmouth as his sole beneficiary. Directory Enquiries gave Henderson her phone number but there was no reply when he rang the house.

*   *   *

Royles got off the bus in the centre of Dartmouth and made his way along the South Embankment towards Bayards Cove and the cottage at Warfleet Creek where he had spent the greater part of his childhood with his aunt. He could not remember a time when Look-Out Cottage had not been his home and he had always turned to Pat whenever a crisis had arisen. She was his bed-rock, and after what had happened at Belmont Court yesterday evening, it was only natural that he should run to her.

The nightmare had started yesterday evening shortly before five o'clock when someone posing as a client had rung the Discount Travel Agency and asked for him by name. In a few terse sentences, the caller had told Royles what he thought of queers and had then described what his friends would do to him if he stayed in London. About forty minutes later when everyone else with the exception of Mr Latif, the office manager, had gone home, the same man had telephoned again, this time to let him hear poor Charlie screaming.

He had been very lucky. If Mr Latif hadn't asked him to check that all the bookings for the day had been confirmed, he would have got the same treatment. By the time he'd arrived home, Charlie had already been carted off to hospital and the neighbours had lost interest, assuming they'd shown any in the first place. Even the solitary police constable who'd responded to the anonymous 999 call which he himself had made from the Discount Agency would have departed had the janitor been quicker at securing the front door to the flat with a padlock and hasp. The officer had wanted to know where he would be spending the night and had been somewhat put out when he'd refused to give an address and phone number.

The constable had thought he was being cagey but in truth he hadn't planned that far ahead. His one idea had been to pack a suitcase and get the hell out of Belmont Court in the shortest possible time. With just twenty pounds in his wallet and a handful of loose change, he'd had to spend the night at the YMCA near the British Museum until the cashpoints opened in the morning. Then he'd drawn a hundred, which had almost cleaned him out, and caught the Plymouth train from Paddington. Alighting at Totnes, he had completed the rest of the journey by bus.

Royles opened the gate in the stone wall and went on down the long flight of wooden steps which led to the cottage below. One of half a dozen houses arranged in a half moon around Warfleet Creek, Look-Out Cottage was the only one occupied all the year round. For as long as he could remember, Pat had had nothing but contempt for the visitors, completely ignoring the fact that her income was derived from the exorbitant rents she charged on two holiday homes across the River Dart in Kingswear. No matter what they did, the summer people were always in the wrong. When he'd telephoned her last night to ask if he could spend a few days at the cottage, she had blamed their fickle ways rather than the recession for the poor season.

Royles grounded his suitcase inside the porch and pressed the bell. Only someone standing a few feet away could have heard the low buzz and he guessed that Pat had been keeping an eye out for him from one of the front rooms.

"Hello, Pat," he said and kissed her on the cheek. "You look marvellous."

It was no exaggeration. She was wearing a man's shirt with a dark blue cravat, tapered trousers which emphasised her slim legs and a pair of low-heeled court shoes. There was a narrow leather belt around her waist and the hair style was definitely boyish. Looking at her unlined face, no one would guess that she was sixty-two.

"I wish I could say the same for you," Pat told him. "If those shadows under your eyes are anything to go by, you've been having far too many late nights."

"Pressure of work."

"So you said on the phone last night."

"I quit my job, Pat; it was either that or a nervous breakdown."

"I thought you liked being with Indus Tours?"

"We parted company a few weeks ago." He left his suitcase in the hall and followed her into the sitting-room. "I was head-hunted by Latif's Discount Travel Agency and they made me an offer I couldn't refuse."

He had concocted the outline of his story before phoning Pat; the embellishments had been added on the journey down from London when he'd mentally prepared himself for the questions she was bound to ask. "I should have known better."

"Money isn't everything, Keith."

"You're so right."

"You're not in trouble with the police, are you?"

Royles told himself there was no way the police or anyone else could have traced him to Dartmouth. Then he recalled Charlie screaming in the background when the man had called him at the office and his stomach suddenly took a nose dive. If Charlie had told them where he worked, what else had they got from him?

"What on earth gave you that idea?" he asked weakly.

"Because I never hear from you these days unless you're in some kind of trouble. I didn't even know you were back in this country until you phoned last night."

"I haven't done anything to be ashamed of. The Discount Agency refused to accept my resignation and they kept on at me to withdraw it. I suppose I should be flattered but the fact is I can't take any more harassment from them."

He wondered if Pat believed him; usually, he could tell what she was thinking but for once her face gave nothing away.

"They haven't been on to you, have they?"

"Of course they haven't."

The more Royles thought about it, the more he was convinced he could forget the skinheads who'd beaten Charlie up. They would lose interest as soon as they learned from the neighbours that he'd left the housing estate. But the police might want a statement from him and Indus Tours had Pat's address on their records.

"No one's telephoned to ask if I'm staying with you?"

"If they did, they must have rung while I was out shopping."

Royles almost sighed out loud; the police weren't after him and that meant the worst was over.

*　　*　　*

Henderson turned into Montgomery Close and pulled up outside number 17. He'd told Judith not to expect him before six but after his abortive attempt to contact Miss Royles, there'd seemed little point in staying on in town. By leaving earlier, he'd also made it back to Stanmore before the evening rush hour began. Collecting his suitcase from the boot, he locked the car, walked up the front path and rang the bell. Judith was at home, her battered old Mini was in the drive, but he had to ring the bell again and keep his finger on the button for some time before she answered the door.

"I thought you were a Jehovah's Witness," Judith said apologetically, then kissed him.

"Do I look like one?"

"No, but I heard they were in the neighbourhood and I wasn't expecting you for a while yet."

"I'm sorry." He stepped inside the hall. "I should have let you know I was going to be early."

"I'm not complaining, Jack. I'm just glad to see you again." She cocked her head to one side. "What happened to the sun tan?"

"You don't get one in hospital."

"I don't know what I'm going to do about you. Someone's always knocking you about. When are you going to get yourself a proper job?"

121

"When are you going to put your degree to work?" he countered.

"Sooner than you may think. You're in the same room as before – okay?"

"Right."

"Oh, by the way, your secretary, Mrs Luckwell, telephoned this afternoon and left a message asking you to call her back." Judith started towards the kitchen. "I don't know what it's about but she insisted on giving me her home number in case you were late. Look on the hall table, you'll find it written down on the back of an old envelope."

Henderson thanked her, went on upstairs to the guest room and dumped his suitcase, then returned to the hall. He had called Sheila Luckwell from Delhi yesterday afternoon to let her know when he would be back and she had told him there was nothing so urgent at the office that it couldn't wait. Evidently something important had cropped up since then. He glanced at his wristwatch, decided that Sheila would have left the office by now and rang her home in Gedling. The slimline warbled twice only before she answered it.

"Hi, Sheila," he said. "I got your message."

"Oh, good. Hang on a moment while I get my notes the right way up." He heard a rustling noise, then Sheila said, "You've got another client. Dudley Spencer called this afternoon after receiving a letter from Colonel Beardsley's solicitors. Apparently his brother-in-law was a good deal wealthier than he'd supposed. His sister had always led him to believe that Beardsley had spent most of her money but evidently that couldn't have been the case."

"How much did he leave?" Henderson asked.

"A cool three hundred and fifty thousand pounds – bonds, stocks, shares, building societies – he was into them all."

With the way the property market was going through the ceiling, a lot of people could put that kind of money together if they were prepared to sell up and move out of London. But Beardsley hadn't been a property owner.

"The thing that angers Mr Spencer is that, apart from a number of small bequests totalling less than a thousand, Colonel Beardsley left all his money to a Mrs Katherine Pascal. Mr Spencer intends to contest the will and wants you to find out all you can about the lady. He's willing to put up a four-figure retainer."

"Fine. Tell him I'm returning to Nottingham tomorrow and will phone as soon as I'm back in town."

"Detective Sergeant Preston would also like to hear from you. He said there'd been an interesting development regarding the break-in you'd reported three weeks ago."

"What about the post-mortem on Prince? Has he heard from the vet?"

"Yes." A pause, then, "I'm afraid Prince had a heart condition and died from a massive coronary induced by a capsule of pentathol. The vet thinks it was an accidental overdose."

What difference did it make even if it was an accident? The intruder had still killed Linda's dog and that was something to be taken into account if ever he caught up with the bastard.

Thanking Sheila, he put the phone down and went through to the kitchen. Judith was standing at the sink contemplating the garden while she peeled the potatoes for dinner, her hands protected by a pair of rubber gloves.

"Would you like me to take over?" he asked.

"I'm almost finished. You can pour me a glass of sherry though. There's a bottle in the cupboard above the fridge, the glasses are on the shelf below. Help yourself to a whisky while you're at it."

"Thanks. When did Lorna and David break up?"

"They came home from school the day after you left for India."

"So where are they then?"

"Out for the day with some friends in Wavell Avenue. Did you get through to Mrs Luckwell?"

"Yes."

"She sounds very nice."

Henderson smiled. It was Judith's ambition to see him married and settled down. Sometimes she was less than subtle about it.

"Sheila Luckwell is forty-two; she has two kids and a roly-poly husband who adores her."

"I see," Judith said in a voice that was intended to make him feel guilty about not confiding in her. The ploy was as old as the hills, but it still worked.

"All right, Judith," he said resignedly. "Beardsley's brother-in-law wants to hire me . . ."

"Beardsley." She spat the name. "I never realised a dead man could cause so much trouble."

"What do you mean?"

"Tim spoke to the Army Record Office at Hayes and asked for Beardsley's personal file from the dead sack. They despatched it all right but somehow Tim's boss got to hear about it and hauled him over the coals. Wanted to know why he'd asked for it and gave him a good roasting for using his appointment to obtain information he wasn't entitled to. He said if it ever happened again, Tim would find himself on an adverse report and that would be the end of his promising career."

"What made Tim ask for the file after I'd told him to forget the whole thing?"

"Well, you know my husband, he has this wilful streak in his psyche. He didn't like the way I'd pressured you to back off, said he was quite capable of looking after himself. We had quite a row about it."

"Christ, I'm sorry. I've really messed things up for you, haven't I?"

"We'll survive." Judith emptied the peelings into the waste disposal and removed the rubber gloves. "It's my fault for interfering; if I'd kept my mouth shut, Tim would have had second thoughts about sending for that bloody file. He would have realised just how much he was chancing his arm and would have invented some little white lie for your benefit."

"I should never have leaned on him in the first place."

"What's done is done, Jack. The thing which is really annoying about the whole sorry business is the fact that there was virtually nothing in the file anyway. Of course Tim didn't actually get his hands on it but his Colonel waved the folder at him and he could see there were hardly any enclosures between the covers. As a matter of fact, Tim thought the file had been weeded."

"When did he tell you he was going to call for Beardsley's file?"

"The day after you'd left for India."

"And when did Tim get hauled over the coals about it?"

Judith frowned. "It must have been a week later when the file finally arrived from Hayes."

A week; plenty of time for someone to put his oar in. But who? One of his brother-in-law's contemporaries with a grudge against him? Or a civil servant at Hayes who believed the requisition was suspect? There were a number of possibilities and all of them were equally valid. He wondered if Tim had any idea who might have shopped him, then decided it was best not to ask.

"What's on your mind, Jack?"

"Nothing at all," he said hastily.

"Then why don't you make yourself comfortable in the lounge while I get on with preparing dinner?"

"Whatever you say." Henderson started towards the hall. "Would it be all right if I used your phone again?" he asked. "Only there's a woman in Dartmouth who was out when I called earlier on and I would like to leave a message with her."

*   *   *

They were sitting out on the terrace watching the yachts rounding One Gun Point as they came up river when the telephone rang. Royles felt his heart skip a beat and gazed fixedly at Pat.

"If it's Latif, I'm not here," he said.

"You answer it," Pat told him. "Your legs are younger than mine."

"Normally I wouldn't hesitate, but you've no idea how Latif has been hounding me since I gave in my notice."

"There's no peace for the wicked," Pat said and launched herself from the deck chair.

Royles gave her a grateful smile, then said, "It doesn't matter who it is, you don't know where I am."

The phone call seemed endless and he sat there, his stomach knotting with tension. He told himself that he was safe in Dartmouth, that no one would bother to come after him now, but he wasn't convinced and he feared the worst when Pat finally returned.

"Who do you know in Nottingham, Keith?" she asked.

Nottingham? Royles frowned, tried to recall if anyone

amongst the countless tourists he'd escorted round India had come from that part of the world.

"No one," he said eventually.

"Well, you do now. His name is Jack Henderson and he's been hired by a Mr Young of Draycott and Draycott to find you. At first I thought he was some kind of high-pressure salesman, so I told him I hadn't seen or heard from you in months. Fortunately, he left me his phone number in case you did contact me."

Royles reluctantly accepted the slip of paper she thrust at him.

"It seems that someone has remembered you in their will," Pat told him drily.

CHAPTER XI

HENDERSON APPLIED the handbrake, left the Escort in first gear to make sure the car was doubly safe on the steep incline, then got out and let himself into the house. 42 Mapperley Hall Drive looked pretty much the same as it had almost three weeks ago even down to the empty bottle on the doorstep which the milkman had neglected to collect. There was no word from the estate agents who were selling the house for him amongst the junk mail that had come through the letter box in his absence, and the gas, electricity and British Telecom bills were an added damper.

Dumping the mail on the hall table, he picked up the phone, rang Spencer and arranged to see him at three o'clock. Then he called the police station in Hyson Green only to learn that Detective Sergeant Preston had been called to a break-in at a betting shop on the Mansfield Road where he'd been since nine o'clock that morning. Knowing Danny of old, he figured Preston wouldn't finish his inquiries until it was time for lunch when he would then retire to the George Inn, his favourite pub in the centre of town.

Henderson's assumption was a hundred per cent correct. Half an hour later, he found Preston occupying his usual position at the bar, perched on a stool with his back to the dividing wall. He was looking very amiable, a condition which invariably owed a lot to the number of whiskies he'd consumed. A contributory factor on this occasion was the presence of a young, blue-eyed, natural blonde with a sensuous figure whom it transpired was a Detective Constable. Henderson bought them a drink and remained on the sidelines while Preston related some long-winded yarn to the girl about the good old days when Henderson had been his partner.

"You want to talk about my burglary now?" Henderson asked him eventually.

"Yeah, why don't we? Remember the car one of the neighbours saw parked outside your house? It had false plates made up by a real pro."

"So?"

"I had a quiet chat with a bent garage owner I know who's into that sort of thing. He swears he didn't make up the plates." Preston swallowed the rest of his whisky and placed the empty glass on the bar. "I was going to suggest that the two of us paid him another visit and went through the old Mutt and Jeff routine but, on reflection, I'm inclined to think he was telling the truth. What interests me is why our burglar went elsewhere to get the plates made up."

"You reckon he's a local man?"

"Got to be, Jack. How else would he have known that your house was up for sale?"

"There are a lot of attractive targets in Mapperley Hall Drive. He could have done my place on the spur of the moment."

"I suppose so," Preston said and stared at his empty glass.

Henderson caught the barman's eye, ordered another straight Scotch for Preston, a vodka and tonic for the woman detective constable and a tomato juice for himself.

"You're a man after my own heart, Jack."

"You trained me," Henderson said and raised his glass.

The DC said 'Cheers', murmured something about the little girls' room and wiggled her way towards the door marked 'Ladies'. Preston studied her pelvic movement with an appreciative eye.

"Great little mover," he said. "I'm showing her the ropes in more ways than one."

"Amenable, is she, Danny?"

"Very friendly. I'm thinking of taking a run out to Clumber Park this afternoon to consolidate our special relationship."

"Have we finished with the break-in?"

"More or less. I seem to recall you saying that nothing really valuable had been stolen?"

"There's nothing wrong with your memory," Henderson said.

"Well, that being the case, I'd like to know why our thief went to so much trouble for so little."

Over ninety per cent of the burglaries that had been committed in Mapperley Hall Drive had been executed by teenage amateurs. Their MO was simple; if no one came to the door after they'd rung the bell, they walked round the back and effected an entry by smashing a window. Their style was strictly smash, grab and run; if they used a vehicle on the job, it was invariably one they'd stolen a few hours beforehand. The man who'd broken into his house had either used his own car or one that he hadn't intended to ditch immediately afterwards, otherwise he wouldn't have gone to the trouble of acquiring a set of false number plates. Furthermore, he'd got hold of a pentathol capsule from somewhere in order to deal with the Alsatian.

"His approach work had the stamp of a pro," Henderson said, thinking aloud. "Kicking the door in is the sort of crudity you'd expect from a tearaway which I reckon is exactly the impression he wanted to convey . . ."

"That's how I see it too," Preston said.

"Why did he want to hoodwink us? If robbery wasn't the motive, what was?"

"You got any enemies, Jack?"

"No more than you. Anyway, he only did a token amount of damage; someone who really harboured a grudge would have wrecked the place."

"Then I give up." Preston glanced at the woman DC who'd returned from the cloakroom and had been listening to their conversation. "You got any ideas, Tracy?" he asked.

"Perhaps the intruder was looking for something he could use against Mr Henderson?"

"Such as what?"

Tracy avoided their gaze, looked down at the floor. "Love letters," she murmured.

"A jealous husband," said Preston. "I like it. Have you been having it off with some married bird, Jack?"

"Tracy's given me an idea – perhaps he planted something?"

"Stolen property? To frame you?"

Henderson shook his head. "More like a bug."

"A bug?" Preston laughed. "What have you done to upset the spooks?"

"Nothing. Who do you know in Special Branch with the nous and the technical equipment to springclean my place?"

"Hey, come on, Jack; that's some favour you're asking."

"Did I say I wanted him to do it? He could give me the benefit of his expert advice, couldn't he? Put me on to one of the security outfits who specialise in protecting firms against industrial espionage."

"I don't know," Preston said, hedging.

"I wouldn't expect him to do it for nothing, Danny. There'd be a consultancy fee."

"How much?"

"You tell me. Fifty? A hundred?"

"Guineas?"

"Got an address in Harley Street, has he?" Henderson said acidly.

"I was only joking."

"I'm not."

"I didn't think you were." Preston frowned at his glass. "Avery might know someone."

"Who's Avery?"

"A detective sergeant, bit of a technical bod."

"Have a word with him and let me know how you make out." Henderson swallowed the rest of his tomato juice.

"Are you going, Jack?" Preston asked.

"Afraid so. Clients are funny; they're apt to get very up-tight if you keep them waiting."

*　　　*　　　*

Dudley Spencer was reclining in a deckchair on the lawn, a straw boater of indeterminate vintage protecting his balding head from the sun. There was a pitcher of lemonade within reach but only one glass on the tray which Henderson correctly surmised had not been put there for his benefit. He was however right in assuming that the upright garden chair with the uncomfortable wooden backrest and seat was meant for him. Spencer waved a languid hand towards it and simultaneously dismissed his housekeeper before she had a chance to introduce him with a curt, "I know it's Mr Henderson – who else were we expecting at three o'clock this afternoon?"

A motor mower was parked near the pond at the bottom of the garden. Four parallel tramlines showed just how much of the grass Spencer had managed to cut.

"Gardener's off sick," he said, as though an explanation was called for. "A sprained ankle or some such nonsense."

"How very inconvenient."

"So is this will my late brother-in-law made in favour of Mrs Katherine Pascal. Drew it up shortly after Nancy died."

"Your sister?"

"Yes. Bit of a scatterbrain but we were very close." Spencer reached into the blazer which was draped across the back of his deckchair and produced a crumpled photostat of the probate. "The Pascal woman lives in Marlow. I'd like you to find out all you can about her. She's obviously a gold-digger; Rupert always did have an eye for a pretty woman and she must have turned his head."

"Do you know this for a fact?"

"There can be no other explanation for what happened. I simply want you to find the evidence to support it. Rupert had no right to leave his money to someone outside the family and I mean to contest the will. I'm not thinking of myself, you understand, I'm doing it for my son, Richard and his family in Australia."

Henderson read the probate order and noted that Katherine Pascal of 'Sunnyside', River's End Way, Marlow was named as the sole executor and principal beneficiary. He presumed Spencer's solicitors had filed a claim against the Estate in accordance with his instructions and had had a rude surprise when the probate officer had replied informing them that Beardsley had made a will. He wondered how much Nancy had actually left her husband and whose lawyers had drawn up her will.

"What advice have you received from your solicitors?" he asked, fishing for information.

"Eastgate, Quayle and Simons aren't very optimistic about the outcome, said we'd have to prove Rupert was incompetent when he made his will."

Eastgate, Quayle and Simons were a highly reputable firm whose offices were in Friar Lane. Henderson knew the junior partner and had done a certain amount of work for him in the past. If they'd handled Nancy's estate, he was pretty sure they would give him a rough idea of how much she had been worth at the time of her death.

"I trust you'll find the enclosed acceptable," Spencer said and gave him an envelope.

Sheila Luckwell had told him that Spencer was prepared to put up a thousand as a retainer but it was still a pleasant surprise to see a cheque with a row of noughts after the initial figure in the box. Except of course he couldn't take Spencer's money, at least not all of it.

"I charge a hundred a day for exclusive service plus expenses," Henderson told him. "It will take me two or three days to compile a biography on Mrs Pascal, by which time I will also be able to advise your solicitors whether or not I think it's worth going on with the investigation. If I consider it would be a waste of my time and your money to do so, I'll submit an itemised account and refund the balance of your retainer."

"When can you start?"

"Now," said Henderson and got to his feet.

"I suppose I ought to get cracking too," Spencer said, eyeing the partly mowed lawn with distaste.

*   *   *

Four-figure retainers didn't exactly fall into Henderson's lap with monotonous regularity. For every Spencer or a Drummond, there were hundreds of repossession orders and inquiries from the Department of Health and Social Security which provided his real bread and butter. As if to remind him of this, Sheila Luckwell had arranged the repossession orders in three separate piles on his desk – the easy to enforce, the not so easy and the downright difficult.

"Detective Sergeant Preston telephoned while you were out," Sheila informed him. "He said to tell you he'd been in touch with Avery who thinks he might be able to do the job himself. Mr Preston also muttered something about not being one to let the grass grow under his feet." She looked up from her notepad. "He sounded a little drunk to me."

"He probably was," Henderson said, then asked her if there had been any other messages.

"No." Sheila nibbled at her bottom lip, uncertain for the moment how to broach the subject. "I was wondering if you would like me to come into the office more than four afternoons a week?"

Her reasons for wanting the extra hours were delivered at machine-gun speed and somewhat incoherently. In a nutshell, they amounted to the fact that her husband, Tony, had suddenly been made redundant and at the age of forty-six, the chances of him getting another job in the immediate future seemed remote. They would lose the use of the company car, they owed eleven hundred and eighty-seven pounds on their credit cards and they had just ninety-two pounds seventy-eight pence in their joint account. They had sat up half the night trying to work out what they could do about the forty thousand mortgage on their house.

"We can work something out," Henderson told her. "If I can't employ you full time, I know a firm of solicitors who'll make up the hours."

"I don't know how to thank you."

Her eyes filled with tears and began to brim over and she nibbled at her bottom lip again. No woman he'd ever known seemed to have a handkerchief at a moment of crisis, and he gave her his and told her not to worry.

Henderson waited until she closed the door to his office behind her, then called Eastgate, Quayle and Simons and spoke to the junior partner. Nancy Beardsley had left her husband exactly two thousand seven hundred and sixty-three pounds. He wondered where the rest of Rupert's small fortune had come from.

*   *   *

The man from British Telecom parked his van opposite number 17 Montgomery Close and got out of the vehicle. Any illegal surveillance job was a chancy business, but this was the second time in three weeks he'd called at the house and he just hoped Century House would see him right if there was a foul-up. The man who planted the bug never went back to retrieve it, that was number one in the rule book and the fact that it was being flouted made him decidedly unhappy. Judith Newman

133

would recognise him the moment she opened the door and she was bright enough to realise the odds against the same engineer returning to the same house to rectify a similar fault were astronomical. To make things worse, her husband was a major in the Royal Signals and knew a thing or two about telecommunications.

He pressed the bell and waited, his mouth dry as dust. An ice cream van turned into the Close and cruised slowly past, the public address system relaying a catchy but repetitive jingle. When it stopped at the bottom of the Close, half a dozen children appeared from nowhere; he hoped the Newman children were among them. As the synthetic clarions fell silent, the door opened behind him and he turned about to face Judith Newman.

"It's me again," he said cheerfully. "You must think I'm the proverbial bad penny but we had this report from the exchange supervisor about your phone being on the blink again."

"I'm impressed," Judith told him.

"You are?"

"It only started to make a whirring noise about an hour ago; British Telecom isn't usually that quick off the mark."

"We have our moments. Also, I happened to be in the area." He gave her one of his infectious smiles that made strangers instinctively warm towards him. "May I come in?"

"Yes, of course. What do you think is wrong with the phone?"

"Hard to say without looking at it. I've got a new one in the van; best thing I can do is make a straight swop."

"What about the extension in the sitting-room?"

"Don't you worry, Mrs Newman, I'll replace that one too if it's necessary. After the trouble you've had, I reckon it's the least we can do."

Replacing both instruments was the quickest and easiest way of springcleaning the house although there was a chance her husband might wonder why British Telecom had been unable to repair the existing ones in situ. If the Major was a busybody, he might ring the Area Manager to satisfy his curiosity and then the fat really would be in the fire because this particular phone tap hadn't been authorised by the Home Office and Customer Enquiries wouldn't have a cover story ready.

Judith Newman was still waiting at the door when he returned from the van with the replacement phones. He didn't mind her breathing down his neck while he changed the one in the hall but he'd rather she was elsewhere when he removed the micro transmitter in the sitting room.

"Black and black," he said, showing her the labels on the two boxes. "Not exactly spoilt for choice, are we?"

"I'm not fussed about the colour so long as we've got a phone that works."

"Right."

"Can I get you something to drink? Tea, coffee – a cold beer?"

"I'd like a cup of coffee."

He would have preferred a beer but it would take Judith Newman longer to make him a cup of coffee and every second counted. As soon as she'd disappeared into the kitchen, he disconnected the phone in the hall and swiftly replaced it, then called out to ask if it was okay if he went into the sitting-room. He didn't bother to wait for her permission.

Five minutes later he was able to enjoy a cup of coffee with Judith Newman in the kitchen, thankful that he'd retrieved the micro transmitter without arousing her suspicion; he was even more thankful that her nine-year-old son hadn't been under his feet asking any number of awkward questions.

*　　　*　　　*

He was twenty-one years old, unemployed, and had two previous convictions for Taking and Driving Away, both of which were now spent and therefore no longer admissible in evidence. Since his last appearance in court, he had stolen a further sixty-one vehicles on behalf of various second-hand dealers who, in most cases, already had a prospective buyer lined up. Brand new Audis, Volkswagens, Citroëns and Toyotas usually ended up on the Continent; Fords, Metros and Vauxhalls that were more than three years old were given a paint job, a log book from an insurance write-off and then sent north.

Side streets were his favourite hunting grounds; they were also his most rewarding ones. The number of people who thought it safe to leave their car unlocked in daylight hours because it was parked in front of the house never ceased to amaze him. On more than one occasion the driver had been obliging enough to leave the keys in the ignition while he nipped back into the house for some last-minute remembered item.

The professional car thief never practised his craft in the same neighbourhood two days on the trot. Yesterday he had visited Caterham, south of the river, where he had drawn a blank; this afternoon he was hoping for better luck in Hampstead. Leaving the Underground station in the High Street, he made his way towards the Heath via Well Walk. The Ford Cortina which caught his eye was parked on the left-hand side of the street some twenty yards short of the T-junction with East Heath Road. The large and elegant houses in the immediate vicinity were built on a plateau well above the level of the sunken road and dated back to the turn of the century when the horseless carriage was still in its infancy. What few garages there were had been dug out of the bank and he thought it likely that the owner of the Cortina had no choice but to leave the car on the street.

Everything was looking good; no one else was about, the Cortina was one of the older models which didn't have a steering lock and the absence of the usual logo on the rear window told him the owner hadn't bothered to have the vehicle made tamper-proof. He slipped a length of thin baling wire between the pillar and the weatherproofing on the nearside door and eased the probe forward until he was able to engage the catch with the slip knot he'd tied at one end. Then he drew on the wire, tightening the noose around the catch before raising it to spring the lock. Opening the door, he leaned across the seats, tripped the catch on the offside door and quickly released the bonnet so that he could hot-wire the ignition and crank the engine. It caught first time and ran sweetly; closing the hood, he got in behind the wheel and pulled out from the kerb.

The car had travelled barely ten feet when the trembler switch was dislodged from its precarious perch on top of the front offside shock absorber. A split second later, the five-pound charge of plastic explosive, which had been anchored to the chassis directly under the driver's seat, detonated with an ear-shattering crump. Most of the blast travelled upwards, reducing the car to fragments as though it were made of the finest bone china. The shock wave shattered every window on both sides of Well Walk for a mean distance of one hundred yards and lifted the tiles on the nearest house. It also stripped the leaves from some of the horse chestnut trees lining the pavements. The ruptured fuel tank containing six gallons of Esso Four Star exploded like a napalm bomb and incinerated a laundry van which at that precise moment happened to be travelling towards East Heath Road.

The emergency services were on the scene within three minutes of the 999 call. There were two fatalities; the driver of the laundry van with third-degree burns on eighty per cent of his body, and a Caucasian, age, sex and identity unknown, whose remains were scattered over a wide area. Sufficient evidence was collected from the scene to enable Forensic to identify some of the components from the trembler switch which had detonated the explosive device.

Also found in the garden of one of the houses in the vicinity was a battered number plate belonging to the Ford Cortina. Although misshapen, the area code, numerals and letter denoting the year the vehicle was first registered were still perfectly recognisable. According to the computer records at Swansea, the Ford belonged to a Miss Alexandra Drummond of 22 Cheyne Walk, London SW3.

Chapter XII

Henderson filled the bowl with cornflakes, sprinkled them with five teaspoonfuls of sugar and added fresh milk from the jug on the kitchen table. Normally he didn't watch TV in the morning but this was Saturday and the weekend was an exception. On Saturdays he rarely went into the office much before ten and then only to sort through the mail. Magazine shows didn't interest him and he did not look at the screen; the television was simply background noise, providing companionship in an otherwise silent house.

His interest was suddenly captured when the programme was interrupted and he heard a newsreader say that two people were now known to have been killed in yesterday's bomb incident in Hampstead. He raised his eyes from the bowl of cornflakes and gazed at the fourteen-inch portable on the worktop beneath the pine store cupboard. White masking tape stretched across the road at stomach height, a pyramid warning sign capped with a flashing blue light, no leaves on the nearby trees, a burnt-out delivery van, scattered bits and pieces of scrap metal, a shallow crater near the kerb: yesterday's lead story in the late evening bulletins, but he'd missed it then. Well Walk: the street name hit him like a blow to the solar plexus.

Jesus: he instinctively reached for his notebook, remembered it was still in his jacket hanging in the wardrobe and ran upstairs to get it. Wagnall, Pamela; he leafed through the pages for her name and telephone number on the way down the stairs. Ignoring the phone in the hall, he went into the kitchen, lifted the extension and dialled 01-435 0056. He listened to the ringing tone, wondered why no one answered it and was beginning to fear the worst when there was a loud click and a woman with a stage version of an upper class accent reeled off her phone number.

"Mrs Wagnall?" he asked politely.

"Yes. Who are you?"

"My name's Henderson . . ."

"Oh, yes, Alex told me about you."

"Is she all right? I've just seen a newsflash on TV – I didn't know about the bombing until a few minutes ago."

"Alex is fine, she wasn't here when it happened."

"Could I speak to her please?"

"I'm afraid she's already left for the office. Can I give her a message?"

"Just tell her I called to find out if she was okay." Henderson paused, then said, "How about you, are you all right?"

"I'm on top of the world." A brittle laugh crackled in his right ear. "I was thinking of having the place redecorated anyway."

"Your house was damaged?"

"The explosion brought half the ceiling down in the dining-room and there are more shards of glass embedded in the wall than I can count. Still, I never did like that wallpaper."

Pamela Wagnall gave another of her brittle laughs, thanked him for his concern, then said she would have to dash. Henderson broke the connection, rang directory enquiries and asked for the phone number of the Finlayson Trust in Bell Yard, London WC1. He could understand shop assistants, police officers, firemen, doctors, nurses, railwaymen, bus drivers and the like having their weekends messed around, but office workers, especially those who were employed by a charitable organisation, were surely not required to be at their desks on a Saturday morning.

The telephone operator told him he wanted 01-242 2445, but as he expected, there was no reply when he rang the number.

*　　　*　　　*

Alexandra didn't care much for the view from the third floor. Westminster Bridge Road was nothing much to look at anyway, but this particular office happened to be on the north side of the building roughly in line with the archway outside Waterloo Station, and all that Walter Tindall could see from the window were the arrivals and departures from the terminus. Not that it bothered him very much; as the chief watchdog, Walter Tindall spent the greater part of each working

139

day locked inside the strong room where the personnel security files were kept. The office was merely a convenient room for interviewing people, although on this occasion Alexandra thought interrogate was a more apposite word.

Like his predecessors, Tindall was on loan from the Security Service, more commonly but inaccurately known as MI5. A former Detective Chief Inspector in the Metropolitan Police Special Branch, he had acquired a reputation for being one of the sharpest interrogators in the business long before he had been recruited by the Security Service in 1978. He was not a man to beat about the bush.

"Do you know what a trembler device is, Miss Drummond?" he asked, coming straight to the point.

"I've seen the drill model which is used for training purposes."

"And for real?"

"It's one means of triggering a booby-trap."

"And booby traps, Miss Drummond, are not laid indiscriminately; they are meant to take out a specific target. The terrorist plants an explosive device in a London department store, tells Scotland Yard where to find it, and calmly informs the incident room that it's due to go off in twenty minutes which gives the police just about enough time to clear the building and cordon off the area. Then in goes an officer from the Bomb Squad to defuse what appears to be a conventional device, only it happens to be booby-trapped and if he isn't very careful, he'll be carried out of there in a body bag. The whole aim of the operation is to kill the bomb disposal expert, not massacre a bunch of civilians." Tindall gazed at her thoughtfully through narrowed slate-grey eyes. "Now, what I want to know is why the IRA put you on their hit list? What have you done to merit such attention?"

"Nothing," Alexandra told him firmly. "I've never had anything to do with the Northern Ireland Desk; the Indian subcontinent is my bailiwick."

"How many of your friends know you're an Analyst Special Intelligence?"

"Those who aren't in the Service believe I work for the Finlayson Trust."

"How about Pamela Wagnall? You two grew up together,

went to the same school and have kept in touch ever since. What does she think you were doing in Islamabad for two years and the Persian Gulf before that?"

"Working for the Foreign Office as a secretary cum personal assistant." Alexandra smiled fleetingly. "There's quite a high turnover among the younger women in the lower administrative grades; most of them leave the Diplomatic Service within six years, either to get married or because they've been offered a better paid job. Pamela accepts that I simply wanted a change when I joined the Finlayson Trust."

"But does she believe it?"

"Pamela is a very loyal, very discreet friend. Whether she actually believes my reasons is immaterial; the point is she would never voice her doubts to another living soul."

"Not even to her merchant banker husband and scion of an Anglo-Irish family?"

Tindall had done his homework and had read her security file from cover to cover looking for a tenuous Irish connection. It was no more than Alexandra had expected of him.

"I'm sure you're aware that Nicholas held a short service commission in the Coldstream Guards before he went into merchant banking. If you haven't already done so, I suggest you ask the Ministry of Defence if he ever served in Northern Ireland. They will tell you that Nicholas did two roulement tours, one in Belfast, the other in Londonderry where he earned himself a Mention in Despatches. He is not, and never has been an IRA sympathiser."

"I never thought he was, Miss Drummond." Tindall inspected his fingernails and grimaced, as though annoyed to find they needed a manicure. "The media think the IRA was responsible; no matter how many times the other side deny it, we'd like them to go on believing that until the incident ceases to be newsworthy. Meanwhile, we can quietly go about our own business of discovering just who would like to see you dead, and why." He raised his head and looked her in the eye. "Have you got any ideas, Alex?"

A few minutes ago it had been Miss Drummond, now it was Alex; Tindall was no longer the interrogator but would have her believe he was a friend and confidant.

"I'm afraid not, Walter," she said, deadpan.

In fact, there were several possibilities – Godfrey Vines, the Director in charge of the South East Asia Bureau, Henry Uxbridge, the Chief of Staff and Graham Oliver, Deputy Director (Operations). Although Beardsley had answered to all three when he was alive, it was inconceivable that the whole triumvirate was corrupt. At the moment, however, Alexandra was unable to narrow the field.

"How long have you been staying with the Wagnalls?" Tindall asked.

"Ever since I found a buyer for my flat in Cheyne Walk. That was almost five weeks ago."

"Presumably you informed your superiors about the change of address?"

"Of course. They need to know where I can be found during silent hours and over weekends. So does the duty officer."

"Let's talk about your car. How often do you use it?"

"Weekends only, when I go house-hunting."

Tindall blinked. "You mean you sold your flat in Cheyne Walk and then started looking, Alex?"

"No, that's not the way it happened. I thought I'd found exactly the right place in Barnes but then, after I'd had the property surveyed, the vendor suddenly decided he didn't want to sell and took the apartment off the market. All my colleagues thought it was a huge joke."

"So everyone knew you would be using your car some time over the weekend?"

"Yes."

"What about your neighbours in Cheyne Walk, Alex? Did they know you were staying with friends in Hampstead?"

"I told the couple next door but I didn't give them the Wagnalls' address."

"They could have got that from the telephone directory," Tindall said.

"Oh, no, they couldn't," said Alexandra. "The Wagnalls aren't listed."

"All the same, I'd better have their names."

"Mark and Rachel Jacobs; he's a broker, she's a housewife."

"Sri Lanka falls within the orbit of the South East Asia Bureau, doesn't it?"

Tindall was off and running on another track. In his eagerness to identify the enemy, Alexandra could read him like a book.

"And Rajiv Gandhi has sent in a peace-keeping force to monitor the ceasefire between the Sri Lankans and the Tamil guerillas. But I'm only concerned with the Indian subcontinent." Alexandra smiled. "Sorry, Walter, but you'll have to look elsewhere for the assassin."

"Could there be a Soviet involvement?" Tindall asked, clutching at another straw.

"There are roughly seventeen hundred Russian instructors and advisers stationed in India, which is hardly surprising considering most of the military hardware is supplied by the USSR. A considerable number of those officers and men are drawn from the GRU and have been tasked to gather military information, but I have yet to cross swords with any of them."

The Indian Government had just purchased forty-eight MIG 29s and, according to informed sources, the Russians had agreed they could manufacture the plane under licence. Soviet technicians would help set up the production lines and they were bound to be accompanied by a strong KGB cell. However, all that was in the future and briefing Tindall at this juncture would only cloud the issue.

"What about Sikh extremists? Have you come up against them, Alex?"

He was close. For a moment, Alexandra wondered if she should tell him about the close ties the South East Asia Bureau appeared to have developed with the separatist movement, then quickly rejected the idea. Tindall would consider it only right to consult Godfrey Vines and the Director would make it very clear that he believed her judgment was seriously at fault, something he'd said to her face when she had tried to appraise him of the situation.

"I'm not a field agent, Walter."

"I know that, but . . ."

"Look, there's virtually a civil war going on in the Punjab, so naturally we're keeping an eye on the area. Among the ethnic minorities living in this country, there are a substantial number of Sikhs and we don't want any extremists coming over here to further their campaign on our streets. What information we get from our sources in India we pass on to Special Branch and MI5 because they're responsible for combating terrorism in the UK. If I was actively involved, one of the local terrorists might be tasked to eliminate me but I am at least one step removed from the arena and they would have a hard time identifying me."

"But it's still a possibility?"

Alexandra nodded. The seed had been planted and with any luck, Tindall would nurture it.

"What prompted you to move out of the flat in Cheyne Walk before contracts were exchanged?" he asked. "Surely it would have been easier to use it as a base instead of moving in with the Wagnalls?"

"I'd already arranged to put my furniture into store before the apartment in Barnes was taken off the market."

"I think you're hiding something from me," Tindall said bluntly. "You could have told the removal people you'd been forced to change your plans and they would have understood. There has to be another reason – someone or something frightened you and you no longer felt safe living alone?"

It was a shrewd guess and not all that far off the mark. Someone had broken into her flat shortly after she had begun to investigate the links which were being forged between the Secret Intelligence Service and the Sikh Independence Movement. Nothing had been taken and, with one exception, the intruder had left everything just as it had been. The exception was the traditional strand of hair which she had placed under her private papers in the centre drawer of the dropleaf bureau. The fact that one evening it was in a slightly different position was all the proof Alexandra had needed; it had confirmed a suspicion that, two days previously, someone had followed her home from the office. Needing a cover story that would stand up should anyone ask her why she had moved in with the Wagnalls, she had put the flat up for sale the following morning.

"I'm still waiting for an answer," Tindall reminded her.

If she mentioned the break-in, he would ask her why she had failed to report it to the branch security officer and there was no wriggling out of that one.

"I moved out because, amongst other things, I was getting

phone calls from a heavy breather in the middle of the night," said Alex. "I thought it was the creepy little biochemist in one of the flats on the ground floor, but I doubt if he was the one who tried to kill me. Perverts don't usually go around planting bombs."

"You're right, they don't. Of course we can have a friendly word with the biochemist but I'm going to recommend we play it safe and put you in quarantine for a week or two."

"Surely that's unnecessary?" Alexandra protested.

"I don't think so."

"Godfrey Vines won't like it."

"Maybe not, but he won't veto my recommendation."

Tindall obviously knew his man. Vines would huff and puff but in the end he would acquiesce. He had reached his ceiling as head of the South East Asia Bureau and knew it. His one remaining ambition was to soldier on to sixty-five in order to qualify for the maximum pension. Grimly determined to keep his nose clean at all costs, he wouldn't dream of rocking the boat.

"Where do you propose to send me?" she asked.

"You'll find out soon enough when you get there." Tindall raised a hand to silence her objections. "I know what you are going to say but a safe house is only safe if its location remains a secret."

"And when do we leave?"

"You'll have an hour to pack a suitcase and make your excuses to the Wagnalls."

Alexandra felt as though the walls were closing in on her. Once Tindall had got her stashed away, it would be ten times more difficult to use Henderson as a bird-dog. She began to wonder just which side the security officer was playing for.

*　　*　　*

The post consisted of the usual kind of dross that arrived on a Saturday morning. Amongst the junk mail addressed to Henderson at the office in St Peter's Gate was a special offer of a twenty-five pound discount on the retail price of a complete set of *The Wide World Encyclopaedia* and an invitation to invest in the Providence Unit Trust. As for the rest, he knew without opening it that the envelope from HM Customs and Excise contained the quarterly Value Added Tax return which had to be submitted by the thirtieth of September. The only bright spot was a brief note from a firm of solicitors in Newark on Trent thanking him for his services and enclosing a cheque for one hundred and seventy-two pounds fifty in settlement of the account.

Henderson went on through to his office, dumped the week's supply of frozen food he'd picked up from Sainsbury's on the spare chair and checked out the answering machine to see if there were any messages. He had hoped that Keith Royles would have called but there was complete silence after the tone signal. He looked at the solitary repossession order in the pending tray and decided the finance company could wait a little while longer for their Peugeot 305. The car had been given to a mother of two small children by her husband not long before he had walked out on her. Subsequently, it transpired the bastard had only made the down payment and she couldn't afford to pay the finance company the hundred and fifty pounds a month the agreement stipulated.

The prospect of having nothing to do and all day to do it in depressed him. Although it was unlikely that Katherine Pascal would agree to see him, he took out his notebook, looked up the number he'd obtained from directory enquiries and dialled it out.

A voice on the telephone can be deceptive and an unreliable guide to a person's age; even so, he got the impression that Katherine Pascal was a good deal younger than her benefactor, Rupert Beardsley. Introducing himself, Henderson told her that he was a claims adjudicator for a life assurance company.

"A life assurance policy is the last thing I need," Katherine Pascal said politely.

"Actually, I'm not trying to sell you anything. The Finlayson Trust effected such a policy on Colonel Beardsley and I understand you are the principal beneficiary in his will?"

"Yes I am, but . . ."

"A Mr Dudley Spencer has filed a claim on the estate."

"Oh yes?"

Henderson thought he detected a note of hostility in her voice and played on it. "Colonel Beardsley's life was assured

146

for twenty thousand pounds; the policy did not attract bonuses but it did have a double indemnity clause relating to war, civil insurrection and unrest. The Trust felt that their representatives occasionally found themselves in dangerous situations and that the next-of-kin should be compensated in the event of any unfortunate incident. The circumstances in which Colonel Beardsley met his death were such that the double idemnity clause is applicable.''

"I see."

Katherine Pascal didn't need a pocket calculator to know that she stood to lose forty thousand pounds and even when she was going to receive eight times that amount under the will, it was still a lot of money.

"The policy isn't subject to Capital Transfer Tax either," Henderson added to wind her up even more.

"I shall contest Mr Spencer's claim to the money."

"Well now, that might be difficult, Mrs Pascal. The Colonel made no provision for the disbursement of this particular sum because he wasn't entitled to do so. The premiums were paid by the Finlayson Trust and the Board of Trustees were extremely rigid in defining who would be regarded as the next-of-kin. However, you may well have a stronger claim than Mr Spencer, which is why I would like to see you."

"When?"

"Would this afternoon be convenient, say around three o'clock?"

Katherine Pascal said she would look forward to meeting him. Had she sounded doubtful or suspicious, Henderson would have suggested she contacted Draycott and Draycott, but it seemed the fear of losing forty thousand pounds was uppermost in her mind.

*   *   *

Royles tried to ignore the phone but it went on ringing as though the caller, despite appearances to the contrary, knew that someone was at home. The sharp, birdlike trill grated on him and left his nerve ends ragged until, unable to stand the racket any longer, he went out into the hall and lifted the receiver.

"Dartmouth 0129," he snapped.

"My name's Quilter," said a harsh voice. "I'm a Detective Inspector with the MPSB. I was beginning to think you weren't going to answer, Mr Royles."

"MPSB?" Royles said uncomprehendingly.

"Metropolitan Police Special Branch. I waited until I saw your aunt leave the house."

"Do you mind telling me what this is all about?" Royles hoped he sounded composed and in control of the situation even though his stomach was churning.

"It's about a man called Jack Henderson. He telephoned your aunt early on Thursday evening and left a message asking you to contact him on a certain number in Nottingham. Am I right?"

"Yes, but how did . . .?"

"He wants to question you about Colonel Beardsley," Quilter continued relentlessly, "and I'm afraid we can't have that."

"Now look here . . ."

"I wouldn't be bothering you, Mr Royles, if this wasn't a serious matter involving the Official Secrets Acts. In the circumstances, we need to put our heads together and decide just how much you can safely tell Mr Henderson in the event you get in touch with him. That's only sensible, isn't it?"

"Yes, I suppose so."

"Good. You'll find me in the beer garden of the Ship Inn across the river in Kingswear. Don't keep me waiting longer than a quarter of an hour."

"How will I recognise you?" Royles asked.

"Don't give it another thought," Quilter told him. "I'll come up and tap you on the shoulder."

Chapter XIII

The Ship Inn on Fore Street was roughly halfway between Kingswear Station and the lower car ferry to Bayards Cove across the river in Dartmouth. There were a dozen or so tables in the beer garden behind the Inn and all of them seemed to be occupied by the yachting crowd from the marina farther up the Dart. Although Royles had no idea what Quilter looked like, he doubted if the Detective Inspector would be wearing rope sole shoes, denims and a T-shirt under an oilskin jacket which appeared to be the standard form of dress for everyone there.

For a man who didn't want to be kept waiting, he thought Quilter was certainly taking his time about making himself known. Then, just as he was beginning to think that he was the victim of an elaborate hoax, someone tapped him on the shoulder and the same harsh voice he'd heard on the telephone said, "Hello Keith, how's the world treating you?"

Royles spun round, his heart thumping. Quilter was roughly the same height as himself but much more compact. There wasn't an ounce of spare flesh on his muscular frame and he immediately classified him as the sort of man for whom, like his friend, Charlie Freeman, fitness training was almost a fetish. He had light brown curly hair, deep-set eyes and a mean, hard-looking face which suggested he got a kick out of hurting people.

"I'm fine," Royles said weakly.

"Good." Quilter smiled, a mechanical grimace that somehow made him seem even more intimidating. "I ran into your old friend, Charlie Freeman, the other day," he continued. "I hate to say it but he didn't look so hot. Still, I understand that nothing has been permanently damaged."

"Are you trying to tell me something?"

"Only that there isn't much I don't know about you." Quilter stared at the nearly empty glass in his right hand. "I think

I'm going to move on to another pub, the service is pretty slow here. You want to come with me?"

"Do I have any choice?"

"Not a lot. My car's parked round the corner."

The car was a dark blue Honda, had a local registration number and had therefore almost certainly been hired from a self drive agency. Quilter ushered him into the front seat, then walked round the car and got in behind the wheel. Before moving off, he produced a warrant card to prove his identity and set Royles' mind at rest. After that, he didn't say another word until they were heading out of town on the B3225 to Brixham.

"Jack Henderson is bad news," Quilter said abruptly. "He likes to call himself a private inquiry agent but in reality he's just a bloody ferret for any investigative journalist who cares to hire him. Right now he's working for a Herbert who's trying to do an exposé on the Secret Intelligence Service."

"Are you saying Colonel Beardsley was a spy?"

"Not exactly. He was a Queen's Messenger but the SIS used him occasionally as a courier."

"I don't see what this has to do with me," Royles said nervously. "I only met the Colonel once."

"Twice. Beardsley denied it of course when you said you thought you'd seen him at some hotel in Rawalpindi."

"The Imperial – so I wasn't mistaken after all. But how did you know?"

"Beardsley called the British High Commission in Delhi from Jaipur to report that he'd been recognised. Hiring Lal as a guide was a blind."

"I don't understand . . ."

"The Colonel was on a delicate mission, he didn't want you to know he was fluent in Hindustani in case you asked him some awkward questions. Unfortunately, Henderson learned that you'd seen Beardsley hobnobbing with some Pakistani businessman in Rawalpindi because Lal told him about it. And if you're wondering how he got on to the Indian guide, there can only be one answer to that question. There has to be a well-placed source inside the SIS who's feeding him with information."

"For what?" Royles asked. "Money?"

Quilter shrugged. "Or to get some advance publicity for a book the source is planning to write under a pseudonym. This much we do know; the man Henderson is working for is determined to prove that British Intelligence is trying to destabilise the Indian Government. According to him, we were behind the assassination of Indira Gandhi and now we are out to get her son, Rajiv. The theory being that we'd like to replace the Gandhi dynasty with someone who isn't so pro-Soviet."

"I can see all that," Royles said uneasily, "but what does Henderson think I can tell him?"

Quilter had an answer for that one too. Henderson was looking for evidence which would prove the SIS were trying to persuade the Pakistanis to supply the Sikh extremists in the Punjab with arms and ammunition. A lot of palms needed greasing to get the operation off the ground and Beardsley had been doing just that the night he'd dined at the Imperial Hotel in Rawalpindi.

"At least, that's Henderson's contention," Quilter continued. "He's going to ask you to identify the Pakistani Beardsley was dining with."

"But I don't know the man from Adam."

Quilter laughed. "That won't bother Henderson; he'll throw a lot of names at you and steer you towards the one he regards as the most suitable. He might even make it worth your while; of course he won't be crude enough to offer you a bribe but there will be a generous allowance to cover travelling expenses and any loss of earnings."

Royles nodded in agreement. Hadn't Henderson already given a broad hint that he could expect a monetary reward? What was it Pat had said after she had spoken to Henderson on the phone? 'It seems someone has remembered you in their will.' You couldn't ask for a broader hint than that.

"There's no way he can induce me to make a false statement."

"Don't you believe it. Henderson's been round to Belmont Court; he knows what those skinheads did to your friend, Charlie Freeman, and he's not above telling them where they can find you if you don't co-operate."

Royles moistened his lips. They had turned off the road to Brixham and were now heading towards Totnes. He wondered vaguely if Quilter intended to double back to Dartmouth on the B3207, but where the Special Branch officer was taking him was the least of his worries.

"What the hell am I going to do?" he whispered.

"We believe it would be best if you went abroad on an extended holiday until this thing blows over. Unless Henderson can come up with something pretty soon, his journalist friend will lose interest and start looking for some alternative issue to investigate."

"Where do you think I'm going to find the money?"

"Open the glove compartment."

Royles did so and took out a bulging brown envelope.

"There's five hundred pounds in there," Quilter told him. "Take it, buy yourself a plane ticket to Cologne. I'll arrange for a colleague to meet you at the airport and put you up for a couple of nights. By that time, I should also be in a position to come up with a long-term solution to the problem." Quilter glanced sideways at him. "Any questions so far?"

"I don't think so."

"What about your passport? Did you leave that behind in Belmont Court?"

Royles shook his head. "I picked it up when I collected some of my things from the flat."

"Good. There's a British Airways flight to Cologne departing from Heathrow at 1725. Make sure you're on it tomorrow without fail. Keep an eye out for my colleague in the airport terminal; he'll be holding up a piece of cardboard with your name on it. Meantime, don't answer the phone in case it's Henderson on the line and don't tell your aunt about this little meeting. Use your imagination, make up some story about being asked to stand in as a guide by a tour operator. Think you can manage that?"

"Yes."

"That's the style. Now I'll run you back to Dartmouth."

"There is one small thing. Could you possibly show me your warrant card again?" Royles smiled apologetically. "You see, I've never been involved in this kind of thing before and I just want to be sure you are who you say you are."

"There's no need to be embarrassed about it," Quilter said affably. "I'd feel the same way in your shoes."

Still smiling, he produced his warrant card. It looked genuine enough to Royles but then he was hardly an expert.

*   *   *

'Sunnyside', River's End Way was the last but one villa in a cul-de-sac of identical houses which looked as though they dated back to the late twenties or early thirties when architects and builders were endeavouring to create their idea of an Englishman's castle for something under a thousand pounds. Katherine Pascal was some fifteen or so years younger than the house in which she lived and was infinitely more charming. Seated opposite her in the sitting-room, Henderson had to admit she wasn't at all his idea of a hard-faced gold-digger.

"You must have thought I was a very grasping person when you phoned me this morning," she said, as though reading his thoughts. "Especially after what I said about contesting Mr Spencer's claim to Rupert's life insurance policy."

"No, not at all; I just put it down to a clash of personalities. From personal experience I know Mr Spencer isn't the easiest man in the world to get along with."

"Yes, well, I've done a lot of thinking since you telephoned and I've come to the conclusion that I'm being greedy. Rupert left me well provided for – why should I begrudge Mr Spencer a share in the estate? If the policy is intended to benefit the next-of-kin, then the money should go to him."

It was the last thing Henderson wanted to hear and it took him some considerable time to persuade Katherine Pascal that the insurance company should be allowed to adjudicate on the matter.

"And I have come all the way from Nottingham to see you," he gently reminded her. "I'd hate the company to think my journey was a complete waste of time. They would refuse to pay the motor mileage allowance and subsistence expenses if they came to that conclusion."

The apologies came thick and fast. How could she have been so thoughtless, but it simply hadn't occurred to her that he would be out of pocket as a result of her quixotic behaviour. She was suitably contrite, and he didn't think it was an act.

Katherine Pascal sounded equally genuine when she asked him to tell her exactly what it was he wanted to know about her friendship with Rupert.

"Well, let's begin at the beginning," said Henderson. "How old a friend was he?"

"We met twelve years ago in June 1975, shortly after I had divorced my husband."

"Did he ever introduce you to Nancy?"

"Ours was a very intimate friendship, Mr Henderson," she said with surprising candour. "To put it bluntly, I was his mistress and we made damn sure Nancy never found out. Had she done so, Rupert would have found himself in Queer Street financially."

"The Colonel lived in Stanhope Square. How did he manage to visit you here in Marlow without his wife getting to know?"

"I've only been living here since the spring of '83."

'Sunnyside' had belonged to Katherine Pascal's mother and she had inherited it on her death. Before that, she had lived in Golders Green, roughly twenty minutes on the Northern Line from the centre of London.

"Rupert travelled a lot and was often away for two or three weeks on end. Sometimes he was in Golders Green with me when Nancy thought he was in India. Of course, he went into the office every day but she knew better than to phone him at work. Rupert didn't socialise with his colleagues and their wives all that much. Occasionally he would invite the odd couple to dinner and inevitably they would talk shop, but he never had any embarrassing moments. Everyone knew that Nancy was an alcoholic and was always getting her dates confused. So if there were any faux pas, he could always use her absent-mindedness to smooth things over. Also Nancy kept pretty much to herself and never coffee-housed with the other Foreign Office wives. She had her own interests; liked to bet on the horses in a big way."

"Were you Foreign Office?" Henderson asked.

"No, I ran the Keith Prowse agency in the West End. Rupert was an avid theatre goer and used to get tickets from us during his lunch hour instead of going to the box office at the theatre. Anyway, that's how we met."

"And became very fond of one another?"

"Yes."

He had hoped that Katherine Pascal would shed some light on Beardsley but she'd told him little that was significant and the man remained an enigma. Although he'd learned that Nancy had been an alcoholic and inveterate gambler, it wasn't the information he'd driven all the way to Marlow for. Yet if he asked any more questions in the same vein, Katherine Pascal would become suspicious.

"Personally, I'm satisfied you have a stronger claim on the insurance policy than Dudley Spencer," he said, adopting a different approach. "But head office may ask me for something more tangible in the way of proof."

"Would that photograph over there do?" she asked.

The photograph was a head and shoulders portrait of Beardsley, recognisable from the duplicate of the one in his passport which Alexandra Drummond had given him.

"Not good enough, I'm afraid," said Henderson. "He hasn't signed it. What we need is something personal in the way of letters, papers or any private documents he may have left in your possession which would show he regarded this house as his real home."

A worried frown appeared only to vanish in almost the next instant. "I think I may have just the proof you want." Katherine Pascal favoured him with a dazzling smile. "Would you excuse me for a moment while I go and fetch it?"

The evidence she eventually produced was somewhat disappointing. It consisted of a clipping from a Sunday newspaper extolling the business philosophy of a Pakistani multi millionaire. Pinned to it was an account in longhand of Beardsley's experiences with an organisation called the Punjab Boundary Force in 1947.

"Do you have anything else belonging to the Colonel, Mrs Pascal?"

Her smile fell away. "I'm afraid not. There were other papers but they haven't been returned to me yet."

"Someone took them away?"

"Yes, one of Rupert's colleagues from the Foreign Office. He said their security department would have to scrutinise his personal papers to make sure none of them came within the scope of Section Two of the Official Secrets Acts. He gave me a receipt for them, it's upstairs in my dressing-table."

"Who is the mysterious 'he', Mrs Pascal?" Henderson saw the doubting expression on her face and attempted to smooth things over. "I mean, it would make it so much easier to establish your claim on the policy if he was prepared to sign a brief statement. He needn't specify what documents had been removed, merely that you had agreed to release various papers belonging to the Colonel."

The doubtful expression was still there and he guessed she had been warned not to divulge the name of the Foreign Office official who'd visited her.

"It could make all the difference," he said, and left it to Katherine Pascal to deduce that preserving the stranger's anonymity was going to cost her forty thousand pounds.

"The man who came to see me was Steven Quilter. He showed me his official pass from the Foreign Office and said I could obtain verification from their security department, which I did."

He would have liked to ask her for a description but that was out of the question. "Did Quilter give you a telephone number?"

"No, he dialled it, then passed the phone and told me what extension to ask for when the switchboard operator answered." Katherine Pascal smiled apologetically. "I'm afraid I've forgotten it now. However, I do recall it was a four figure number beginning with a six."

"Don't worry, I'll find it."

Tim Newman could do a little digging on his behalf. He wasn't exactly sure what his brother-in-law did at Stanmore but he knew it had something to do with the selection of officers for various staff appointments including Assistant Military Attachés in embassies around the world. If Tim didn't have the telephone number of the Foreign Office Security Department at his fingertips, he could certainly obtain it without arousing suspicion. And he didn't see how his sister could object; it wasn't the same as asking Tim to get hold of someone's personal file.

"It's almost four o'clock," Katherine Pascal suddenly announced. "I'm going to make myself a cup of tea. Will you join me, Mr Henderson, or would you prefer something stronger?"

Henderson said it was very kind of her to offer but he ought to be making tracks, a somewhat thin excuse which she readily accepted without making the slightest attempt to persuade him to change his mind.

*   *   *

Sicklemere Ford was roughly midway between Walsham le Willows and Bodwell Ash, eleven miles south-east of Thetford which itself lay on the fringe of the Army's field firing area at Stanford. The smallest hamlet in Norfolk with a population of forty-six men, women and children, it consisted of sixteen cottages, a pub called the Old Smithy, a general store cum sub post office and three outlying farms.

Hereward's Farm was on the outskirts of the hamlet, a good quarter of a mile from the nearest cottage. Classified as a Grade 3 safe house, it was one of several reception centres up and down the country where guests were accommodated in the short term while Head Office made up their minds what to do with them. Those guests who were considered to be at risk or potentially hostile were subsequently moved on to either a Grade 2 or Grade 1 haven. Both categories offered maximum protection, the only difference between them being the fact that the spartan accommodation and harsh régime at a Grade 1 establishment was meant to intimidate any person unfortunate enough to be sent there. It was not unknown for a guest to progress from 3 to 2 to 1.

Alexandra Drummond thought she would either be returned to the fold within a week or transferred to a more secure abode. Everything depended on Tindall, what he made of her, who he reported to, what sort of man he was. He had been very distant with her on the journey down to Sicklemere Ford and even when he had conversed with her it had always been on the subject of the trembler switch. Nothing was going to convince him that the man who'd planted the bomb had been out to inflict the maximum number of casualties on the population at large. Had that been the case, he would have chosen a busy shopping centre like Oxford Street. Furthermore, the explosive device would have been initiated either with a time delay fuse or by a short

157

wave radio transmission. To Tindall's way of thinking, it had been a deliberate attack against a specific target. If Alexandra herself wasn't the target, it had to be someone else who lived in Well Walk and, even more incredibly, the assassin had then made a cock of it by booby-trapping the wrong Ford Cortina.

Alexandra walked over to the bedroom window and gazed out over the flat unbroken countryside. It was hard to imagine a more isolated community. Apart from a Dodge transit van provided by the local education authority to collect the school-children, there were only two buses a day into Thetford. Tindall had given express instructions to the distaff that she was not to use the telephone at the farmhouse and although she was free to go for a walk, there wasn't a public call box in Sicklemere Ford.

There was of course nothing to stop her asking one of the local residents if she could use their phone, but it would only get back to the distaff. Tindall would want to know why she had ignored his instructions and things could snowball from there. If she had been kept under surveillance for any length of time, there was a strong possibility that her clandestine meetings with Henderson had been photographed. All the opposition had to do was provide Tindall with evidence to show that there had been a serious leakage of information from the South East Asia Bureau and she would end up in a Grade 1 safe house. No one was going to bring any charges under the Official Secrets Acts; in her twilight world, the benefit of the doubt went to the State and they would simply do enough to thoroughly discredit her.

Alexandra moved away from the window and began to unpack the suitcase she had brought with her. The fact that she had come within a hair's breadth of being murdered would be turned round and used against her – she had been supplying information to a Hostile Intelligence Service and had decided to call it a day – when they had tried to blackmail her, she had let it be known that, in exchange for a guarantee of immunity from prosecution, she would identify the case officer who'd been running her and would blow the whole network – rather than allow that to happen, the HIS had attempted to silence her.

Was it so far-fetched? Alexandra knew of far more outlandish scenarios which had been taken seriously, but where Tindall was concerned, she thought the security officer would want to confront her with some tangible evidence before he sanctioned a hostile interrogation at a detention centre.

Alexandra reckoned she was safe for the moment, but the same could not be said for Henderson and she had a guilty feeling about him. He was the innocent dupe and the one most at risk. She just hoped that he would get in touch with Pamela Wagnall and would be sharp enough to appreciate the significance of the message she had left with her.

*   *   *

Quilter left his car in St James Square near the London Reference Library, took a cab as far as the Adelphi Theatre in The Strand, then walked the rest of the way to the offices of the Finlayson Trust in Bell Yard. Except for the West End, the centre of London was invariably dead on a Saturday evening and no one saw him enter the office from the alleyway directly behind the narrow, Dickensian-type building. Pausing only to switch off the burglar alarm inside the door, he climbed the staircase to the attic room on the fourth floor which he had been allocated by the office manager on instructions from the Board of Trustees.

Nowadays, the Finlayson Trust was a charitable organisation in name only. By the beginning of 1947 its financial resources had been practically exhausted; it was still making grants in aid forty years later because it was now funded by the Foreign and Commonwealth Office on behalf of Century House. Neither the office staff nor the bona fide members of the Board of Trustees were aware of this arrangement. As far as they were concerned, the strangers who occupied the rooms in the attic from time to time were working for the Trust on a purely voluntary basis. When Quilter had joined the staff ten weeks ago, the office manager had been told that he was an expert in the field of adult education. Quilter had given him no reason to disbelieve the cover story; using material supplied by his associates, he had kept the small typing pool busy on a plan to improve the literacy of peasant farmers in the Mainpuri District of Uttar Pradesh. Alexandra Drummond knew different, but she had been led to believe that he was on temporary loan to the Sri Lankan Desk from the Royal Navy, and like any well-indoctrinated analyst from Century House, she had a proper regard for the need-to-know principle.

Quilter unlocked the door to his office and walked inside. The first thing he noticed was an orange warning light on the telephone which indicated there was a message for him on the answering machine. Rewinding the tape to the starting point, he inserted the crypto fill gun into the receiver slot and pressed it home. In the field of cipher equipment, the scrambler of World War Two vintage was the equivalent of the plane the Wright Brothers designed. The technological revolution since then was such that a telephone answering machine was now available which automatically encoded a clear text message. No one could unlock the code unless they possessed an electronic fill gun with the correct key for the day. Any unauthorised person who attempted to do so would simply hear a continuous burr after the tone signal.

He listened to the sound of his own voice inviting the caller to leave a message, then a woman with a low-pitched voice said: "This is Katherine Pascal. I hope you will get back to me, Mr Quilter, because I hate talking to a machine. However, the fact is that a Mr Jack Henderson called on me today. He said he was a claims adjudicator for a Life Assurance Company and that they were liable for a forty-thousand-pound double indemnity claim on Rupert's life policy. He also told me that the premiums had been paid by the Finlayson Trust and that I would be entitled to the money if I could show that Colonel Beardsley regarded me as his next-of-kin. Mr Henderson asked me if I had any papers belonging to him which might infer that he looked upon my house as his home . . ."

There was a long agonising pause and even though Quilter could guess what she was about to tell him, it still came as a nasty shock.

"So I gave him an article about a Pakistani entrepreneur which Rupert had cut out of a Sunday colour supplement and pinned to some notes he'd made about his experiences with the Punjab Boundary Force. I hope this was all right . . .?"

It was all wrong. The clipping featured Ahmad Bashir Khan and included a photograph. Everyone who'd done business with him could look forward to spending the next thirty years in jail if Henderson ever showed the article to Keith Royles.

Chapter XIV

His name was Ahmad Bashir Khan. The photograph had been taken in the library of his London home against a background of floor to ceiling bookshelves chock-a-block with leather-bound volumes. Henderson thought he was about five foot seven but as he was sitting in a wing chair, it was difficult to judge his height with any accuracy. Khan had sleek black hair parted arrow straight on the left side, brown unsmiling eyes which were set close together and a round solemn-looking face. It was evident that Ahmad Khan indulged in all the luxuries of a capitalist society, such things as handmade shoes and a beautifully cut suit which, despite the undoubted skill of a Savile Row tailor, could not disguise the plump thighs and a waist that was beginning to show signs of flabbiness.

Ahmad Bashir Khan was forty-nine. He had been born in Jinda, a small village in the East Punjab, and had arrived in England in the spring of 1957 with a little over nineteen pounds in his pocket which equated to his age. A distant relative had given him a job as a shop assistant in a men's outfitters and the extra cash he'd earned in his spare time, moonlighting as a mini-cab driver, he'd put on deposit with Barclays. Within five years and with a little help from the bank, he'd accumulated enough money to buy a small newsagents in the Handsworth district of Birmingham. It had been the first of a chain he'd subsequently established throughout the Midlands.

Like most successful entrepreneurs, Ahmad Khan had diversified into such fast-moving consumer items as electrical goods, food and clothing. By the time he was thirty, he'd acquired his first million and a suitable wife who was destined to bear him the son he'd always wanted after producing three daughters. Money begat money and the second million had arrived in less than a quarter of the time it had taken him to amass the first. By 1980, when the article had appeared, Ahmad

Khan possessed a town house in London's Eaton Square, a farm in Gloucestershire, a villa outside Nice and a chalet in the Swiss ski resort of Crans Montana. In addition to a yacht, he owned two Rolls Royces, a Cadillac and a customised Ford Mustang. It was, Henderson thought, no mean achievement for someone who had fled the Punjab after being orphaned at the age of eight and had then spent the next eleven years of his life as a beggar on the streets of Karachi.

The notes which Beardsley had attached to the clipping didn't mention Ahmad Bashir Khan by name but there was an obvious connection. On the night of the nineteenth of August 1947, three days after the declaration of Independence, the Rajputana Rifles along with other regiments of the old Indian Army had been drafted into East Punjab to restore law and order.

Following the division of the subcontinent, the biggest migration in history had begun. Every Hindu in the predominately Muslim West Punjab had wanted to move east; every Muslim had wanted to leave the Hindu dominated East Punjab. At the insistence of the politicians, a multi-racial army had been broken up into nationalist components. Hindus and Muslims who'd served together and fought in the same regiment had suddenly become strangers at best, enemies at worst. The police force in East Punjab, which had been predominately Muslim, had been disarmed well before Independence Day and for months before that, every civil servant had become thoroughly partisan through looking over their shoulders towards their future political masters in either Karachi or Delhi.

The killing had begun on Independence Day near Amritsar. A mob of Sikhs had seized, stripped and raped a number of Muslim women whom they had subsequently paraded naked through the streets before murdering them. That same night, across the border in West Punjab, Muslims had burned down a Sikh temple, incinerating the twenty or so people who had taken refuge there.

The first massacre Beardsley had witnessed had occurred eighteen miles from Ambala where a trainload of refugees had been ambushed. A section of the track had been ripped up, forcing the driver to effect an emergency halt; then, as the train had screeched to a standstill, the six-car unit had been raked by Bren gun fire. Later that same day, he had taken to the air in a Lysander to reconnoitre the area and had seen the long accusing fingers of black smoke rising in the still air from the burning villages. And everywhere, the caravans had been on the move, men, women, children, bullock carts and cattle. Some columns had been well organised and had moved with disciplined purpose; others had been strung out, the stragglers in the rear at the mercy of marauding bands of armed men who'd harried and picked them off one by one.

Ahmad Bashir Khan had been part of that nightmare and had survived even though his parents had been murdered almost in front of his eyes. The journalist who'd interviewed him hadn't said so, but Henderson reckoned Beardsley would never have pinned the clipping to the notes he'd made forty years ago if that hadn't been the case. He was equally certain that Khan was the man whom Royles had seen dining with Beardsley at the Imperial Hotel in Rawalpindi. Proving it would be easy enough if only he could get hold of Royles.

Henderson loaded the breakfast things into the dishwasher, then used the extension in the kitchen to call Dartmouth.

"Miss Royles?" he said, recognising her voice when she answered the phone. "My name's Henderson. I'm the man who rang last Thursday and left a message for your nephew."

"I remember."

"Good. I was hoping he would have contacted me before now."

"What makes you think I've seen him, Mr Henderson?"

Her guarded response told him a great deal. Pat Royles was clearly the sort of woman who found it difficult to lie convincingly.

"Because I've traced Keith to Dartmouth and I can't think where else he would stay."

"Keith is a grown man. I can't make him phone you if he doesn't want to."

"Of course you can't. Listen, I'll drive down; there's a photograph I'd like him to see, and I could do with a short break."

"You'll be wasting your time, Mr Henderson. My nephew's no longer here."

"May I ask when he left?"

163

"He caught a train to London early yesterday morning. It seems the travel company he used to work for telephoned on Saturday while I was out shopping and begged him to stand in for the courier in charge of the Grand European Tour who'd been taken seriously ill."

Royles had indicated that he was leaving from Heathrow but she had no idea where he was going. This wasn't an insuperable problem to Henderson's way of thinking. All he had to do was get hold of a railway timetable, look up the departures from Totnes and add on a couple of hours for delays. British Rail had a habit of digging up half their track on a Sunday and Royles had probably been routed all over the place. It would take him another fifty minutes to get to Heathrow from the centre of London, and no experienced traveller, especially one as experienced as Royles, would hang around the airport terminal longer than was strictly necessary. One hour after checking in he'd be on his way. Given a reasonable time span, Henderson was sure his friendly travel agent at Thomas Cook could provide him with a list of all the airline departures to various destinations in Europe.

Leaving the house, Henderson drove into Nottingham, parked the Ford Escort in the multi-storey below the City Hospital and walked to his office in St Peter's Gate. There were no appointments in his desk diary, the only mail was a final reminder from East Midlands Electricity and no one had rung the office on Sunday to leave a message for him on the answering machine.

Judith telephoned him some ten minutes later with the number of the Foreign Office security department which he'd asked his brother-in-law to obtain. When he rang them up, no one there had ever heard of Quilter. Security departments were notoriously secretive but in this instance, he was sure they weren't lying to him.

Ahmad Bashir Khan and Steven Quilter: he ought to try both names on Alexandra, but going through Young would involve too many explanations. Lifting the receiver, he called Pamela Wagnall instead.

Although she sounded more composed than when he had spoken to her on Saturday, there was still an underlying note of tension in her voice. He managed to get as far as asking her if she would mind passing a message to Alexandra before she interrupted him.

"I don't know when I'll be seeing her again."

"You mean she's no longer staying with you?"

"Not exactly, although Alex has gone away. The Trust felt she was very run down and needed a rest so they packed her off to a nursing home."

"Whereabouts?"

"I don't know," Pamela Wagnall said, then added, "she didn't tell me."

"Her illness is a bit sudden, isn't it? I mean, Alexandra seemed all right when I saw her on Thursday."

"She's suffering from delayed shock, Mr Henderson. It was her car they blew up."

"Christ."

"She also asked me to tell you that she's very satisfied with your accounts and will be writing to thank you herself when she is feeling better."

"What accounts?"

"I don't know, Mr Henderson," Pamela Wagnall said irritably. "I expect she didn't want to talk about her private affairs in front of one of her colleagues."

"Where did all this happen?"

"Here in my house – and don't ask me his name because we weren't introduced."

A dozen questions sprang to mind but she was gone before he could ask a single one.

*   *   *

They arrived in two cars, Walter Tindall and Henry Uxbridge, the Chief of Staff, in one, the Special Branch team in the other. At least, Alexandra assumed the two youngish looking men and the flaxen haired girl in jeans who remained outside with their Rover 3500 were Special Branch. Henry Uxbridge was wearing a suitably grave expression although there was nothing unusual about that. An anaemic, round-shouldered man in his late fifties Henry always looked sour as though life and the people around him were a source of constant disappointment. A colourless, fussy and pedantic individual who liked things to be neat and tidy, he was in many ways an ideal Chief of Staff, an appointment he'd held for many years and was likely to go on holding until the day he retired. Alexandra sometimes wondered if this was the reason he was so embittered.

Tindall and Uxbridge ranged themselves on one side of the oak table in the breakfast room and invited Alexandra to take one of the dining chairs facing them. The whole atmosphere was reminiscent of a Judicial Inquiry, an impression that was heightened by the slow, very deliberate way Tindall opened his government-issue briefcase and produced a clutch of glossy photographs for her inspection.

"Who is this man, Alex?" he asked.

"Jack Henderson." Some of the photographs had been taken the day she had met him outside India House, the rest showed him walking through Lincoln's Inn Fields. "He's a private detective," she added.

"Is he working for you?"

"Yes. I hired him to find out what he could about Colonel Beardsley's financial affairs. I had reason to believe that Rupert was involved in wholesale bribery and corruption."

"Did you report this to your superiors?"

"Indeed I did." Alexandra gazed at Uxbridge. "But you wouldn't listen to me, would you, Henry?"

"I never pay any attention to idle speculation. The only evidence you managed to come up with consisted of an unattributable consignment note and a photocopy of a letter addressed to 'Rupert Sahib' of the British High Commission in Delhi which you inferred had been written by an Indian Customs Officer . . ."

"Which you were determined to keep off the file."

"Because there was nothing in it," Uxbridge said testily.

"Lawrence Goodman thought there was, otherwise he wouldn't have bothered to send it on."

"He was simply covering himself." Uxbridge wrinkled his nose as though he'd become aware of an unpleasant smell. "Anyway, we didn't motor all the way down here from London to listen to your pet theory."

"Maybe not," Tindall intervened, "but I'd still like to hear it." He smiled at Alexandra. "As concisely as possible," he added.

"Have you ever heard of a company called QRX Industrial Tools and Dies Limited?"

"No."

"I'm not surprised, Walter. It isn't listed in any trade directory. I first heard about QRX from Lawrence Goodman in October '85 after a gang of armed men broke into a boxcar in the sidings at Jhansi and stole a large packing crate. We don't know what it contained but it must have been pretty valuable because they didn't hesitate to murder a railwayman who was unfortunate enough to arrive on the scene at exactly the wrong moment."

His body had been found by the track the following morning surrounded by other miscellaneous items of freight which the robbers had had to unload before they'd been able to get at the particular crate they'd wanted. In their haste to get the job done quickly, one of the consignment labels on the crate had been ripped off. The note had indicated that the goods had been addressed to a non-existent firm in a non-existent road in Ambala up in the Punjab. That the crate, along with the other containers had ended up in Jhansi instead had been due to a simple error; there had been a mix-up in the marshalling yards at Bombay and the boxcar had been hooked on to the wrong freight train.

"The Indian Port Authorities were unable to ascertain where the crate had come from, nor did they ever discover which ship it had arrived on."

"And that's it?" Tindall asked.

"There's the letter which was addressed to 'Rupert Sahib', British High Commission, Delhi. It arrived on the twenty-ninth of January this year and was opened by the Second Secretary, Commerce, whose Christian name also happened to be Rupert. He read the letter and was sufficiently disturbed by the implications to pass it on to Lawrence Goodman."

The author had preferred to remain anonymous, his signature had been illegible and he had deliberately omitted his own address. His usage of English had been flowery and only semi-literate but there had been no mistaking the thrust of the writer's complaint or his occupation. The disgruntled customs officer had wanted to know why he hadn't been rewarded for clearing the machine tools from QRX. He'd also accused Rupert of going behind his back to find another port of entry in order to avoid paying the money he owed him.

"There was an eighteen-month interval between the robbery and the letter," Tindall observed. "I find it hard to believe the customs officer would have waited that long for his kick-back."

"We've no way of telling how many other letters he may have written."

"What made you fasten on to Colonel Beardsley, Alex? It's got to be more than just a Christian name."

She had already learned that Tindall was at his most dangerous when he was being chummy. But how could she tell him that she had never trusted Rupert? There had been something about the man which had made her skin crawl, so much so that right from the day they had first met, she had been on the look out for anything that would confirm her suspicions.

"It was mainly chemistry to begin with, then I discovered he'd lied to me about certain things in his private life."

"Such as?"

"Rupert was always telling people how devoted he'd been to Nancy but he'd had a mistress called Katherine Pascal long before his wife died."

Tindall raised a questioning eyebrow at Uxbridge. "Did you know about this?" he asked.

"Yes, so did Graham Oliver. Rupert consulted us before he told Godfrey Vines, the Director in charge of the South East Asia Bureau. We all knew that Nancy was a lush and that the marriage was on the rocks. The Director took the view that since Beardsley had been quite open with us about his extra-marital relationship with Mrs Pascal, he wasn't vulnerable to pressure."

It was another way of saying he couldn't be blackmailed, but it had been his financial affairs rather than his sexual peccadilloes which had bothered Alexandra.

"Rupert left over three hundred thousand pounds in his will," she said.

"I'm not surprised," Uxbridge told her loftily. "We always knew he was quite well-to-do."

"The money was on Nancy's side of the family."

"Then he probably inherited it from her."

"She had only two and a half thousand to her name when she died in 1983. Rupert must certainly have had the Midas touch to make that little bit of capital grow the way it did in four years."

Uxbridge frowned. "When was the last time we looked at his Positive Vetting clearance, Walter?"

"A quinquennial review was carried out in 1983."

Alexandra guessed that Tindall had pulled Beardsley's security file from the non-effective cabinet and had read it from cover to cover.

"Your vetting people would have gone into his financial position at the time, wouldn't they?"

"The last subject interview was done in September 1978."

Alexandra thought Tindall had managed to evade the question quite neatly. Although a PV clearance was reviewed every five years, the subject himself was only interviewed every ten years. In 1983, the vetting unit had simply obtained reports from Beardsley's superiors before revalidating his security clearance. And what Vines, Oliver and Uxbridge had known about Rupert's financial affairs had probably been conveyed in such well-worn phrases as 'Lives within his means', 'Follows a modest life-style' or, more prosaically, 'No known debts'. She also knew that the subject interview would have been less inquisitive in 1978 than it was nowadays. Nine years ago, the field investigating officer would merely have satisfied himself that Beardsley wasn't actually in debt.

"We should have worked on Dudley Spencer, Rupert's brother-in-law," Alexandra said. "It still wouldn't take much effort to make him ask his solicitors for a detailed statement of Beardsley's financial affairs."

"But no one would listen to you?" Tindall suggested.

"Unfortunately not."

"So you took the law into your own hands and briefed Mr Henderson?"

"I hired him."

"No matter how you choose to put it, you knowingly committed a major breach of security."

"That's stretching it a bit."

"And that wasn't the only leakage of information, was it?"

Here we go, Alexandra thought. "What else am I supposed to have done?" she asked.

"Someone has been keeping the Indian authorities extremely well informed about the attitude of Her Majesty's Government towards Sikh extremists in the UK."

"I didn't know we had an attitude." Alexandra smiled wryly. "Anyway, surely you can do better than that?"

Tindall most certainly could. In the last few months, a number of well-placed informants serving in the Indian Army had been arrested and charged with espionage following a tip-off from London. Delhi was also aware that both the Command and Logistic nets of their peace-keeping force in Sri Lanka were being monitored by the Secret Intelligence Service.

"All the files containing this information passed across your desk," Tindall said in conclusion.

"Among others. I'm not the only desk officer to have seen the material."

"Quite so, but you're the only one whose clandestine behaviour has come to our notice."

"You're not saying you're going to have me arrested?"

"We hope it won't come to that, Alex. However, there are a number of questions which must be put to you and this is not the place to do it."

"I presume you have somewhere more suitable in mind?"

Tindall had, but he was not prepared to enlighten her. Nor was the flaxen-haired girl from Special Branch who stayed with her while she packed her suitcase.

Chapter XV

Henderson parked the Ford Escort in the first available space by the kerbside, which happened to be at the top end of Well Walk, then made his way down the hill towards the Heath. Three days after the incident, no one would have known that two men had been killed by a bomb in this quiet, leafy side street. The charred wreckage of the laundry van had been towed away and only a few bare trees and a black square of freshly laid asphalt marked the spot where the crater had been.

He'd had no difficulty in persuading himself that he should follow up his telephone conversation with Pamela Wagnall. There was nothing to keep him in Nottingham; he had worked out a not-before/not-after time based on the Sunday service from Totnes to London which British Rail Enquiries had given him, and it was now up to his travel agent to produce a list of airline departures from Heathrow.

Henderson climbed the steps leading to the terraced garden above and rang the bell inside the porch of the Edwardian house. Pamela Wagnall wasn't expecting him; had he telephoned to say he proposed to drive up to London, he had a feeling she would have made sure that she was out when he called at the house. The rather sickly looking smile which twisted her mouth after he had introduced himself tended to confirm that his supposition had been correct.

"What brings you to London, Mr Henderson?" she asked in a voice that sounded cagey.

"I'm hoping you can help me. The message Alexandra left with you didn't make sense and I can't help feeling she hoped I'd be able to read between the lines."

"Well, I don't know that I can . . ."

Pamela Wagnall wanted to get rid of him and she wasn't going to invite him inside if she could help it.

"Why don't you want to get involved?" he asked.

The colour rose in her face. "You're being impertinent . . ."

"Someone wants to kill Alexandra because it sure as hell wasn't a coincidence when her car was destroyed by a bomb. You think so too; that's why you want to stay out of it. You're frightened they will come after you."

"That's absurd . . ."

"Did she ever mention a Steven Quilter?"

"No, who's he?"

"A removal man. He tidied up after Beardsley, cleared everything out of the Colonel's love nest down in Marlow and probably did the same for him at his flat in Stanhope Square. The lady-friend in Marlow thinks Quilter is with the Foreign Office Security Department but they've never heard of him."

"I think you'd better come in," Pamela Wagnall said and opened the door wider. "We'll have to use my husband's study, the rooms facing Well Walk are still in a mess."

The study was at the back of the house looking out on to a small walled garden enclosing a lawn the size of a hearth rug. It was furnished like an office with an executive desk, a three-drawer filing cabinet, a word processor and a swivel chair on wheels. The only other item of furniture was a ladder-back chair which looked as though it belonged in the kitchen.

"My husband's a merchant banker." Pamela Wagnall indicated he should take the swivel chair while she perched herself on the ladder-back. "Now, what else can I tell you?"

"Who accompanied Alexandra when she left here on Saturday?"

"I've already told you, Mr Henderson – we weren't introduced."

"Could you describe him then?"

"Fairly tall, lean, pushing fifty, more grey hairs than black, face shaped like a bird – narrow and pointed."

"That's a very good description," Henderson told her, smiling.

"I'm not entirely unobservant."

"I never thought you were. I don't suppose you can give me the names of any of Alexandra's colleagues, can you?"

"Alex never talked about her job with the Finlayson Trust except to say that it was very boring."

"Did she get in touch with her parents to let them know where she was going?"

"They live in Spain."

"When I first met her, Alexandra told me that she was the youngest of four."

"Yes, she is."

Pamela Wagnall might be observant but she wasn't going to volunteer any information, and her manner suggested that she resented him prodding her.

"Who threw the book at you?" he asked. "The man who came here with Alexandra?"

"I don't know what you're talking about."

"He quoted the Official Secrets Acts at you, didn't he? Told you not to say anything or else they would make life difficult for your husband." Henderson raised a hand to silence her before she started telling him just how wrong he was. "I'm sorry, obviously there are things you can't talk about but the members of her family can't be a state secret, can they?"

"Hardly."

"Look, I may be an ex-policeman from the sticks but I do know the Finlayson Trust is not a charitable organisation. I think it's an adjunct of the SIS, Century House, MI6 or whatever it is they like to call themselves. Alexandra discovered that something very odd was going on in her department but no one wanted to know about it, so she hired me to start a fire. Unfortunately, the blaze got out of control and she's trying to warn me off. Meanwhile she's in danger of getting burned. If Alexandra isn't already under arrest, she soon will be. You can't spring her, Mrs Wagnall, neither can I, but maybe her family can."

"I suppose Alex's father might still have some influence . . ."

"All right, let's start with him."

Fergus Drummond had been a High Court Judge whose clerk, acting on his instructions, had ensured that he had spent the greater part of his working life on the Western Circuit within easy motoring distance of the family home near Cheltenham. A man of considerable independent means, he had been blessed with an acid sense of humour and had been happiest when demolishing barristers, especially those from London whom he'd considered were getting above themselves. There were three sons of whom the eldest was now living in New Zealand. Harvey, the middle son, was a doctor married to another doctor and practising in Manchester, while Andrew, who was regarded as the most affable and least ambitious, was a PE teacher at a comprehensive school in Leicester. But Pamela Wagnall was right; with the possible exception of the father, none of them seemed in a position to make the government sit up and take notice.

"Does Alexandra have any influential friends?" Henderson asked.

"She's unattached at the moment."

"What has that got to do with it?"

"It happens to be the answer to the question you'd really like to ask me." She studied him thoughtfully, a knowing smile at the corners of her mouth. "Admit it, you've got a thing about Alex."

Henderson shook his head. "You're mistaken, I've only met her three times." But even to his own ears, his voice lacked conviction.

"Derek Mancroft is in a position to unlock a few doors for her."

"Derek Mancroft? What does he do for a living?"

"He's a rising star in the Home Office. He used to have the spare key to Alex's flat in Cheyne Walk, then last November they had this big row and she told him to return it. He's married of course; lives in Wimbledon and won't ask his wife for a divorce on religious grounds. Dear Derek is a devout Catholic – when it suits him."

Son of a bitch, Henderson thought, and hoped his anger didn't show.

"Somehow I don't think he will put himself out to help Alex."

"We'll see about that."

"Yes, Mr Henderson, I rather think you will."

Pamela Wagnall uncrossed her legs and leaned forward in the chair in a way which was clearly intended to let him know that she felt it was time he thought of leaving. Taking the hint, Henderson got to his feet a split second before she did and told her how grateful he was at least twice before they reached the front door.

He walked back up the hill, got into the car and sat there for several minutes unable to decide whether he should approach Mancroft for help or concentrate on Royles. He spun a coin to settle the issue on a heads or tails basis, found that the monarch was right side up and promptly drove out to Heathrow. He would probably have done the same had it come up tails.

He parked the Ford Escort in the short-stay multi-storey opposite the European Terminal, then used one of the pay-phones in the main concourse to ring his friendly travel agent in Nottingham. The list of scheduled departures between 1630 and 1830 hours on Sunday was dauntingly long. Aeroflot, Air Austria, Air France, British Airways, KLM, SAS, Swissair, Iberian, Malev, Lot, Lufthansa, Air Italia, Sabena: just about every European airline operating into and out of Heathrow was represented. Even when those from the Eastern Bloc were eliminated, there was still a formidable number left. He started with the British Airways desk for no other reason than it happened to be the nearest.

He pitched the usual 'stray dog' routine, how he had been hired by the family to trace Keith Royles and why he had reason to believe the missing person had left Heathrow yesterday evening on a BA flight to an unknown destination in Europe. It was a long, complicated, but far more believable story than the truth. The girl on duty at the information desk didn't question it, neither did her supervisor who decided she liked the look of Henderson, especially his open face and friendly smile. There was, of course, more than one BA flight between 1630 and 1830; after a great deal of cross checking, the supervisor came up with the information that Royles had been a passenger on BA Flight 744 departing at 1725 hours for Cologne.

Derek Mancroft was the one man he knew of with enough clout to ask his West German counterpart to put a trace on Royles. Pamela Wagnall had told him where Mancroft lived but his private phone number wasn't listed and only a senior police officer could prise that out of Directory Enquiries. By no stretch of the imagination could Detective Sergeant Preston be described as a senior officer; he was, however, on better than nodding terms with the Assistant Chief Constable and the Chief Superintendent in charge of the Force Research Unit.

*　　*　　*

Vines had two offices, one in Bell Yard, the other on the eighth floor of Century House where he spent the greater part of the week in splendid isolation from the desk officers of the South East Asia Bureau. He did of course show himself in Bell Yard on Mondays, Wednesdays and Fridays between the hours of nine thirty and eleven when he chaired the tri-weekly staff meetings. But any subordinate who wished to see him privately had to brief Henry Uxbridge first, then make an appointment with the PA. As the Chief Investigating Officer, Tindall only had to contend with the PA.

This was the second time in three days that Tindall had had a tête-à-tête with Godfrey Vines; before that they had scarcely been on nodding terms. His knowledge of the man was limited to the information contained between the covers of the Bureau Chief's security file and that didn't amount to a great deal. Born at Hastings in Sussex on the eleventh of October 1927, Vines had been called up for National Service on his eighteenth birthday, had subsequently been commissioned into the Royal Artillery and had served out his term with the Occupation Forces in Austria. Thereafter, his life had followed an equally well-ordered pattern.

While still reading English at Queens College, Oxford, he had been recruited by the Foreign Office acting on behalf of the Secret Intelligence Service and had made a reputation for himself as an expert on the Far East. His field experience had been gained in Malaya during counter insurgency operations against the Communist terrorists in the early fifties, followed by the confrontation with Indonesia in Borneo some fourteen years later. Since then, he had been stationed in London and had gradually worked his way up the ladder to head the South East Asia Bureau. Along the way, he had acquired a wife, three children and a house in Oxford within commuting distance of London.

Vines looked soft and plump, like a cat overfed by its doting owner. Although nearly sixty, his face was smooth and unlined but what was left of his hair formed a fringe, more white than grey, with a few strands carefully trained across a pink scalp. Tindall found it hard to like the man but greeted him with a polite smile.

"Will this take long?" Vines asked before he had a chance to settle himself in one of the armchairs provided for visitors. "Only the Cabinet Office is pressing me for a damage assessment."

Tindall thought it was hardly a propitious start and it wiped the smile from his face. "You're satisfied that Miss Drummond has been passing information to the KGB?"

"It's possible she has been using an intermediary," Vines said without committing himself to a definite opinion.

"The man with her in the photograph is Jack Henderson, a private investigator and former CID officer with the Nottinghamshire Constabulary. Everyone speaks very highly of him."

"So they did about Philby until he disappeared from Beirut."

"Quite. When did you begin to suspect that Miss Drummond was working for the KGB – sir?"

The 'sir' was very much an afterthought occasioned by a frosty look from Vines which told him the Bureau chief was very conscious of his status.

"Tuesday, May thirteenth, 1986, exactly seventy-two hours after we had learned that a number of high-ranking officers in the Indian Army who had been supplying us with information had been arrested."

It was obvious to Tindall that Vines had anticipated the line he would take and had prepared himself accordingly. Even someone blessed with a phenomenal memory would be hard pressed to recall the exact day and date fifteen months later.

"The matter had been discussed at some length during the staff meeting the day before when Miss Drummond had argued that no one in London had marked their cards." Vines frowned as though trying to recall the thrust of her case, then said, "She based her contention on the fact that not all the members of the Kohinoor Circle had been rounded up."

"Kohinoor?" Tindall muttered as if talking to himself.

"They were named after the Kohinoor diamond because we regarded the Circle as the brightest jewel in the crown.

Kohinoor also means Mountain of Light, which was equally apposite. Anyway, Henry Uxbridge, my Chief of Staff, and Graham Oliver, the Deputy Director of Operations came to see me the following afternoon. There had been other leaks besides the Kohinoor Circle and they had been looking for a common denominator. Miss Drummond had come to their notice because the internal register of classified documents showed that, excluding Uxbridge, Oliver and myself, she was the one person who'd had constant access to the relevant files. Indeed, she had taken them out more times than the rest of us put together. After due consideration, I therefore decided to place her under surveillance."

But Vines had not alerted him. He had kept it within the family and Uxbridge had borrowed a few watchdogs from other departments of Century House to keep an eye on the prime suspect. MI5 might run their vetting organisation for them but when the chips were down, it was all too evident that the SIS regarded his team as a bunch of interlopers. However, that was ancient history now; five pounds of gelignite had put Tindall in the driving seat and he wasn't about to score a few debating points when there were more important questions that needed to be answered.

"Miss Drummond has made certain allegations about the late Colonel Beardsley . . ."

"Yes. Apparently Rupert is supposed to have bribed an Indian Customs Officer. The accusation was made after his death and without a shred of evidence to back it up."

"When did you first hear about it?" Tindall paused, then added "sir" just in time.

"Miss Drummond saw me by appointment on Wednesday the twentieth of May. This was, of course, several days after she had been placed under surveillance and you may draw your own conclusions from that."

"It was my understanding that she had raised the matter with your Chief of Staff prior to that?"

"Yes, I believe she did. Henry wasn't impressed with her case either but she insisted on seeing me."

Tindall noted the careful response, the sudden reference to Uxbridge by his Christian name as though, like the Chief of Staff, he was a member of the inner cabinet who ran the South

East Asia Bureau. He could understand now how Vines had got as far as he had in the Service. He was the sort of man who was wise after the event but invariably managed to convince his superiors that he had seen trouble coming and had taken what pre-emptive measures he could. It was a tactical ploy which had evidently served him well in the early years; once he'd been made an Assistant Director and had had to make his own decisions, it had no longer worked for him. Tindall thought it explained why he hadn't gone any farther.

"Is it fair to say that you had complete faith in Colonel Beardsley and trusted him implicitly?" Tindall asked.

"I had no reason to doubt his integrity and he was very highly regarded by his superiors in the Foreign Office proper."

"Beardsley really was a Queen's Messenger?"

"Oh yes. We borrowed him from time to time, quite frequently in fact – but he was always their man."

It was an example of the way Vines endeavoured to protect himself. If Beardsley had been involved in some kind of racket, no one was going to accuse him of failing to know what his subordinates were up to. But anyone who felt that insecure was open to manipulation.

"The QRX Industrial Tools and Dies incident?" Tindall said, adopting a different approach. "What did you make of it at the time?"

"We were completely baffled," Vines told him with disarming candour. "A missing crate, a consignment note from a non-existent company to a non-existent address, and a dead railwayman; obviously something was being smuggled into the country and it must have been extremely valuable, but we'd no idea what the cargo was nor could we even hazard a guess. The Indian authorities sent a photocopy of the invoice to the British High Commission to see if we could identify the company. They also posed the same question to the Americans who weren't able to help them either."

"And the letter to Rupert?"

"You get a lot of begging letters in India," said Vines. "There is a scribe in most villages of any size who will compose one for you in English for a few annas. The tale of woe lists all the tragedies that have befallen the bearer of the note and, as the reader, you are expected to contribute a little something to relieve his or her distress. The letter addressed to Rupert was however in a different category; it was sent through the post and the general tone was threatening. I think it was a warning shot; the author had performed a service for which he hadn't been rewarded and if the money wasn't forthcoming, there would be another more compromising note."

Vines was sitting on the fence again. One minute he seemed to be siding with his Chief of Staff and Deputy Director, then in the next breath he seemed to imply that there might be something to Alexandra Drummond's theory after all.

"Why did he write only the one note?" Tindall asked, knowing he would get the obvious answer.

"I imagine the anonymous Rupert paid him off."

"Or maybe he was no longer able to post a letter?"

"What do you mean?"

"I'm curious to know the wastage rate amongst Customs and Excise officers in Bombay," said Tindall. "I cabled Goodman and asked him to find out."

*   *   *

The signal from London was classified SECRET UK EYES ONLY and was prefaced Personal for Goodman from SOSFA which was the official abbreviation for Secretary of State Foreign Affairs. Naturally the Foreign Secretary hadn't even seen the cable let alone approved it; SOSFA was simply the umbrella Century House liked to shelter under. Goodman didn't hesitate to show it to Manik Bhose because fifteen months after the Kohinoor Circle had been rounded up, he was still trying to mend a few fences with the Permanent Under Secretary. Oddly enough, the process had begun with Beardsley; the Indian Government had been embarrassed by his abduction and subsequent accidental death, which Goodman had exploited to the full. He had made Manik Bhose feel even more obligated by alerting him to the fact that Beardsley's family had hired a private investigator to look into the circumstances of his death.

"You're taking a risk, aren't you, Lawrence?" Manik asked, looking up from the cable. "What would your people do to you if they discovered I'd seen this?"

"I asked London to downgrade it to RESTRICTED and remove the UK caveat. I said we would never get the information they wanted unless I could brief you. Of course, if London chooses to ignore my request, I'll be looking for another job, assuming I'm not fated to spend the next thirty years inside."

"You've been standing out in the sun too long, that's your trouble, Lawrence."

"Will you provide the answers to the questions they've asked?"

"You want to know how many Customs and Excise officers employed in Bombay have left the service voluntarily or for other reasons since the first of June 1985?"

"Plus the same for Calcutta."

"What exactly does London mean by 'other reasons'?"

"Dismissal, imprisonment, sudden death," Goodman told him laconically.

"Would you say this signal has something to do with the incident at Jhansi fifteen months ago?"

"I should think it has everything to do with it," said Goodman.

CHAPTER XVI

THE SPECIAL BRANCH team were not unfriendly but while they had been willing to talk about everything else under the sun, they had refused point blank to say where they were taking her. What they'd hoped to gain from their secretiveness was still a mystery to Alexandra. No attempt had been made to blindfold her and they'd stuck to the main roads heading roughly north west through Thetford, King's Lynn, Grantham and Nottingham, so that she had guessed the safe house was somewhere in the Peak District of Derbyshire long before they'd reached Matlock.

The safe house was a large Victorian granite building high up in the sheep country of the Dales, a good ten miles from the Spa town. A brass plate on one of the stone gateposts indicated that it was the 'Moorlands Residential Training Centre'. The local tradesmen believed 'Moorlands' was a private educational establishment specialising in business studies for mature students. Only the permanent staff and visiting interrogators were allowed into Matlock; the former passed themselves off as tutors while the latter, whose faces were always changing, were thought to be students.

Alexandra didn't know how many other guests of Her Majesty's Government were currently in residence, nor did it seem likely that she would find out from the staff. As soon as they arrived at 'Moorlands', she was taken off to the library for a preliminary interrogation by the flaxen-haired girl from Special Branch.

"My name is Louise," she said, introducing herself a little late in the day. "However, most people call me Lou."

"Really? Most people call me Miss Drummond until they know me well."

"Oh, I'm sure we are going to become the best of friends," Louise said, cheerfully ignoring the snub.

"I guess you have to be an optimist in your job. Incidentally, how long have you been a policewoman?"

"More years than I care to remember."

At the age of eighteen she had joined the WRAC, subsequently rebadging to the Royal Military Police after completing her basic training at Guildford. She had left the army at the six-year point and joined the Metropolitan Police. Her previous experience in Belfast where she had been employed in an undercover job had made her a natural for the Special Branch. But none of this was relevant to the present situation and she had no intention of allowing Alexandra Drummond to distract her from the main purpose of the interview.

"Let's talk about Jack Henderson." Louise opened the notebook she had taken from her shoulderbag and uncapped a biro. "We'd like to know what made you choose him?"

"I was told he was a good detective. People who know Mr Henderson well say that he never gives up on a case. Tenacious was how they described him. And incorruptible, the sort of man who makes a staunch friend but a bad enemy."

"Why did you have to go so far afield? Couldn't you have found a private investigator with the same qualities nearer home?"

"I've already explained my reasons to Mr Tindall."

"I'd like to hear them too, Alex."

Of course Louise would, and afterwards she would compare notes with Tindall hoping to find some inconsistency in her story which they could exploit the next time they quizzed her.

"Beardsley came from Nottingham; it seemed a good idea to hire a local man to look into his background."

"I see. So who put you on to Mr Henderson?"

Alexandra hesitated, wondered if Special Branch would subject Young to a lengthy interrogation if she gave them his name.

"Look, we want to believe you, Alex, but how can we if you won't be honest with us?" Louise gazed at her with a concerned expression which, in the circumstances, seemed a touch hypocritical. "You've got to trust us."

But not all the way, Alexandra thought, and decided to give her an edited version of the truth.

"The sale of my flat in Cheyne Walk is being handled by a

Mr Young of Draycott and Draycott. I told him that I believed the charitable organisation I work for was being ripped off by one of the trustees and asked if he could recommend a private investigator in the Nottingham area. He said he would make some enquiries and phoned back a few days later to say that Mr Henderson was probably the sort of man I was looking for. I made an appointment to see him, took a day's leave and went up to Nottingham."

"Who else knew about it?"

"No one. I told Henry Uxbridge I was taking the day off to go house-hunting."

"You didn't confide in Pamela Wagnall?"

"I didn't want anyone to know what I was up to."

"Did Mr Young ever phone you at the office, Alex?"

"Yes, several times. There are two phones on my desk; one is on the Ptarmigan Crypto network, the other is an ordinary British Telecom line and that's the number I gave Mr Young. He was very discreet, if anyone had been listening in they would have thought Mr Henderson was a surveyor."

"And Henderson didn't know your phone number?"

Alexandra shook her head. Without Young realising it, she had used him as a cut out during normal working hours. Evenings and weekends, Henderson could ring her at the Wagnalls, but there was no harm in that. It didn't jeopardise the arrangements she had made which were intended to ensure that no one in the South East Asia Bureau should know they were in contact or see them together. But clearly this security measure hadn't worked and someone had had forewarning of their every move.

"Would you have known if your phone had been bugged?" Louise asked.

"I took it apart every morning and it was clean. Unfortunately, I didn't have the technical resources to sweep the office and obviously I couldn't ask for them."

"Seems to me the surveillance team did a pretty good job on you."

"Yes, well, I expect they've already received an accolade from Henry Uxbridge."

"Or Graham Oliver?"

Alexandra stared at the flaxen-haired girl. "Are you telling me it was the Deputy Director of Operations who recruited them?"

"According to Mr Tindall, he's the one who recommended that you should be kept under surveillance."

"And I thought it was Henry. It just shows how wrong one can be."

"Has Mr Henderson been doing any better? I mean, is there any chance of him getting a result?"

In police jargon, getting a result meant you'd wrapped up the case and a conviction was a foregone conclusion. Unless his luck had suddenly changed, Henderson hadn't got very far in spite of all his hard work.

"He's come up with one promising lead."

"Are you going to share it with us?"

"I don't see why not."

In a few short sentences, Alexandra told her about Keith Royles, who he was, what he did for a living and how he had apparently crossed swords with Beardsley when the latter had denied he'd seen him dining with a Pakistani businessman at the Imperial Hotel in Rawalpindi.

"Royles left Indus Tours and came home after receiving a telegram from his boyfriend. Someone learned that Henderson was looking for him and arranged for several musclemen to call at the flat where he was living. They put the boyfriend in hospital then told Royles they would do the same to him if he showed his face in Belmont Court again. At least, we think that was the message they gave him because Royles left town in a hurry and didn't tell anyone where he was going. I asked Mr Henderson to find him."

"Why?"

Alexandra looked to her right and gazed through the window at the hard court on the west side of the house where two men in tracksuits were knocking up. Both players were sacrificing accuracy in favour of speed and were over-hitting more often than not. Metaphorically speaking, Alexandra had a feeling that she was about to do the same.

"I want to question Mr Royles about the Pakistani who was dining with Rupert Beardsley. And I also want to show him the gallery of faces who have come to our notice and see if he recognises anyone."

"Who are these faces, Alex?"

"Politicians, agitators, shady money men, Communists, suspected terrorists of one kind or another . . ."

Her voice tailed away, silenced by the sceptical look in the blonde girl's eyes. Alexandra didn't blame her; had their positions been reversed, she would have been just as doubtful. There were too many suppositions and not enough facts in her case against Beardsley. She might believe that Royles had been given his marching orders because he knew too much but, after all, he was a homosexual and in a neighbourhood like Belmont Court, queer-bashing was practically a sporting pastime.

"You've really got a thing about Colonel Beardsley, haven't you, Alex? The guy may be dead but you're still going after him."

"You're wrong. I'm gunning for his associates and Rupert is going to lead me to them."

"From the grave?"

"Yes, with a little help from Royles."

"I might have guessed there would be a proviso." Louise stared at her thoughtfully for some moments, then said, "I think I'd like a word with my colleagues. Would you excuse me for a few minutes, Alex?"

"Don't hurry yourself on my account," Alexandra told her drily, "I'm not going anywhere."

The tennis twins were playing in real earnest now, both men using their speed and stamina to cover the court whenever they failed to anticipate where the ball was going. They were, she assumed, substitutes for guard dogs; 'Moorlands' was supposed to be an educational establishment and a couple of Dobermans would look out of place to the locals.

Louise returned a few minutes later with a telephone and a long extension cord which she plugged into the bayonet socket above the skirting board near the window.

"My colleagues would like you to call Mr Henderson," she said brightly.

"Give me one good reason?"

"He's looking for Royles and we're quite good at tracing missing persons. Besides, a little mutual co-operation wouldn't do your case any harm either."

"What do you want me to say to him?"

186

"Ask him how he's doing, whether he's had any joy in tracing Royles. Hell, Alex, you don't need any guidance from me."

Alexandra glanced at her wristwatch, saw that it was almost six thirty and rang his private number. There was no reply.

"Seems he's not at home," she said and held the receiver at arm's length so that Louise could hear it ringing out. "I could try his office and leave a message on the answering machine."

"You must think I was born yesterday," Louise said and yanked the bayonet plug from the socket to disconnect the phone.

*   *   *

Mancroft lived in the up-market area of Wimbledon in a large mock-Georgian house halfway down St Mary's Road. After Preston had understandably refused to obtain his home address and unlisted phone number, Henderson had finally run him to ground with the help of a young local government officer. Recalling that Pamela Wagnall had told him Mancroft lived in Wimbledon, he'd driven there from Heathrow and more by luck than judgment, had arrived at the Town Hall before it closed at five. Provided Mancroft hadn't moved away from the area, Henderson knew that his name and address would appear somewhere on the Electoral Roll, which any citizen had a right to see any time he liked during normal office hours. The problem lay in knowing where to look for his name; fortunately, the local government officer had been in Wimbledon long enough to say which were the most desirable residential areas. With the field narrowed to a couple of wards, it had then taken Henderson less than ten minutes to find Mancroft's address.

Nine to five hours didn't apply to a rising star like Mancroft; civil servants who wanted to go all the way stayed at their desks long after everyone else had gone home. Henderson had thought Mancroft was unlikely to be an exception and had killed an hour and a half at a snack bar before he'd started looking for St Mary's Road. When eventually he found the street, he parked the Ford Escort up the hill from the house. At a quarter to seven he got out of the car, walked back down the road and rang the front door bell. The woman who answered it was in her early forties, had lacklustre brown hair and the beginnings of a double chin.

"My name's Henderson," he told her. "I'm making inquiries about a Miss Alexandra Drummond, a former colleague of your husband. I don't suppose he's home yet?"

"I'm afraid not – this is about the time he usually leaves the office." Mrs Mancroft peered at the laminated card bearing the logo of the Gold Seal Inquiry Agency which he was holding up and seemed reassured. "Would you like to come back in twenty minutes? He shouldn't be longer than that."

"Thank you."

"May I ask what you want to see him about?"

"Positive Vetting," said Henderson. "Miss Drummond nominated your husband as a referee."

Henderson returned to the car, put a tape on the stereo and sat there listening to Bert Kampfert. He had told Mrs Mancroft enough to make it difficult for her husband to refuse to see him. Positive Vetting was government business and Mancroft would need to come up with a cast-iron excuse for avoiding him otherwise his wife might begin to suspect that his relationship with Alexandra Drummond was less than kosher.

A police car appeared in the rear view mirror and he wondered if the officers were going to stop and question him but at the last moment, the driver tripped the indicator and went on up the hill. Shortly afterwards, a black Rover limousine swept into the driveway of the house. Henderson gave the Home Office man a few minutes to greet his wife and hear the bad news, then got out of the car and walked back down the hill again.

Derek Mancroft was a swarthy man of medium height whose dark hair looked as though it had been permed. He was not exactly overjoyed to see Henderson.

"Now, what is all this nonsense about?" he demanded once they were alone in the small room off the hall which he used as a snug.

"Nonsense is the right word," Henderson said icily. "On Saturday afternoon, some twenty-four hours after an attempt had been made on her life, Miss Drummond was taken into protective custody. No charges appear to have been preferred and as far as anyone can tell, she has not been able to consult a solicitor."

"I don't see what this has to do with me . . ."

"Yesterday evening, a Mr Keith Royles boarded British Airways Flight 744 to Cologne. The people who tried to kill Miss Drummond didn't want him around because he knows too much about the late Colonel Beardsley. So they put the fear of God into Royles and made him run."

"I still don't see . . ."

"You are going to have a word with the people who are holding Miss Drummond and inform them that if I don't hear from her within the next forty-eight hours, she will become a household name because her picture is going to appear in all the tabloids."

"Are you trying to threaten me, Mr Henderson?"

"Then you are going to ask your West German counterpart to put a trace on Keith Royles." Henderson tore a page from his pocket notebook and gave it to Mancroft. "This is a description of him which I jotted down while waiting for you to come home. I personally have never met the guy but it's what he looks like according to those who have. I imagine you'll have no difficulty in obtaining his photograph from the passport office."

Mancroft reduced the page to confetti, tearing it in half, again and again. Then he dropped the pieces into a waste-paper basket.

"That's what I think of your threats. Now I think you'd better go before I decide to call the police."

"You shouldn't have done that," Henderson said calmly. "The date and place of his birth were on that page. You'll need that information if you're to obtain his passport photograph."

"Get out. Get out of my house." His voice hissed, the colour rose in his face.

"You'd better get down on your hands and knees and stick those pieces together," Henderson told him quietly, "because if you fail to deliver, I'm going to heap so much shit on you, the stink will still be there when they put you in your coffin. I know all about your affair with Miss Drummond and how being a devout Catholic stopped you from divorcing your wife to marry her, and I'm telling you the tabloids will have a field day. I can just see the headlines – 'Beautiful Spy Disappears – Home Office Lover Says Not Guilty'. How do you suppose Mrs Mancroft will like that?"

"You bastard."

"I know," said Henderson. "But I'm working at being one; with you it just comes naturally."

* * *

Quilter listened to the phone ringing at the other end of the line, thumb and fingers of his right hand drumming the desk top in mounting impatience. Ahmad Bashir Khan was probably lounging by the swimming pool on the terrace of his hilltop villa overlooking Cannes while enjoying the mint julep he permitted himself at sunset; but there was a houseful of servants and even if they were French, they weren't all deaf for Christ sake. He let the phone ring another minute, then, just as he was about to hang up, someone finally deigned to answer it.

The arrogant, haughty voice belonged to the butler, a fifty-year-old Parisian with delusions of grandeur who acted as though he was doing Khan a favour by condescending to work for him. Quilter had met him only the once and had been irritated by the man's superciliousness.

"My name's Quilter," he said brusquely. "I'm the managing director of QRX Industrial Tools and Dies. Mr Khan is expecting my call."

"If Monsieur will kindly wait a minute."

Time seemed to have little meaning for the Frenchman and Quilter suspected it would be several minutes. From his small office on Paternoster Row, he could see the dome of St Paul's. Below him, the usually busy precinct was deserted, the last of the tourists and city workers long since departed. So also had the junior partners of Steven Quilter and Associates, Charter and Supply Specialists. They provided the legitimate front behind which he operated and it was their proud boast that they could charter anything from a luxury ocean-going yacht to a jumbo jet at a cheaper rate than any of their competitors. Quilter handled the less reputable side of the business and for a remunerative fee would supply anything from a ZB298 radar to a 120 mm mortar. Ahmad Bashir Khan was one of his more important clients.

There was a faint clatter as someone picked up the phone, then, to his relief, Khan said, "Good evening, Mr Quilter, how are you keeping?"

"I'm fine," Quilter told him, "especially now that I've heard from my West German colleague. To all intents and purposes, that little problem we spoke about has been solved."

"Good." Khan cleared his throat. "May I ask when you plan to deliver the next consignment of industrial tools?"

"We've had a spot of trouble with the labour force but the union has accepted our offer and the dispute has been settled. Things should therefore be back to normal by the end of next week."

Henderson was still around but the Drummond girl was locked up in a safe house near Matlock and without her to point him in the right direction, he was just an unguided missile.

"That soon?"

"We aim to please," Quilter said and hung up.

The little problem he'd referred to was Keith Royles and in a few hours from now, he would no longer be a threat. Long after he had been consigned to a watery grave, the postcards from Bonn, Baden Baden, Munich, Salzburg and Vienna would continue to arrive at 'Look-Out Cottage' to give the impression that he was still alive.

*　　　*　　　*

The postcard showed the Olympic Stadium in Munich. On the back, Royles wrote 'Arrived here Thursday. Tomorrow we go on to Salzburg where we spend two nights before making our way to Vienna. Trip going well with few complaints from the tourists, but they are one of the best groups I've escorted. Love, K.'

He had already written two other cards, one allegedly in Bonn, the other from Baden Baden, and he was running out of inspiration. He'd never been much of a correspondent and Pat was going to think it very odd when a series of postcards dropped through her letter box, but he assumed Quilter and Immelmann knew what they were doing.

Franz Immelmann had met him at Cologne Airport. For some reason, Royles had thought he would be roughly his size but at six feet two, the German towered over him. However, like many big men, and Immelmann weighed all of two hundred pounds, he was modest, quietly spoken and easy-going. He had short blond hair, a round open face and a mouth which seemed permanently on the point of breaking out in a smile.

From Cologne they had motored south, following the Rhine before turning off the autobahn some forty-six kilometres from Freiburg to head cross country on minor roads to this chalet somewhere in the heart of the Black Forest. It had been pitch dark when they'd arrived on Sunday evening and even now, twenty-four hours later, he still had no idea where they were. Franz had told him the area was famous for its wild boar and that the chalet was actually a hunting lodge. According to him, the log cabin belonged to a wealthy industrialist in Frankfurt who, because of his friendship with the Herr Direktor, occasionally loaned it to the BND, the West German equivalent of the Special Branch.

As a hide-out, the lodge obviously had a lot going for it; the nearest village was at least fifteen kilometres away, there were no other cabins in this part of the forest and the building couldn't be seen from the road. As a guest house, it definitely had its limitations. There was no electricity or running water, the lavatory was an earth closet and the only cooking facility was a wood-burning stove. The accommodation consisted of two sparsely furnished bedrooms and one large, equally spartan communal room. Fortunately, he wouldn't be staying there much longer; Franz had driven into Offenburg to phone Quilter and, with any luck, perhaps the Special Branch officer would have already made alternative arrangements for him.

Royles looked up from the table. The evening was drawing in fast, hastened by the thunderstorm in the distance which was steadily coming their way. Pushing the postcards away from him, he got up and went into the curtained-off alcove which served as the kitchen, storeroom and larder to see to the pressure lamps. All five had been filled that morning; nevertheless, pumping them up to full pressure and lighting each mantle was still a lengthy and messy business. He was just hanging the fifth and last one from a beam above the table when Franz Immelmann returned from Offenburg.

"We have wine, Rösti potatoes and schnitzels," the German said, holding up a string bag so that he could see the purchases.

Royles jumped down from the table. "Did you speak to Mr Quilter?" he asked.

"But of course." Immelmann went into the alcove, put the groceries on the draining board, then found two glasses in the cupboard above the sink and uncorked one of the bottles. "Niersteiner Gutes Domtal," he said, glancing over his shoulder. "Not a bad year either."

"For Christ sake," Royles protested. "What did Quilter have to say?"

"Relax, everything has been taken care of. Tomorrow you will be moving on to Crans Montana where Detective Inspector Quilter will be waiting for you. A Mr Khan has offered to look after you."

"Who is this Mr Khan?"

"A man who owes Mr Quilter a favour. You will be quite safe with him." Immelmann poured the wine, gave one glass to Royles, then raised his to salute him. "Prost."

"Cheers."

"Tell me, Keith, have you written the postcards to your aunt?"

"Yes, all three of them."

Immelmann put down his glass. "That is good. They will lay a false trail for Mr Henderson to follow."

"You think he'll call on my aunt?"

"Oh, yes. Mr Quilter says he is a very persistent fellow." Immelmann clapped his hands, rubbed them together. "But let us not worry about him. Tonight we eat, drink and be merry, eh?"

"Yes."

"For tomorrow we must part." Immelmann smiled regretfully. "We hardly know each other," he said, "but I think I am going to miss you, Keith."

"Me too," Royles said and felt his pulses quicken.

Outside, the thunder rumbled and presently it began to rain.

Chapter XVII

IMMELMANN DUMPED his suitcase on the back seat of the Mercedes, then returned to the chalet with the packet of bin liners he'd bought at the supermarket in Offenburg. A man noted for being methodical, he opened the packet with a pair of nail scissors, removed one of the black polythene bags and carefully unfolded it. Placing the bin liner near the stove, he opened the fire door and raked the ashes into the pan below the bars. As soon as he was satisfied the stove was completely empty, he removed the pan and slowly emptied the ashes into the bin liner. From a cursory inspection, he couldn't see any trace of man-made fibres, but there was no telling what a forensic scientist would have found under a microscope.

He opened a second bin liner, went into the kitchen alcove and cleared everything out of the cupboard. Two empty wine bottles, yesterday's loaf of bread, 500 grams of sugar, the remains of a packet of butter, breakfast cereal, a can of peaches and a jar of coffee went into the polythene bag. So did a litre carton of milk after he'd emptied the contents down the sink. That done, he tied the neck of the bin liner in a knot, did the same with the one containing the ashes from the fire and carried both out to the car.

Immelmann went back into the chalet again to check out the bedrooms. The one he'd slept in was squared away like a barrack room, the individual biscuits of the three-piece mattress piled one on top of the other in front of the headboard, the duvet folded to conform with the overall symmetry. Even the pillow had been dressed off in line with the forward edge of the duvet. The room was, in fact, exactly as he'd found it late on Sunday evening.

The one Royles had occupied was equally neat and tidy but that was because he had tidied up after the Englishman.

194

Immelmann sniffed the air and was satisfied that there was no trace now of the cloying scent Royles had sprayed himself with before retiring to bed to await his lover. He closed the window which he had opened after the storm was over in order to ventilate the room, then rubbed the catch with a handkerchief to obliterate his fingerprints.

For the third and last time, he left the chalet and walked over to the Mercedes. Taking a bunch of car keys out of his pocket, he unlocked and opened the boot. Royles was lying on his right side, the suitcase he'd brought from England wedged behind him. His knees were touching his stomach and his head was bowed as though in prayer. Although death had occurred eight hours ago, his face was still purple. Rigor mortis had set in and the body would be difficult to carry in the foetal position but given the cubic capacity of the boot, it had been the only way of transporting the corpse to its ultimate destination at the bottom of the Bodensee. Immelmann picked up the polythene bags he'd left by the offside rear wheel and placed them lengthways on top of the body to conceal it from view, then slammed the lid down and locked it.

Thus far, everything had gone smoothly. Even strangling the Englishman had been easier than he had expected. Royles had drunk too much wine over dinner and with only a little encouragement from him, had completely misread all the signs. The simpering fool had actually believed he was interested in his body and had minced off to his bedroom, wiggling his ass like some fifty-mark whore on the Reeperbahn in Hamburg. When he had walked into the room a few minutes later, Royles had changed into a pair of silk pyjamas and had bathed himself in scent. Observing his apparent embarrassment, the English-man had walked forward and taking hold of his hand, had led him towards the bed. In turning about to back into him, Royles had been his own executioner; looping the picture cord around his neck, Immelmann had garotted him before he had time to cry out.

At the moment of death, Royles had fouled himself and cleaning up the mess had been the worst thing he'd had to do. The silk pyjamas had gone into the stove along with the rest of his clothes, toiletries and shaving tackle. Immelmann had kept the suitcase mainly on account of the trouble he'd had destroying the shoes. There were no initials on the suitcase, it wasn't an expensive model and since he had burned the labels and airline baggage check, no one would be able to tell who it had originally belonged to.

It had still been raining when Immelmann had carried the body out to the car and this had meant he'd had to wash the floor down to remove his muddy footprints, but that had been unavoidable. Had he waited for the rain to stop, the corpse would have become too rigid to squeeze into the boot.

Immelmann came to with a start, uncertain for a split second where he was. He wondered how long he had been sitting there wool-gathering behind the wheel of the Mercedes and vented his anger in a stream of expletives. Then reason prevailed and he calmed down. It was a good hundred and sixty kilometres to the Bodensee and even a minor traffic accident would be a disaster. He checked to make sure the postcards Royles had written were on him, then started the engine and drove out of the forest clearing.

*   *   *

Danny Preston was the last person Henderson expected to find on his doorstep at seven forty-five in the morning. To have a visitor at that hour was unusual enough but two was unheard of.

"This is Detective Sergeant Avery, Jack," Preston said. "He's the expert on electronic surveillance I told you about."

"Nice to meet you," Henderson said as they shook hands.

Sizing him up, Henderson reckoned Avery was a small compact man roughly five feet seven and weighing something in the region of a hundred and fifty pounds. He had dark, wiry hair, pale blue eyes and a chin that could have been chiselled out of stone. The faintly nervous smile on his lips was at odds with the strong-looking face.

"Well, aren't you going to invite us in?" Preston asked. "I mean, you did know we were coming to debug your house this morning?"

Henderson moved aside and let the two men into the hall. "No," he said, "I can't say I did."

"I rang your office yesterday evening and left a message on the answering machine. Ten to one, you didn't go near the place."

"You're right. Fact is, I didn't get back from London until ten o'clock last night."

"Perhaps we should make it another day?" Avery suggested.

"Not on your life," Preston told him. "I had enough trouble setting up this date with you without going through that shemozzle again. Let's get the job done now."

Avery looked to Henderson. "Is it okay with you?" he asked.

"Sure."

"I see the phone's in the hall. Do you have an extension elsewhere in the house?"

"There's one in the kitchen."

"Danny tells me you live alone?"

"What's that got to do with it?" Henderson asked.

"I need to know how many rooms are in use," Avery explained.

"I eat in the kitchen and sleep in the small bedroom at the back of the house. I can't remember the last time I entertained anyone at home but sometimes I move the TV into the lounge and watch it in comfort."

Avery opened the zipper bag he'd been carrying and took out a cylindrical, hypersensitive microphone and a head-set. "You can hear a pin drop with this little job," he said. "It works like a metal detector. Forget what you may have heard; there is no such thing as a totally passive sensor. They all emit a signal and if there's a bug around here, this gubbins will screech like hell."

Avery started in the hall and checked out the lounge-diner before moving on to the kitchen and utility room. He was upstairs working on the small back bedroom when the phone rang. In a morning that was already full of surprises, to find he had Alexandra Drummond on the line was really only par for the course.

"Are you okay?" Henderson asked.

"I'm fine, the rest is doing me good."

The innuendo wasn't lost on him. For rest, substitute custody. He thought it would do no harm to let her warders know he was on to them.

"I'm glad Mancroft was quick off the mark," he said.

"Mancroft? Do you mean Derek Mancroft?"

"Yes, your friend in the Home Office."

"How is he involved?" Her voice was faint and sounded as though she was out of breath.

"I called at his house in Wimbledon yesterday evening and told him your picture would be in all the tabloids if I didn't hear from you within the next forty-eight hours. I guess he took it to heart."

"How did you know . . .?"

"I saw Pamela Wagnall," Henderson said, cutting Alexandra off in mid-sentence. "She told me all about him."

"My God, you're amazing, you know that?"

Her voice was more incredulous than breathless now and he could picture her shaking her head.

"That isn't what Mancroft called me but then he was a touch upset."

"I'm sure he was," Alexandra said drily. "Did you have as much joy with Mr Royles?"

"I think Royles is trying to avoid me; he flew out to Cologne on Sunday evening. However, I persuaded your friend, Derek Mancroft to put a trace on him."

"You must have really put the wind up Derek."

"Well, he also agreed that you could see a solicitor whenever you wanted to."

"Actually, I tried to get in touch with you early yesterday evening but obviously you were still in London."

It was, Henderson realised, a way of telling him that her phone call hadn't come about as a result of Mancroft's intervention. His instincts also told him that Alex, as he had now started to think of her, was not an entirely free agent. If he was right, a third party would be listening to their conversation, ready to pull the plug on her the moment she stepped out of line.

"Have you ever heard of a Mr Quilter?" he asked.

"Yes. I think his first name is Steven; he's an expert in the field of adult education and is preparing a paper on behalf of the Trust to do with improving literacy amongst the peasant farmers of Uttar Pradesh."

Although Henderson had no experience of the Intelligence

world, it sounded to him like a well-rehearsed cover story to explain what Quilter was doing.

"Katherine Pascal is under the impression that he's a Foreign Office security man."

"It has to be someone with the same surname."

"The Foreign Office say they don't have a Mr Quilter working for them. So – are you going to tell the chairman of the Finlayson Trust about this impostor or shall I?"

"I think you'd better leave it to me, Mr Henderson."

"All right, I'll keep working on Royles. You want to give me the phone number of the place where you're staying?"

The third party wasn't going to have that. As though someone had cut the wires, the phone suddenly went dead.

"Problems?" Preston asked, raising an eyebrow.

"Just a bad connection."

"In more ways than one, Jack. Sure you aren't out of your depth?"

"If I am, I'm in good company." Henderson heard the sound of footsteps on the staircase and went out into the hall. "All finished?" he asked, looking up at Avery.

"Yes, your house is as clean as a whistle. If the place was bugged, someone must have come back and removed the evidence."

"You didn't look at the extension in the kitchen."

"There's no need to."

Eavesdropping had been developed to a fine art and the days when it was necessary to take a phone apart were long gone. The latest technology was a wire mike so thin it was practically invisible to the naked eye and a battery-powered transmitter no bigger than a thumb tack.

"Of course, we could be up against an external directional probe," Avery said, warming to his subject, "but that's big league stuff. The eavesdroppers would need to establish a base across the street or in one of the houses backing on to this property and no private enterprise outfit could set up such an operation. The Home Office could but I would have known about it."

"And you haven't heard a dicky-bird?" said Preston.

"Right." Avery laughed. "All the same, it would be one hell of a joke if you'd called me in to remove a bug I'd planted!"

Preston agreed it would be very droll though his chuckle sounded a little forced. Henderson then asked if he could show his appreciation in some small way and reached for his wallet, but the Special Branch man wouldn't hear of it.

"Listen, I did it as a favour to Danny and the world's in a sorry state if you can't do a good turn for a friend."

"Well, it's very good of you."

Avery moved down the hall towards the zipper bag he'd left near the front door and packed the detector equipment away. "It's time I was on my way," he muttered. "I'm supposed to attend a meeting in Leicester at ten thirty."

Henderson shook hands, thanked him again for what he'd done and saw him out of the house.

"Avery's a likeable bloke," Preston said, after watching him drive off down the hill.

"What's he doing in Leicester? Surely that's outside his bailiwick?"

"Avery is no longer with the Nottinghamshire Constabulary; he was transferred to the Regional Task Force about eighteen months ago and is employed in their Counter Extremist Cell. PIRA, the PLF, ETA, Action Directe and the Red Army Faction; any terrorist group you care to name, they're after them. He's got a lot on his plate; that's why he's a difficult man to pin down. Matter of fact, I've lost count of the number of phone calls it took me to get him to agree to this particular date."

"I owe you, Danny."

"Your credit's good," Preston said and lifted a hand in farewell.

Henderson collected his jacket from the bedroom, checked to make sure he hadn't left his car keys on the chest of drawers before he walked out of the house, then closed the front door behind him. As he moved round to the garage, the retired school-teacher across the road called to him from her front garden and said she was so pleased he had found a buyer at last.

Curious to know what she meant, Henderson crossed the street to have a word with her.

"The man who left your house a few minutes ago in the dark blue car," she said. "He was there on Saturday with his wife."

"Are you sure?" he asked.

"Quite sure, Mr Henderson. I remember thinking at the time that his car was the same colour as the one I saw the day your house was burgled."

*   *   *

Tindall had never met Graham Oliver before. Although familiar with his security file, Tindall's predecessor had carried out the third quinquennial vetting review and the Deputy Director (Operations) rarely visited Century House. Whenever he did, it was always to see Vines and the rest of the hierarchy on the eighth floor. Conversely, this morning was one of the few times Tindall had called round to the Finlayson Trust in Bell Yard.

Slightly younger than the other Grade 6 officers of his seniority, Oliver would be forty in May '88. Unlike his colleagues, he was not a product of Oxbridge but had obtained a First in Law at Bristol. He had also been married and divorced twice which, despite all the glowing reports he had received over the years from his superiors, raised doubts about his judgment and stability. In Tindall's eyes, everyone was entitled to one major error but two was downright careless. And, like marriage, it took more than one person to make a divorce. Tindall, however, had not crossed the river to discuss Oliver's marital problems with him; he was much more concerned to know what the Deputy Director made of Alexandra Drummond.

"I understand she is an expert on the Indian subcontinent?" Tindall said, broaching the subject.

"Alex is certainly very knowledgeable," Oliver conceded. "She compiled a rogues' gallery of Sikh extremists who want a separate state in the Punjab."

"That would be Khalistan?"

Oliver nodded. "I can see you've been doing your homework," he said good-humouredly.

"I've still got a lot to learn. For instance, who is technically responsible for monitoring the activities of Sikh extremists in the UK?"

"Your lot," said Oliver, "MI5, the Security Service. Of course, there is a great deal of cross fertilisation and we've been able to pass on a few names as a result of the sources we've cultivated in India."

"Alex led me to understand that she wasn't concerned with the UK end?"

"It isn't exactly a closed book to her, Walter; she does see the relevant files from time to time. But Alex is right in saying that, as an analyst, she isn't involved in obtaining the information. Rupert Beardsley was the man who did that. Although officially a Queen's Messenger, he was one of the best field agents we had. The number of people he knew in India was quite phenomenal, but then he'd been going there for years and was a sahib from the old days of the Raj."

And had been born half a century too late to have seen the best of it. Some men would say that Beardsley had been denied the opportunity to make a name for himself, though the DSO and MC he'd won in Burma should have stood him in good stead when he'd transferred to the British Army after Independence.

"I would have expected Beardsley to go much farther than he did." Tindall raised a quizzical eyebrow. "Any idea why he left the Army prematurely to become a Queen's Messenger?"

"Rupert had to resign his commission; he was having it away with the wife of a junior officer under his command and they were caught in flagrante delicto on the Mess billiard table one ladies' guest night. The Army Board frowns on that sort of thing, especially when the aggrieved husband sues for divorce and cites a brother officer as the co-respondent. So he had to go. However, Rupert was not without influential friends and they got him a job with the Foreign Office. We sent for his personal file from the Army and laundered it when he started working indirectly for us."

"What else did you find in it?" Tindall was sure there had to be something more than just a messy divorce.

"The laundering was done long before my time, but I understand Rupert was quite a womaniser in his younger days. And he certainly lived it up for a man who was dependent on his army pay."

"He was a bit of a security risk, wasn't he? What on earth persuaded the SIS to use him?"

"Because he was head and shoulders above everyone else. To all intents and purposes, he was the Kohinoor Circle; he recruited every man."

"The brightest jewel in the crown," Tindall murmured.

"Quite. At least, Godfrey Vines was apt to describe the Circle in those terms." Oliver shrugged. "Personally, I think that's going a bit over the top. Rupert may have nobbled some up-and-coming young staff officers in their Directorate of Military Intelligence but all they ever gave us were the names of Sikh extremists who were thought to be living in this country. They never gave us a thing on any of the Soviet advisers and there are several thousand of them attached to the Indian Army and Air Force."

"So why would Alex betray them?"

"I don't believe she did. Instead of looking for a potential mole, we should give their counter intelligence people credit for doing a good job."

"But it was you who recommended that Alex should be kept under surveillance," Tindall pointed out.

"Actually, I merely concurred with the recommendation. It was Godfrey Vines and Henry Uxbridge who wanted it done. For various reasons they no longer trusted her and I felt a surveillance operation would help to clear the air. Unfortunately, it did nothing of the kind. As for the photographs, they merely proved that we should have called in the professionals instead of trying to do the job ourselves." Oliver smiled wryly. "Godfrey wanted to drop the problem in your lap; I'm the genius who talked him out of it."

"Why?"

"Because I thought a witch hunt was just what the KGB wanted."

According to Oliver, no one in the Kohinoor Circle would admit to betraying their country. All those involved had firmly believed that in passing information about known Sikh terrorists to a friendly power, they were merely doing what the Indian Government should have done. Their attitude had ruffled politicians and civil servants alike; playing on this, the KGB had suggested the Indian Government should attribute the success of their counter intelligence operation to inside information from a British source.

"What about the allegation that we were monitoring their command net in Sri Lanka?" Tindall asked.

"Every country uses communications intelligence; they

didn't need a source to know that we were eavesdropping on them."

"Are you giving Alex a clean bill of health then?"

"I don't believe she's a double agent," Oliver said carefully.

In his eyes, Alexandra Drummond was something else. She was intelligent, ambitious and single-minded.

"I think Rupert may well have been up to his neck in shady deals, exporting duty-free liquor to India, importing ivory and other prohibited goods," he went on, "but Alex is determined to prove that he and certain unknown officers of the South East Asia Bureau were running some kind of unauthorised and highly profitable operation."

"Would she bend the facts to that end?"

Oliver thought about it long and hard, his forehead creased in deep furrows. "I think she could persuade herself that her interpretation of the facts was the unadulterated truth."

It was almost impossible to get a straight answer out of Oliver but he was in good company. Vines was the arch dissembler while Uxbridge was his staunch disciple.

"As I've already said, Mr Tindall, she's a very ambitious lady who intends to go all the way."

"And how far is that?"

"We have a woman Prime Minister," said Oliver. "Why not a woman at the head of the Secret Intelligence Service?"

Chapter XVIII

ALEXANDRA THOUGHT the routine at 'Moorlands' had been modelled on the lines of a maximum security prison. Shortly after she had spoken to Henderson on the phone, she had been escorted back to her room by one of the Special Branch officers and locked in. Although there were no bars, the window couldn't be opened from the inside and the only means of ventilation was a small grille just below the ceiling. The room itself was furnished on spartan lines which would not have offended the ascetic tastes of a Trappist monk. She had nothing to read, nothing to listen to, nothing to look at, and the oppressive silence was intended to undermine her powers of resistance to interrogation.

The exercise period had begun at twelve fifteen but without a wristwatch, she had to take what Louise told her on trust. The flaxen-haired girl wasn't in a communicative mood either and they had walked round the tennis court a good half a dozen times before she finally decided to speak.

"Tindall has told us to let you go," Louise said abruptly.

"What?"

"You're free to leave whenever you like."

Alexandra stopped in her tracks and grabbed Louise by the arm. "When did you hear this?"

"About an hour ago."

"Well, you took your time about passing it on."

Louise shook her off and walked on. "Tindall wanted to brief me using the secure link to Century House."

"Why the big secret?"

"He's not giving you a clean bill of health, Alex, even though Vines, Uxbridge and Oliver spoke up for you. The fact is, what we have on you wouldn't stand up in court and you're in danger of becoming a cause célèbre. You can put that down to Henderson."

"He's a good man to have on one's side," Alexandra said. "Even better than I'd been led to expect."

"One way or another, he's certainly making life difficult for us. Not that it's going to be easy for you. Tindall has suspended all your clearances indefinitely which means you will be denied access to all information classified Restricted and above."

"It also means that effectively I'm out of a job. Even the duty roster is classified."

"Tough luck. I imagine you are familiar with the appeals procedure?"

Alexandra nodded. Every government servant in her position had the right to appeal to an independent tribunal but she couldn't see what good that would do. If the Prosecution Service were not going to charge her with an offence under the Official Secrets Acts, the government were duty bound to offer her alternative employment in the same grade. The trouble was that bodies like the Department of Health and Social Security had little use for a trained Intelligence Analyst, nor would she be enthusiastic about accepting a routine administrative post.

"You don't have to take the first job you're offered, Alex. The Foreign Office will continue to pay your present salary for six months from the date of your suspension."

"Thanks for the tip."

"Mr Tindall also instructed me to find out where you intend going when you leave 'Moorlands'."

"You can tell Walter I haven't made up my mind yet."

"I know how you must feel, but it's for your own good." Louise smiled apologetically. "Someone tried to kill you and it's our job to make sure they don't succeed should they try again."

And they probably would, Alexandra thought. It also crossed her mind that Tindall was using her as the bait to draw the killer out into the open.

"I'll probably stop off in Nottingham on my way back to London. I might even spend the night there, depending on how long it takes me to get in touch with Mr Henderson."

"We'd like to be kept informed of all your movements, Alex." Louise reached inside the anorak she was wearing and brought out a slip of paper. "Day or night, just ring this number and leave a message for me. Whatever you do, don't phone anyone at Century House."

"I take your point." Vines, Uxbridge, Oliver and the rest of her colleagues were to be kept in the dark. Tindall didn't want any of them to know where she was.

"I'm afraid there's more," Louise said, embarrassed. "We'd appreciate it if you found somewhere else to live rather than with the Wagnalls. It's reasonable to assume the opposition will be watching the house to see if you return."

Considering the amount of damage that had been done to her house, Alexandra doubted if Pamela Wagnall would mind all that much if she moved out. She might even greet the news with a profound sense of relief.

"I don't think that's going to be a problem," Alexandra said drily.

"Good. I thought I would drive into Chesterfield after lunch and drop you off at the station, if that's convenient?"

"Suits me."

"We'll have a minder watching your back the whole time." Louise reached into the anorak again and handed her a small, nondescript brooch. "It would help if you wore this all the time."

No larger than a fingernail, the brooch looked like a regimental crest. The flaxen-haired girl didn't have to tell Alexandra it was an audio beacon.

*   *   *

Henderson walked through the Victoria Centre, entered Jeavons Department Store and followed the directional signs for their accounts office. With great reluctance, Preston had given him Avery's telephone number on the Regional Task Force; with even greater reluctance, he had told him where he could find Mrs Avery. Ordinarily, he wouldn't have bothered her but Avery hadn't responded to any of the messages he'd left for him and the clerical officer to whom Henderson had spoken had confirmed that the meeting in Leicester had broken up around noon.

The accounts section resembled a high street bank; choosing a vacant window, he told the woman behind the glass partition that he wanted to see Mrs Avery and was informed that it was her lunch hour. Politely declining her offer of assistance, he elected to wait for Mrs Avery and sat down in one of the easy chairs in the centre of the room. A little while later, a small, pert-looking brunette in high heels and wearing a blouse and skirt, emerged from the staff room to his left and walked purposefully towards him.

"I'm Mrs Avery," she said briskly. "How can I help you?"

"My name's Henderson," he told her and stood up. "I live in Mapperley Hall Drive."

"Oh yes?"

She tried to sound casual but it didn't come off. She knew why he had sought her out and was afraid. The way she clenched her hands, digging the nails into the palms told him so.

"Look, I'm not a greedy man. The asking price on my house may be eighty thousand but I'm open to a reasonable offer."

"I don't know what you're talking about. I was told you were making inquiries about a budget account."

"Please don't play games with me, Mrs Avery; my estate agent described you to a T. He said your husband rang the office just before lunch on Saturday and made an appointment to view the house at two thirty. Naturally, he used a different name."

"I'm not going to stand here listening to this nonsense a minute longer." Her voice was muted and lacked any kind of bite.

"A retired school-teacher lives opposite me. She's a lonely person and spends an inordinate amount of time looking after her front garden on the offchance that neighbours and passers-by might stop for a chat. This morning she called me over to say how pleased she was that I'd found a buyer for the house. This was a few minutes after she'd seen your husband drive off."

"If you don't leave this instant, Mr Henderson, I'm going to call the supervisor and have you removed . . ."

"She recognised your husband and remembered seeing him at the house on Saturday. She is also positive it was his car she saw parked by the kerbside the afternoon my place was burgled."

"Don't be ridiculous . . ."

"What he did was certainly stupid," Henderson said calmly. "Someone ordered him to put a phone tap on me; since it hadn't been authorised by the Home Office, he had to force his way into the house to make it seem like a burglary and to quiet my dog, he overdosed him. I feel badly enough about that but the fact remains that breaking and entering is still a crime."

"I'm aware of that, Mr Henderson."

"Good. I hope you also realise that no one is going to stand by him when the balloon goes up?"

"What do you want me to do?"

Total capitulation, sudden but not unexpected.

"I've left several messages for your husband asking him to get in touch with me but he's playing hard to get. I want you to make him see reason."

"I'll try, but he can be very stubborn . . ."

"So can I," said Henderson. "I'm going to be away from my office for a couple of hours visiting a client in Southwell. You've got until four thirty to convince him that talking to me is the only option he's got."

"What happens if he refuses?"

"I make an official complaint to the police. If they fail to charge him with breaking and entering, I'll instruct my solicitor to bring a private prosecution."

*   *   *

The man phoned at three twenty-eight. Quilter knew the precise time because he had just returned from a highly successful business lunch at the Silver Chalice in Holborn. Bad news always has a greater impact than good; years after the event, most people of his age group could remember exactly where they were and what they were doing when they heard the news of Kennedy's assassination. On a lesser, more personal level, Quilter would remember the precise minute the man told him that the Security Service was aware of his existence.

"What the hell do you mean?" he snapped.

"They have your name," the man said. "Henderson got it from Katherine Pascal and gave it to Alex who subsequently passed it on to our compliant MI5 representative."

"Jesus."

"I've done my best to limit the damage. Tindall believes you are a member of the team we organised to keep Alexandra Drummond under surveillance. The story will hold up because that's exactly what you were doing."

"It will fall apart when Tindall questions the others and learns they've never heard of me."

"We can cover that, Steven. The team were aware they were being supplied with information by a source close to Alexandra Drummond; they didn't need to know the identity of the source."

Quilter thought it made sense but for one small thing. Tindall would soon discover his lack of any kind of security clearance and would want to know why the Bureau had employed someone to carry out a highly sensitive task who wasn't positively vetted.

"Suppose Tindall brings up the question of my security status or lack of one?" Quilter asked. "How are you going to field that question?"

"It takes approximately four months to clear an individual for constant access to Top Secret and we couldn't afford to wait. There was no way we could make yours a priority case for clearance without drawing attention to you, which might have alerted Alex. We'll make two other points to Tindall. First, you were cleared for Top Secret while you were in the Marines and again when you were seconded to Century House; secondly, steps were taken to ensure you didn't have access to highly classified information."

It could work. The man would have a breach of security recorded against him in his personal dossier but he was unlikely to lose any sleep over that. A hundred thousand a year paid into a numbered Swiss bank account was more than adequate compensation for any adverse comment which could affect his chances of future promotion, assuming he had any.

"There's a chance that Tindall will be forced to release Alex. It seems Henderson has got one of the big shots at the Home Office by the short and curlies and writs will start flying about like confetti if Tindall doesn't produce her body within the next forty-eight hours."

"Shit. You promised me that woman wouldn't be released

before she had been thoroughly discredited. You said, 'By the time we have finished with Alex, resigning from the Service will seem to her the most sensible thing she could do.' What happened to that copper-bottomed guarantee?"

"The situation has changed, Steven."

And in more than one way it appeared. Somehow or other, Henderson had traced Royles to Heathrow and knew he'd boarded the BA flight to Cologne. An official request to the West German authorities in Bonn, asking them to trace Royles was already on its way and it was only a question of time before the Polizei had copies of his passport photograph to help them with their inquiries.

Royles was dead. In a few hours from now his body would be resting on the bottom of the Bodensee, both feet embedded in concrete. But what if the police stopped Immelmann for some reason and asked him to open the boot of his Mercedes? Quilter put the thought out of his mind. Nothing was going to happen to Franz; he was not the kind of man to drink and drive and had never been involved in a traffic accident.

"Just keep your head down until this thing blows over and you'll be all right, Steven."

"Let's hope you're right," Quilter said and hung up.

The man could afford to be laid back; he wasn't in the direct line of fire like Immelmann and himself. If the police really started asking around, someone who'd been at Cologne Airport on Sunday evening might recall seeing Franz there holding up a home-made sign with Royles' name on it. And under-estimating Henderson had also been an error; contrary to what he'd previously believed, the private investigator didn't need Alexandra Drummond to point him in the right direction. Against all expectations, he had traced Royles to Cologne; if the trail went cold on him there, he would get in touch with Pat Royles again to see if she knew which tour company her nephew was supposed to be working for.

Quilter sat there hunched over his desk like a man in a deep hypnotic trance. Henderson would have to be stopped before he got too close to him; where and when were the only two questions that occupied his mind.

*　　　*　　　*

Henderson turned into St Peter's Gate and immediately stepped up his pace as though reaching the office a few moments earlier would make all the difference. Spencer had kept him in Southwell a good hour longer than he'd anticipated and he wondered if Avery had tried to get in touch with him during his absence. Although it was after five twenty, he wasn't surprised to find that Sheila Luckwell hadn't departed for home. An extremely conscientious person, she had never been a clock watcher; if there was work still to be done, she would stay on after her normal office hours to complete it. She was even-tempered, efficient and concerned to keep the business on a sound financial basis.

The old-fashioned look she gave him as he entered the office was, he thought, a sign that she still felt he had acted quixotically in returning the greater part of the retainer Spencer had paid him. However, there was no way he could dig up enough evidence to show that the money willed to Katherine Pascal belonged to the Spencer family and, in his view, it was morally wrong to continue with the investigation until the retainer was exhausted. Sheila had been right about one thing though; convincing Spencer he shouldn't waste his money had been an uphill struggle.

"Any messages?" Henderson asked, ignoring her frown.

"A Mr Avery phoned twice, once at four thirty, then again half an hour later before he left to keep a previous appointment. He said he would call you again when he got back to his office around six fifteen."

"Thanks."

Four thirty on the dot. Mrs Avery had made her husband see reason all right; punctuality in this instance was a sign of a nervous man.

"You have a visitor," Sheila told him in a low voice.

"Who?"

"Miss Drummond. She's the reason I stayed on." Sheila stood up, eased the dust cover over the typewriter on her desk, then checked to make sure she hadn't forgotten anything.

"How long has she been waiting?" he asked.

"About an hour. Don't worry, Jack, I looked after her, gave her a cup of tea and all that."

"Thanks again."

"Don't mention it. Try not to lose your head."

Sound advice, he thought, but it was too late in the day to heed it now. With hindsight, it was obvious to him that he'd lost his head the afternoon Alexandra had walked into his office and no matter what happened in the future, he would never be quite the same man again. Mouth a little dry at the prospect of seeing her again, Henderson went next door.

"Hello, Miss Drummond," he said woodenly. "I'm glad they finally came to their senses and let you go. Your friend Mancroft must have a lot of clout."

The smile vanished from her lips. "He has a certain amount of influence," she said in a glacial voice that chilled him to the bone.

"I'm sorry, I didn't mean to sound disapproving." He groaned aloud. "Oh God, that's even worse."

The smile made a welcome re-appearance. "Don't you think it's about time you called me Alex?"

"Yes, maybe it is. Anyway, I'm very glad to see you again. Where were they holding you?"

"At a place called 'Moorlands'; it's in the Peak District near Matlock."

"Have they cleared you?"

Alexandra shook her head. "I doubt if they ever will. Six months from now, I'll be out of the South East Asia Bureau and looking for another job."

It was the first time she had dropped the pretence of working for a charitable organisation and the shared confidence was, he thought, a tangible sign of her trust in him.

"I thought I was being really clever, Jack, but the people I work for must have been watching me for months and I'm afraid I led them straight to you."

"Yes, I guess they had a marker out on me before you'd even signed the cheque for my retainer."

He told her then about Avery and why he was sure Special Branch had bugged his telephone.

"They did Judith's too, or so I learned when I rang her this morning."

"Judith?"

"My sister. Her husband's a major in the Royal Signals and is a staff officer in the Military Secretary's Department.

An engineer from British Telecom called at their house in Stanmore, ostensibly to rectify a fault on the line. This was just before I went out to India; three weeks later, the same man returned to deal with a similar fault. I asked Judith to check with the area manager of British Telecom to see if he knew anything about it. Apparently he didn't."

"They didn't leave much to chance, did they?" said Alexandra.

"No. When did Quilter arrive on the scene?"

"A few days after we had learned that Rupert was dead. I'd submitted a paper to Vines drawing his attention to the number of Sikh extremists Rupert was in touch with, many of whom were suspected terrorists."

"And he hadn't cultivated them for the purpose of obtaining information. Right?"

"I believe Rupert was helping to supply them with arms. Until I knew differently, I thought he'd used Nancy's money to make the initial purchase and was only just beginning to recoup his outlay when he was accidentally killed by the dacoits."

"I reckon he had a financial backer," said Henderson.

"Really?" Alexandra gazed at him thoughtfully. "Who do you have in mind?"

"Does Ahmad Bashir Khan feature in this rogues' gallery of yours?"

"No, Khan is a Muslim name, not a Sikh."

"I think he could be the banker."

Henderson told her about the newspaper article which Beardsley had kept and how as a boy of nine, Khan had seen his parents murdered by a Hindu mob. He left nothing out, the years of grinding poverty which had followed after Khan had fled to Pakistan, the beggar on the streets of Karachi, the barely literate teenager with a smattering of English starting again in Handsworth. And of the subsequent rags to riches saga.

"He wants revenge," Henderson said. "Supplying the Sikh terrorists in the Punjab with arms and ammunition is his way of extracting it. Goodman told me that the Sikhs constitute a disproportionately large element of the Indian Army; every time a Hindu mob goes on the rampage after an incident brings their eventual disaffection that one step nearer."

"Khan is the Pakistani businessman Beardsley was dining with at the Imperial Hotel in Rawalpindi?"

"I'd bet on it," Henderson said.

"Rupert was the Mr Fix It, the man who greased the right palms in India to ensure the goods weren't intercepted along the way. It's the wheeler-dealers I want, the greedy high-priced help within the South East Asia Bureau who obtained the weapons for a large consideration."

"Do you have any idea who they are?"

"Uxbridge was my number one choice, now I'm not so sure Oliver and Vines aren't implicated. What we need is a connecting link to the people at the top."

The phone rang, cutting Alexandra off before she had time to expand on her theme. Henderson answered it, listened attentively to the caller, grunting non-committally whenever there was a pause, then said he'd be there at six thirty and hung up.

"That was Avery. He wants me to meet him in a lay-by south of Plumtree on the A606."

"Can I go with you?"

"There's nothing I'd like better," said Henderson, "but he's not going to come clean in front of a witness. If you give me a phone number, I'll get in touch with you after the meet."

"I'm staying at the Savoy Hotel here in Nottingham."

"I'll call in on the way home then."

He had just enough time to run Alexandra back to her hotel, but she wouldn't hear of it. In the end, he walked her to the Market Square, flagged down a passing cab, then continued on to the multi-storey car park near the City Hospital via Friar Lane and the pedestrian underpass beneath Maid Marion Way.

It was the quiet period, the evening rush hour had finished and there was still some time to go before the night people appeared on the town. There were roughly a dozen vehicles on the third level where he had left the Ford Escort and no one else about when he arrived, except for the two men who had been waiting for him in the lea of a Dodge Transit van. But that was really pure supposition on his part because he never saw them coming.

He had the key in the door lock when they struck. One man

pinioned his arms in a bear hug from behind and swung him round to meet a short arm jab; the second man delivered it, powering a vicious right into the pit of his stomach. A wave of nausea engulfed him and there was a stabbing pain in the left side of his chest as though he was having a heart attack. His legs were already folding at the knees when a left hook exploded against his jaw. Still holding him with one arm, the second man pressed a first aid field dressing over his nose and mouth. There was the same sickly, cloying smell Henderson associated with hospitals, then the ground gave way beneath his feet and he fell into a black hole.

*   *   *

"Can you hear me?"

The voice seemed a long way off to Henderson and fuzzy too.

"I think so."

His own voice sounded equally fuzzy and now he came to think about it, his tongue felt as though it had been coated with a thick white paste.

"Here, take a swig of this, it'll do you the world of good."

The Good Samaritan placed a hip flask in his hands and helped raise it to his lips. Henderson swallowed a draught, enjoyed the warm glow from the alcohol as it went down.

"Hey, steady on, old chap, that's Chivas Regal you're gulping and we don't want you drunk in charge, do we?"

But if anything, the Good Samaritan tipped the flask even farther back and some of the liquid ran down Henderson's chin. It was only withdrawn when he started coughing and spluttering.

"Feeling better?"

"On top of the world."

Except Henderson didn't know what he was doing sitting on the floor of the garage, his back resting against the car. He stood up, walked unsteadily round to the driver's side and got in. Seat belt on, click clunk every trip. Or was it clunk click?

"Are you really sure you're fit to drive?" the Good Samaritan asked and helped him push the ignition key into the right slot.

"Of course I am."

He could do anything, write a sonnet, compose a hit tune,

climb Everest, win a hatful of gold medals at the Seoul Olympics. He started up and gunned the engine.

"This is not the start of the Le Mans Twenty-four Hours," the Good Samaritan told him mildly.

"You're wrong there," Henderson yelled and slammed the door.

He shifted into reverse, let the clutch engage and shot out of the parking space. Then he put the wheel hard over to the left, hit the brakes, slammed the gear stick into first and took off like a rocket. He was in third before he reached the first hairpin bend and went through it like a dream, tyres screaming. In top now, foot hard down on the straight, racing change into third, stab the brakes, then foot down again coming out of the second bend. Shit, was he or was he not the best bloody Grand Prix driver on the circuit? Into the final straight now, look for the chequered flag and do a gentle lap of honour.

Still doing close on twenty miles an hour, he went through the barrier by the ticket office, snapping the metal arm as if it were matchwood. Completely out of control, he shot across the road, clipped the rear end of a Montego parked by the kerbside, mounted the pavement and crashed into the side of a building. The horn started blaring as though sounding a discordant Last Post.

CHAPTER XIX

HENDERSON OPENED his eyes, rolled over on to his back and stared blankly at the ceiling. He felt rough, hung over like a man who had just come to after a two-day binge except that no one was tapping away inside his skull with a hammer. His brain was also a long way from being addled which was how he knew immediately that he had spent the night in a cell. It was, after all, standard procedure when dealing with a drunk to remove his shoes, belt and tie before placing him in the recovery position to ensure he didn't drown in his own vomit.

The police had obviously banged him up for driving under the influence but there could well be other and more serious charges. Some Good Samaritan had revived him after he had been knocked out and he vaguely remembered driving off in the Ford Escort but that was all. He wondered how many hours had passed since he had left the office with Alexandra and rapidly discovered that the police had removed his wristwatch. The only light in his cell came from a seventy-five watt bulb, making it impossible to tell night from day. He rubbed his jaw, feeling how much beard he had, and winced as his fingers encountered the bruise he'd collected in the course of a very brief and one-sided brawl.

Henderson swung both feet clear of the raised bedboard and sat up, his back supported by the wall. In his own mind, he was sure someone was watching him through the spyhole; consequently he wasn't surprised when a few moments later the door opened and the duty sergeant beckoned him to come out.

"Feeling better this morning, are we?"

"I'm okay."

"Good. Your Brief's here."

"Who?"

"Leonard Simons of Eastgate, Quayle and Simons. Somehow I don't think you're his favourite client right now, especially at seven thirty on a grey and windy morning." The sergeant handed him his belt, shoes and tie. "You'd better put these on," he said. "We don't want any unwarranted remarks about police brutality, do we?"

Despite his immaculate grey pinstripe, conservative tie and shirt, Leonard Simons looked as though he had just dragged himself out of bed, still half asleep. His eyelids were drooping and the way he kept tightening his jaw suggested he was finding it difficult not to yawn.

"How did you know I was here?" Henderson asked.

"Miss Drummond told me, and don't ask how she knew because it's a long, complicated story and it's best coming from her."

"She's here?"

"In a manner of speaking. Actually, she's waiting in my car round the corner."

"That's the good news," said Henderson. "Now tell me the bad."

The duty sergeant was more than willing to do that. The police, he informed Henderson, were going to charge him with driving under the influence, reckless driving, assault occasioning actual bodily harm and criminal damage. Apart from the drink-related offences, he had lashed out at one of the ambulance men who had been called to the scene of the accident and had caught him a glancing blow on the shoulder. The criminal damage was the pane of glass he'd broken in the police station when he had picked up a fire extinguisher and hurled it at the window. He had also told the police officer investigating the traffic accident exactly what he could do with his little plastic bag and subsequently, on arrival at the police station in Sherwood Street, he'd refused to provide a specimen. Not that a blood alcohol test was really necessary; the officers had smelt the whisky on his breath and it had taken the combined efforts of four constables to subdue him.

"We're going to fix you up with a date to see the Beaks," the duty sergeant said, winding up. "Of course, the way things are at the Magistrates' Court, you'll have to wait at least a fortnight."

"That should give you plenty of time to identify the goons who set me up."

"What are you talking about?"

"The two bent coppers from Special Branch who were waiting for me in the multi-storey car park."

"You want to take your client home now?" the duty sergeant asked Simons.

"Yes, I do."

Henderson felt a hand pluck his sleeve above the elbow and shook it off. "They shouldn't be difficult to trace, sergeant," he said icily. "Avery can't have that many friends willing to go out on a limb for him."

"Leave it be, Jack." This time Simons took a firm grip on his arm. "Save your defence for later. Just sign for your personal belongings and let's get out of here."

His jacket looked the worse for wear and one of the buttons was missing. His wristwatch however had survived the fracas and was still working.

"The same can't be said for the Ford Escort," the duty sergeant told him with a good deal of pleasure. "It's a complete write-off."

"Shit."

"And you're well and truly in it. Still, you might want the keys as a souvenir."

Henderson slipped them into his pocket. By the time he was finished, replacing his car was going to cost the police authority a bomb. Meantime, he would have to rent a vehicle, an expense which was not covered by his current insurance policy. Expensive as that would be, he was going to find himself in an even worse financial state if the magistrates banned him from driving for twelve months.

"What do you reckon to my chances, Leonard?" he asked Simons as they walked out of the station.

"Anything up to four hundred pounds and an eighteen month disqualification."

"Thanks," said Henderson, "you've made my day."

"One has to be realistic about these things," Simons observed loftily.

"You wouldn't be quite so sanguine if your living was at stake."

"Get Mrs Luckwell to drive you around."

There was, Henderson thought, always a solution to every problem. Provided of course you had the money and people were still putting business your way.

Alexandra was waiting for them in Burton Street. She had managed to get hold of a cab which brought an appreciative smile from Simons because it meant that he didn't have to offer her a lift to the Savoy Hotel. To Henderson, he appeared even more relieved to hear that he didn't have to run him back to his house in Mapperley Hall Drive.

"There are some things we need to talk about in private," Alex said after the solicitor had driven off in his BMW.

Henderson nodded. "Thanks for springing me. I'm sorry Leonard was a touch grouchy; usually he doesn't surface before nine."

"He wasn't exactly overjoyed." Alex looked him over with a critical eye. "You're not as badly damaged as I feared."

"I'll survive."

"I'm sure you will. Do you have anything edible at your place?"

Up front, the West Indian cab driver was all ears and in no hurry to find out where they wanted to go.

"There are some eggs in the fridge and hopefully the sliced bread hasn't got green mould on it yet."

"Good, we'll talk over breakfast."

Alexandra leaned forward, tapped the cab driver on the shoulder and gave him the address. After that, she didn't say another word until they were inside the house.

"You want to tell me what happened?" she asked.

"I didn't get to see Avery," Henderson said tersely, "that's the bottom line."

"And the rest?"

"Two of his friends were waiting for me in the multi-storey. No one else was around when I showed up to collect my car so they jumped me there and then instead of later. One of them subsequently played the Good Samaritan and revived me with a stiff whisky laced with LSD."

"Could you recognise them again?"

"I never saw their faces; everything happened too fast."

"Then how do you know they were Avery's friends?"

"Instinct and training tell me so. If you're a copper, you don't have too many friends outside the Force because the godfathers don't like you fraternising with civilians. So policemen tend to stick together and in the process become closer to one another than most families. I was leaning on Avery and his friends decided to do something about it because they could see he was getting jittery. Solidarity is the name of the game; but not all of them set me up out of pure friendship. At least one man believed there was a real possibility he would find himself in the mire with Avery."

"Really?"

Henderson thought he detected an element of doubt in her voice which needed to be answered.

"Avery had a partner keeping tabs on me while he broke into my house. Both of them were aware that it was an illegal job, but it wouldn't have been the first surveillance operation Special Branch had mounted on the nod without a warrant from the Home Secretary and it didn't bother them until things started to go wrong. They knew no one in your Service was going to stand by them; discrediting me before the roof caved in on them was their only hope."

"They could have killed you," Alex said.

Henderson shrugged. "They were angry and frightened; that's a dangerous and potentially lethal combination. I should know, it's the way I feel right now."

"You're going to take another crack at Avery."

He didn't have to say anything. Alex could read his mind and already knew the answer.

"I think you're being very foolhardy, Jack. You're in enough trouble as it is."

"If you feel like eating, you'll find the eggs in the fridge. I'm going upstairs for a quick shower and change of clothes."

He wasn't open to persuasion. Avery had set him up and he was going after the Detective Sergeant. Nothing she could say would deflect him from that and, if she was honest with herself, it suited her purpose to let him confront Avery. She could however ensure there were no hostile witnesses around when the encounter occurred.

*　　*　　*

The phone started ringing seconds after Avery walked into the office. There was nothing unusual about that; on some occasions, the switchboard had actually buzzed him when he was halfway between Nottingham and the Regional Task Force Headquarters at Newark and he'd had to stop and use the nearest landline. But he couldn't remember the last time a woman with a voice which conjured up such exciting possibilities had rung him at that hour of the morning.

"Detective Sergeant Avery?"

"That's me," he said happily. "What can I do for you?"

"I'm Alexandra Drummond. I assume you've heard of me?"

Suddenly his day was ruined and he felt apprehensive. "I don't know why you should think so," he blustered.

"You'll have to do better than that, Mr Avery."

"Maybe you aren't aware of it, but deliberately wasting the time of a police officer is a criminal offence."

"And you could end up in prison for breaking and entering . . ."

"I've had enough of this, Miss Drummond, I'm going to hang up."

"I wouldn't do that if I were you. There are two witnesses who can place you at 42 Mapperley Hall Drive – a retired school-teacher living opposite and the estate agent, to whom incidentally you gave a false name."

"Go tell it to the Chief Constable . . ."

"Before I do that, I think you should phone Century House and ask to speak to Mr Walter Tindall – his extension is 2154."

Tindall. The name didn't mean a damn thing to him but he knew she wouldn't have rattled off a bogus extension. Whatever else she was, Alexandra Drummond was no fool. If she was bluffing, giving him a false number was the quickest way to have it called.

"He's on loan to us from BOX," she continued.

BOX, the 'in house' okay phrase for the Security Service, more popularly known by the media as MI5 even though they had been divorced from Military Intelligence since 1931 when the Army had wisely decided they weren't in the business of keeping an eye on political subversives.

"You're in it way over your head, Mr Avery. An illegal

surveillance operation is bad enough but attempted murder is something else."

"What are you talking about?"

"Remember the car that was blown to pieces in Hampstead last Friday? It belonged to me. Of course, I'm not saying you were directly involved but I'm pretty sure we have sufficient evidence of irregularities to persuade the Chief Constable that he should refer the matter to Complaints and Discipline for further investigation. And where do you suppose they will start looking?"

At his house, and they wouldn't need a search warrant either. Avery thought about the synthesised receiver in the spare bedroom and knew it was all the evidence Complaints and Discipline needed to crucify him. Electronic surveillance devices were supposed to be held in a central stores depot belonging to British Telecom; the rules also stated the equipment could only be released on written authority from the Home Secretary. Worse still, the synthesised receiver manufactured by Racal Communications Limited was not standard issue and was therefore an indication that he had been involved in a considerable number of illegal operations.

"It doesn't have to end in tears, Mr Avery. If you cooperate, I'll make sure Mr Tindall keeps your name out of it."

"You scratch my back and I'll scratch yours?"

"That's the most satisfactory way of guaranteeing your immunity from prosecution."

"All right, what do you want from me?" he asked resignedly.

"Some answers face to face."

"Where and when?"

Alexandra Drummond gave him detailed instructions, then said, "Eleven o'clock sharp, and this time, come alone."

*　　　*　　　*

The telex from Bonn which was delivered to Mancroft shortly after he arrived at the office had been received by the duty clerk at 2105 hours. Unclassified and carrying only a routine precedence, it would have been passed to central registry for action had not the opening sentence named Mancroft as the intended recipient. He had not expected his request for assistance to produce anything other than a negative feed-back but elements of GSG9 based at Cologne Airport had proved him wrong. It seemed there had been a familiar face among the milling crowd waiting to meet British Airways Flight 744 on Sunday evening whom one of the officers from the Anti-Terrorist Squad had subsequently identified as Franz Immelmann, an arms dealer from Frankfurt.

Immelmann was regarded as friendly; with his contacts in the Arab world, he was a valuable source of information and was on first name terms with the Deputy Chief of the Counter Extremist Intelligence Cell co-located with the Interpol communications centre at Wiesbaden. However, despite his quasi official status, the arms dealer was still kept under discreet surveillance, but only within the confines of the Federal Republic. What he did abroad was apparently of no concern to the West German authorities; they were merely interested to learn who he did business with at home.

The warrant officer on plainclothes duty in the concourse had noticed that Immelmann was holding a card against his chest as a means of identification but had been unable to see the name written on it. According to Bonn, the stranger who eventually went up to Immelmann and introduced himself had closely resembled the description of Keith Royles which Mancroft had sent them. In view of the fact that the two men had left the airport before the warrant officer could put a tail on them, Bonn was understandably anxious to know what the Home Office had on Keith Royles.

Mancroft scowled; officially the Home Office had never heard of Keith Royles and what Henderson had told him about the man was next to damn all. He had allowed himself to be intimidated by a third-rate private detective and now his whole career was in jeopardy. An informal off-the-record appeal for assistance had suddenly become official business and since the duty clerk had logged the incoming telex, there was no concealing it now. To cover himself and head off the awkward questions the Permanent Under Secretary was bound to ask, he would need to muddy the waters by involving Century House. Although he'd never had any dealings with Vines before, it wasn't difficult for a man in his position to obtain the phone number of the Director in charge of the South East Asia Bureau.

"I believe we have a mutual interest," he told Vines. "A Miss Alexandra Drummond?"

"She works for me," Vines admitted cautiously. "How did you come to meet her?"

Mancroft wondered if he was being devious or just playing it close to the chest.

"Someone tried to kill her with a car bomb and got the driver of a laundry van instead. Remember?"

"I thought you chaps at the Home Office left that sort of thing to the police?"

"Usually we do, but sometimes a murder investigation goes political and before you know it, we're involved." Mancroft paused, then said, "Have your people got anything going with a West German arms dealer called Franz Immelmann?"

"No, definitely not."

"I hope no one is trying to hide something nasty under the carpet because the West German authorities have identified Mr Keith Royles as the man whom Immelmann met off the British Airways flight to Cologne on Sunday evening."

"I don't see the connection," Vines said petulantly.

"Royles is a courier, he gets his instructions from Miss Drummond through a man called Henderson. At least, that's how the police are beginning to see it. The question is, what can we tell Bonn about Royles?"

Vines suggested they switched to secure means, waited until Mancroft had keyed in the crypto setting for the day, then said, "Precious little. Graham Oliver, my Deputy Director Operations is here with me and he can tell you better than I what little information we do have on Royles."

Graham Oliver could not have been more open or more helpful. He confirmed everything Henderson had already told him about Royles and while he couldn't prove it, he had a pretty good idea why the former guide had met Immelmann in Cologne.

"Alex would dearly love to prove that the late Colonel Beardsley was involved in gun running. To do that, she needs an arms dealer whom she can link to our former colleague. I fancy she picked Immelmann out of a hat; Royles however had met Rupert Beardsley on a couple of occasions in India and she is using him to establish the connection."

Mancroft thought it was believable except for one small point. "Someone tried to kill her."

"To be frank, that bothers me too," said Oliver. "It only makes sense if we regard it as an entirely separate and unrelated incident. Alex has committed several minor breaches of security in the last few months; I think she became equally careless about her own security and the Provos identified her as an Intelligence Officer. They don't care that she has no connection with the Irish Desk; she works for Century House and that's good enough for them."

It was a good enough reason for Mancroft too. "So what can I tell Bonn about Royles?" he asked, reverting to his original question.

Oliver said he would be only too happy to give him a laundered profile.

* * *

Alexandra turned off the A614 to Bawtry at Ollerton and, guided by Henderson, went on down an unmarked track which led to a picnic area in the forest roughly a hundred yards from the main road. Moments later, a dark blue Rover swept into the clearing and parked some distance from them behind a clump of bushes.

"I see our guard dogs are still with us," Henderson said.

The Rover had been sitting on their tail ever since they had collected the Ford Sierra from the Hertz Rental Agency in Nottingham and the continued presence of the Special Branch team was beginning to annoy him.

"Trust me, I know what I'm doing."

Hadn't he already backed her all the way? Who had allowed himself to be talked into setting up this rendezvous with Avery on the edge of Sherwood Forest when he'd wanted to have it out with the bastard in his office at Task Force Headquarters? And then there was the flaxen-haired Louise, the wonder girl from Special Branch, and her nameless companion. Inviting them along had been a mistake, probably a big one.

"There's nothing to worry about, Jack. Avery won't duck out."

"Who said he would?" But all the same, her knack of reading his thoughts was becoming a disconcerting habit.

Avery arrived in a Mazda saloon at twelve minutes past eleven, almost a quarter of an hour later than Alex had stipulated. He was full of excuses and was suitably apologetic.

"The traffic was nose to tail in Sherwood."

"It always is," Henderson told him. "How many phone calls have you made since Miss Drummond rang?"

"What are you getting at?"

"You're only here now because London won't let you shelter under their umbrella."

Avery ignored him and turned to Alex. "Why have you brought Henderson along?" he said heatedly. "I thought we were going to have a quiet chat, just you and me."

"For the record, there are two Special Branch officers in a Rover the other side of the clearing. They photographed you as you got out of your car to meet us and they're listening to our conversation now with a directional strobe."

"What is this?"

"A none too subtle reminder that you are in serious trouble."

"You think I don't know that?" Avery snapped.

"Why don't you tell me who instructed you to set up an electronic surveillance on Mr Henderson?"

"It was done on the nod almost a month ago. The Detective Chief Inspector in charge of our small team calls me into his office one morning and says the Security Service is on to a major espionage ring and Task Force has been asked to provide a couple of officers to assist them with their investigation. It's all hush hush and he doesn't know any more than I've just told you. London is calling the shots and I'll get my instructions direct from them. So far as my DCI is concerned, I'm no longer working for the Regional Task Force."

The Investigating Officer had rung Avery at home. Identifying himself only by his first name, he had briefed Avery and then given him the number of an answering service he was to phone whenever he had anything to report. Henderson's name, home and business addresses had arrived in the post a day or so later with his passport photograph.

"And not having a warrant didn't bother you at all?" Henderson said.

"Christ, MI5 might just as well throw in the towel if they

had to obtain a warrant from the Home Secretary every time they wanted to open a letter, enter a house or bug a phone. Putting you under surveillance was part of a large scale operation which had been unofficially sanctioned."

Large scale? Well, they had certainly gone after his sister Judith and her husband. Henderson glanced sideways at Alex and wondered if she had unintentionally put the Security Service on to them. Leonard Simons knew his brother-in-law was in the Army and it was odds on that he was the man who had recommended him when she had got Young to find her a reliable private detective in the Nottingham area. On the other hand, it could well have been him who had pointed MI5 in their direction when he'd phoned Judith to ask if she could give him a bed for the night.

"I'd like the phone number of this answering service," Alex said coldly.

Avery gave it to her unhesitatingly, then said, "Am I in the clear now?"

"You will be when I have the names of the two officers who assaulted Mr Henderson."

"I figured you would say that." Avery reached inside his jacket and brought out a sealed envelope. "Their names are in there."

"Thank you."

"Just don't expect me to give evidence against them."

"Nobody's asking you to, Mr Avery."

"Good. That's us square then?"

Henderson waited for Alex to deny it. The bastard had broken into his house, killed Linda's dog and slashed her clothes to ribbons. Two of his friends had used him as a punchbag before setting him up on a drink-driving offence and all Alex could do was nod her head. The anger welled inside Henderson and erupted like a volcano; clenching his fist, he smashed it into Avery's stomach directly below the breastbone. His face a doughy grey, the Special Branch man buckled at the knees, sank down on to his haunches and vomited into his lap.

"We are now," Henderson said grimly.

The flaxen-haired girl and her companion came running but they weren't needed. Before they had a chance to intervene, Alex had grabbed his arm and dragged him away.

"You crazy man," she said angrily. "What do you think you achieved by hitting him?"

"I evened up the score."

"Get in the car and don't say another bloody word."

He didn't argue; his anger had evaporated so that he was now deflated and not a little ashamed of his lack of self-control. Leaving Alex to sort things out, Henderson walked over to the Ford Sierra and got in. When she joined him a few minutes later, her tight-lipped expression appeared to have taken root. No words were exchanged until they were well on the way back to Nottingham and then it was Henderson who broke the oppressive silence.

"I guess I'm in the doghouse."

"Why? Because you hit Avery?" Alex shook her head. "I think I would have done the same."

"Then why so grim?"

"That phone number Avery gave me could only have been activated by Henry Uxbridge, our Chief of Staff."

"So?"

"Henry may be a disappointed man because he's reached his ceiling but he's no crook. The truth is that he lacks the imagination to be one. Henry has never been an innovator; he's just a methodical staff officer who's very good at dotting the 'i's and crossing the 't's."

It seemed Uxbridge was also loyal, unquestioning and painstakingly thorough, three attributes which Henderson thought made him the perfect foil.

CHAPTER XX

DELHI, FIVE P.M.; a slight haze in the azure sky, the sun dipping towards the horizon, but still a blast furnace of heat that sapped Goodman's energy and left him feeling languorous and devitalised. In the days of the Raj, long before World War Two, the Viceroy and senior administrative officers of the Indian Civil Service, together with their supporting staffs, would have left the capital for Simla in the foothills of the Himalayas, there to remain from May to September until the hot season was over. Fifty years later, air-conditioning had arrived and the government stayed put. The only problem was how to move from one cool building to the next without becoming like a piece of chewed string in the process. Goodman's second-hand Renault was not fitted with an air-conditioning unit and none of the limousines belonging to the British High Commission had been available. Consequently, he arrived at Manik Bhose's office in the Secretariat North Block with his shirt clinging to his back and every pore oozing sweat.

"Good of you to spare me the time," Manik said, waving him to a chair. "I could have given you the information over the phone but there are a number of implications my Minister has said he would like me to discuss with you. I'm referring of course to the UK Eyes Only signal you received the other day and our subsequent discussion about former members of the Customs and Excise Service in Bombay."

"Quite." Goodman was sitting directly in the path of the chilled air coming from the Westinghouse unit which was positioned on the outside wall to his left and rear. But that wasn't the only reason why he felt cold and clammy; in his experience, senior civil servants only quoted their Minister when they had something unpleasant to say.

"You wanted to know how many Customs and Excise officers had left the service voluntarily since the first of June 1985 or had been dismissed, imprisoned or met with sudden death . . ." Manik glanced at the topmost file in his pending tray as if to refresh his memory. "There were no premature retirements and no one was sentenced to a term of imprisonment. However, one senior officer was killed in a plane crash in which eight other passengers died, and two more were killed in traffic accidents, one of whom had suffered a massive coronary moments before he drove straight into an oncoming bus. The other victim was knocked down by a truck as he was crossing a busy thoroughfare in Bombay. He had retired from the service in January of this year on a full pension. Prior to his retirement, his lifestyle and assets, which included a small villa, were entirely in keeping with the standard of living a government official on his salary would enjoy. Finally, there was no evidence of foul play and the truck driver was sentenced to four years' imprisonment for involuntary manslaughter."

"What about dismissals?" Goodman asked.

"The dockyard police were collecting evidence against one officer whom they suspected was accepting bribes but he was rushed into hospital and died from typhoid fever before charges could be brought against him. His name was Salman Bedi and his command of English was about as quaint as the man who wrote to 'Rupert Sahib'."

"Really?"

"His widow, though understandably grief-stricken, was well provided for. There are grounds for thinking she would have been even better off had Bedi been less generous towards her relatives. As a would-be entrepreneur, he had the unfortunate knack of backing one loss-maker after another." Manik paused, then delivered the punch line. "As you may have already guessed, QRX Industrial Tools and Dies were among the firms who contributed to his private pension fund."

"On how regular a basis?" Goodman asked.

"Somewhat infrequently. As a matter of fact, the police are reasonably sure that Bedi only cleared two consignments from QRX. Of course, when you are supplying terrorists with arms and ammunition, it's only prudent to use several ports of entry. Bedi knew this, that's why he complained to 'Rupert Sahib'."

"That's a pretty large assumption, isn't it?"

"My Minister can think of no other explanation, Lawrence.

Indeed, he's convinced the British Secret Service can tell us which other ports are being used by QRX, as well as naming those Customs and Excise officials who are on the company's payroll."

"I'm afraid your Minister is very much mistaken if . . ."

Manik smiled wearily, raised a hand to silence him. "I think so too but he won't listen to me. And it's my sad duty to inform you that you will be declared persona non grata unless we have the names of those Customs officers and the ports of entry within the next forty-eight hours."

"We're not in a position to do that."

"My Minister is convinced otherwise."

"I don't believe it," Goodman said incredulously, "you showed him the photocopy of the UK Eyes Only signal I gave you."

"Forty-eight hours, Lawrence," Manik said and made a helpless gesture.

Two days: Goodman thought he might as well start packing now. His wife wouldn't mind; Judy had never liked India and it simply wouldn't occur to her that getting himself expelled was unlikely to do his career much good. And all this for one lousy name; he found himself hoping that Tindall's future would be similarly blighted. He stood up, moved stiffly towards the door, then turned about.

"I'm sorry our friendship has to end like this, Manik. Do give my regards to your wife, Madhu, the next time you see her, whenever that might be."

It was hardly the definitive parting shot, and not in his nature to be deliberately unkind, but all the same, he got some satisfaction out of knowing that he had succeeded in wounding Manik Bhose.

*   *   *

The depression which had settled over the Midlands was only a shade less than the atmosphere Henderson encountered when he walked into the office a few minutes before twelve thirty. Sheila Luckwell had already heard about the drink-drive incident from Danny Preston when he had phoned her earlier on to explain why he would be late in, and nothing had happened since then to alter her opinion that he would have no one but himself to blame if the Gold Seal Inquiry Agency were to collapse about their ears.

"This may be a one man organisation, Jack, but we need more than one client to survive."

"And you've been drumming up a few," he said, eyeing her notebook.

"A Mr and Mrs Glaisher; their seventeen-year-old daughter has run off with a barman who's heavily married with four children and is old enough to be her father. They want you to find her and bring her back; I assured them you would get on to it right away."

"Did you now."

"You'll find the case notes and their cheque for five hundred pounds as a retainer in your in-tray."

"You have been efficient," he said drily.

"Also a batch of repossession orders."

"Anything else?"

There was a momentary hesitation before Sheila told him that a Mr Keith Royles had telephoned from somewhere in Switzerland.

"I asked if I could take a message and he said he was on his way to Crans Montana and would call again between twelve thirty and one o'clock our time."

Crans Montana: Ahmad Bashir Khan had a chalet there; he remembered it being mentioned in the magazine article Katherine Pascal had given him.

"Perhaps you'd like to read yourself into the Glaisher case while you're waiting for him to phone back?"

"I might just do that, Sheila."

Henderson went through to his own office. He had arranged to meet Alex for lunch at one fifteen and he rang the Savoy Hotel to warn her that he might be late. In the event, Royles came through at twelve forty-five.

"My name's Keith Royles," he said, nervously clearing his throat. "I spoke to your secretary about an hour and a half ago . . ."

"Yes, she told me."

"I've been thinking about the message you left with my aunt and wondering whether I should get in touch with you."

234

"I'm glad you finally did."

"Are you working on behalf of a journalist, Mr Henderson?"

"No. What on earth gave you that idea?"

"Detective Inspector Quilter said you were. He came to see me when I was staying in Dartmouth. According to him, you are trying to dig up a load of dirt on Colonel Rupert Beardsley and will go to any lengths to get it. He said if I refused to cooperate, you would threaten to let those skinheads who put Charlie Freeman in hospital know where they could find me."

"And you believed him?"

"I'd no reason to doubt Mr Quilter's word, especially after he had shown me his warrant card."

"Did he tell you who he was with?" Henderson asked.

"The Metropolitan Special Branch."

Quilter was something of a chameleon; he had led Katherine Pascal to believe he was with the security department of the Foreign and Commonwealth Office, now he was passing himself off as a police officer.

"He told me State Security was involved and suggested it would be a good idea if I left England for a prolonged holiday on the Continent. I was given five hundred pounds in cash towards my expenses and told to be on the British Airways flight to Cologne departing at 1725 hours on Sunday evening."

"Anyone meet you at the airport?"

"Yes, a West German police officer; arrangements had been made to take me on to a safe house. I told my aunt a travel agency had asked me to fill in for one of their guides on the Grand European Tour who'd suddenly been taken ill. I've sent her a number of postcards to prove it."

"If they're looking after you that well," said Henderson, "what prompted you to get in touch with me?"

"I'm running out of cash," Royles told him candidly. "My German friend is happy to chauffeur me around but I have to pick up the bills and they've dumped me at this villa in Crans Montana and the woman who owns it is asking for a fortnight's rent in advance. Quilter was supposed to meet us in Basel on Tuesday night with a bagful of cash but he didn't show up. Instead, he called the hotel where we were staying and told Franz to bring me on here."

"Franz?"

"My West German friend, I don't know his surname. The thing is, Franz said it was not his problem any more and pushed off back to Germany soon after we got here, leaving me stranded high and dry." Royles cleared his throat again. "So I sort of wondered if we couldn't get together?"

Royles was looking for another hand-out. His motives for wanting to get in touch with him were however irrelevant; the only thing that mattered to Henderson was the fact that contact had finally been established.

"There's a photograph I'd like you to see, Mr Royles. I think you'll recognise the subject at a glance."

"Is that all?"

Henderson thought he sounded disappointed. "Don't worry, I'll make it worth your while. Now tell me exactly where I can find you."

There was a repetitive pinging sound as Royles fed a handful of coins into the pay box, then he proceeded to give him very clear and very concise directions. After he had hung up, Henderson called Miss Royles in Dartmouth and learned that her nephew had indeed sent her a postcard from Bonn.

* * *

Quilter backed out of the pay-phone kiosk in the main concourse at Zürich Hauptbahnhof and made his way towards the restaurant near the indicator board beyond the mini shopping precinct. Immelmann was sitting in a corner booth at the back of the room opposite the entrance. As he moved towards him, the German raised his hand and signalled the waitress to bring two more beers.

"Well, what happened?" Immelmann demanded.

"Henderson bought it, just as I said he would."

"Amazing. The man shouldn't be allowed out on his own if he's that gullible."

"He thought I was Keith Royles . . ." Quilter broke off while the waitress placed their beers in front of them and tucked the bill under the ashtray, then went on, "Henderson had no reason to suspect I was an impostor; he's never met Royles nor even spoken to him on the phone. I said I had been advised by Special Branch to give him a wide berth and that they had paid me to go abroad. I also told him that, on their instructions, I'd sold my aunt a pack of lies about a tour company urgently needing a replacement guide and how I was keeping up the pretence by sending her postcards from all our mythical destinations."

"So when can we expect to see him?"

"Tonight, or the early hours of tomorrow morning depending on what flight he's on."

"That soon?" Immelmann scowled. "I don't like it, Steven, he's too eager."

Quilter lit a cigarette. There were a number of things Franz didn't like, beginning with his phone call yesterday evening when he had told him that further extreme measures would have to be taken before they could consider themselves safe. He had caught Immelmann at his weekend villa on the shores of the Bodensee near Lindau before he'd had time to dump Royles into the lake, and the German had damn nearly blown a fuse when he'd told him about the threat posed by Henderson.

"Of course Henderson is eager," Quilter said impatiently, "he thinks he's cracked it."

"And you think he will if we don't take him out?"

"You can bet on it, Franz."

"You have somewhere in mind to do this thing?"

Quilter nodded. "Crans Montana."

"Are you crazy? That's where Ahmad Khan lives." Immelmann leaned forward, dropped his voice to a murmur. "We will be pointing a finger at ourselves."

"You would prefer we chose some other location?"

"Natürlich," Immelmann said, lapsing into German.

"There is a small problem. Henderson is going to catch the first plane he can from Heathrow and since he himself doesn't know his flight number, estimated time of arrival and destination yet, where the hell are we going to lie in wait for him? Zürich, Geneva or Basel? You tell me – he could arrive at any one of those airports."

There were other factors Quilter had had to take into account. A hit had to be planned with the same kind of attention to detail that went into laying an ambush. You had to look at the lie of the land and choose a killing ground which the intended victim couldn't avoid and where there was plenty of cover to conceal the marksman as he lay in wait.

"The chalet Khan owns in Crans Montana is the ideal site," he continued. "Take it from me, I've been there and know the area well." Quilter stubbed out his cigarette. "The chalet is on the outskirts of town, there isn't another property within half a mile and Khan only uses the place during the winter. It's locked up for the rest of the year, but of course a handyman drops by once a week to make sure it's still there."

"When?" Immelmann asked.

"Every Monday."

"I still don't like it, Steven."

Patiently, as though dealing with a somewhat dense adolescent, Quilter explained why there was no alternative. Henderson had to disappear without trace and that meant he had to be eliminated before he left too many footprints.

"And what about our footprints?"

"We aren't going to leave any, Franz."

He had flown to Zürich as Harold Paige, utilising the blank passport Uxbridge had provided for emergencies when they'd decided to monitor the Drummond woman. The same Harold Paige would hire a car from the Hertz agency in town, paying the rental charge in cash. Immelmann could then leave his Mercedes in a parking lot, safe in the knowledge that no one would be able to trace his subsequent movements.

"You forget one thing," Immelmann told him. "I'm empty handed, so are you."

Quilter calculated how long it would take Henderson to drive down from Nottingham and added on the longest flight time from Heathrow, then said, "You're an arms dealer, Franz, you've got four hours in which to make a buy."

Chapter XXI

There were the usual filing trays on the desk – In, Out and Pending. Tindall had heard it said of Uxbridge that he prided himself on being on top of the paperwork and having a photographic memory. At five minutes past three that afternoon, the In and Pending trays were empty; Tindall hoped his other proud boast was equally justified.

"Steven Quilter," he said abruptly. "What can you tell me about him?"

"Ex Royal Marine, served with 3 Commando Brigade, finished his time with the Special Boat Section and left at the nine-year point in 1976. Special skills listed as combat radioman, small arms instructor and assault pioneer . . ."

"What's that?"

"It means he had been trained how to lay, breach or lift a minefield, rig boobytraps, blow things up."

An assault pioneer: Tindall believed he didn't have to look any further for the man who had moulded five pounds of plastic explosive and a trembler to the chassis of the Ford Cortina belonging to Alexandra Drummond.

"We took him on as an instructor when he left the Marines," Uxbridge continued. "We gave him a five-year contract and sent him down to our training school near Petersfield. Steven was an ideal choice; he was an experienced staff sergeant, he had received outstanding gradings in his last four confidential reports, he held a current positive vetting clearance and had earned a special commendation from Graham Oliver."

"For doing what?"

"I'm not allowed to tell you."

"I'm cleared for Top Secret, Atomal, Cosmic and Codeword – what more do you want?"

"It's the 'Need to Know' principle."

"And I need to know," Tindall said firmly. "Ring the Director General if you're in doubt."

Uxbridge reached for the telephone, then abruptly changed his mind. "I don't think we need to bother him. After all, what happened in 1975 is ancient history now."

In those days, Oliver had been the British Resident in Tripoli when the Chief of Staff of the IRA's Belfast Brigade had arrived in town with his personal bodyguard on an arms buying mission. The bodyguard had been the former altarboy, Sean McBride who had killed his first man before his seventeenth birthday in 1971 and had subsequently become the chief enforcer for the Turf Lodge area. By 1974, the Royal Ulster Constabulary's Special Branch had incontrovertible evidence that he had executed at least six informers, all of whom he'd maimed before delivering the coup de grâce. Quilter had given McBride a taste of his own medicine when some of the hawks running the Irish Desk in Century House had decided to take a hand in the negotiations.

"Quilter could have killed the Chief of Staff while he was at it but Graham Oliver thought it would be more effective if the hero was allowed to go back home to Northern Ireland, pissing himself every step of the way."

It did not automatically follow that a man was a killer because he knew how to make a car bomb. To take another person's life in cold blood called for a degree of callousness and ruthless indifference to suffering not found in most people; the Libyan incident was proof that Quilter possessed these negative qualities in abundance.

"We wanted to renew his contract but Steven was being head-hunted by a private security company and he decided to sample life on the outside." A bleak smile appeared fleetingly. "The truth is, the Service couldn't pay him enough. Neither it seemed could the security firm; within eighteen months of leaving us, Steven had set himself up as a general broker, a sort of Mr Fix It."

Tindall wondered how many others had felt the Foreign Office was not paying them enough. Beardsley for one of course, but what of Vines? And Oliver? And Uxbridge?

"When was the last time Beardsley attended a course at the training school?"

"We never sent Rupert to Petersfield. Quilter accompanied him on one of his trips to India and Sri Lanka; they were away for ten weeks altogether. That's how they got to know one another."

Uxbridge had anticipated his question with uncanny perception, so much so that Tindall wondered how much credence he should give to the Chief of Staff's testimony from there on.

"Quilter lost his security clearance the day he left Century House, yet he was the man the South East Asia Bureau turned to when it was decided to put Alex Drummond under surveillance. Whose bright idea was that?"

"I can't honestly remember; his name came up in conversation and we unanimously decided he was the best man to have on the inside. It was then my job to put the surveillance team together."

"And you got Quilter's address from Admin?"

Uxbridge looked inordinately pleased with himself. "I didn't have to go to them; I knew he had an office in Paternoster Row."

"How come?"

"I like to keep in touch with former officers of the Bureau; there's always a chance they'll come up with some useful titbit of information."

The bleeper Tindall carried in his jacket pocket emitted a high-pitched warble. Smiling apologetically, he asked Uxbridge if he could use the phone to call his security section in Century House. Moments later, Tindall was listening to a tape-recorded message from the Special Branch team in Nottingham.

"It seems Mr Royles has surfaced," he told Uxbridge. "He called Henderson about an hour ago, said you people had persuaded him to take a long holiday abroad. Apparently, Franz is looking after him."

"Franz?"

"Franz Immelmann."

There was a long pause. Not an eyelid flickered, not a muscle moved. Finally, Uxbridge said, "I don't believe I've heard of him."

"He's an arms dealer."

The information had come from Mancroft at the Home

241

Office. Tindall didn't pretend to know how they had become involved or made the connection; what mattered was the fact that, after sitting on the information for several hours, Vines had finally decided to pass it on to him.

Vines hadn't been on the take; in wanting a quiet life until he retired, he had simply closed his eyes and ears to what was going on around him. Now, with the storm about to break, he had hurriedly put up an umbrella to protect himself from the downpour. Tindall believed he knew the identity of the man inside the South East Asia Bureau who had covered for Beardsley and the others; proving it was an altogether different matter.

"I think you'd better give me the address of Quilter's office," he said.

*   *   *

Khan's mountain retreat had been built on a natural shelf roughly two hundred feet below the road from Crans Montana to Aminona. The chalet itself had cost a small fortune but, as he'd told Quilter many times, that had been nothing compared with what the municipal authority had charged for constructing the all-weather track which had made it possible for him to live in splendid isolation from the rest of the village. Right now however, the Pakistani was sunning himself on the Riviera and he and Immelmann had the place to themselves. But not for much longer; in another hour or so, Henderson would be joining them.

"The light's going," Immelmann said tensely.

The sun was dipping behind the mountains now and the whole of the valley was already in deep shadow. Within a matter of minutes it would be dark, a situation that would persist throughout the night since the moon was in the last quarter.

"It won't make any difference to us," Quilter said. "Henderson will use his main beams on that track."

"Provided he's driving."

"There aren't any trains to Crans Montana and he sure as hell won't come on foot."

Henderson would probably fly to Geneva, then drive to

the mountain resort via Montreux, Aigle and Sion, a distance of roughly one hundred miles. But no matter which airport he arrived at, he would have to hire a car and there was no alternative route to Crans Montana other than by way of Aigle.

"Suppose Henderson parks his car in the village and walks down the hillside?"

"He won't do that, Franz, I told him to ignore the sign."

Khan had erected a notice board at the road and track junction which said 'Private – No Thoroughfare' in French, German and English.

"Didn't you tell me that Henderson is unpredictable?"

"Yes, but . . ."

"No buts. Let's assume he follows our example and leaves his car in a side street off the main square."

Quilter knew it was useless to point out that they had arrived in broad daylight and couldn't afford to be seen at the chalet with their BMW whereas Henderson would be arriving after dark. Immelmann wanted to consider the worst case and would not allow himself to be side-tracked.

"Then we've got a problem, Franz . . ."

"We certainly have."

"But not an insuperable one," Quilter added.

Killing Henderson would be simple enough. The moment he stepped out of his car, Immelmann would drop him with a single shot from the 5.56 mm SG543 Manurhin assault rifle he'd acquired in Zürich. Then they would zip up his body in the sleeping bag they'd also bought along the way and slip a couple of polythene bin liners around the torso to prevent any blood seeping through on to the upholstery of the car. No stranger to the area, Quilter knew of a disused salt mine at Bex on the way to Montreux where no one would ever find the body. But if Henderson was to disappear without a trace, his car had to be returned to the rental agency.

"Of course, I'm not saying it isn't a time-consuming one," he continued. "Obviously we will have to collect the BMW before we can remove the body; then you'll have to drop me off in the village and carry on while I look for his car."

"What's that saying you English have about a hayrick?"

"A hayrick? Do you mean like trying to find a needle in

243

a haystack?'' said Quilter. "It won't be as difficult as that. Henderson will have the keys on him and the rental agency's logo will be somewhere on the vehicle.''

"It's still a goddamned mess.''

Immelmann was right about that. The whole operation had started to come unstuck the day Beardsley had gone missing and Mr Bloody Graham Oliver in his massive conceit, had decided he could use the system to muzzle the Drummond bitch.

"If we are not careful, Steven, you and I will be left with the babies.''

There were times when the correct idiom eluded Immelmann but his meaning was clear enough.

"No one is going to do that to me,'' Quilter said.

He had given Oliver a copy of the letter he'd deposited with his bank for safe keeping. In it he had described the legitimate Intelligence-gathering operation Beardsley had helped to run and the list of Sikh extremists he had acquired as a result of his frequent liaison visits to India. It was all there, the snippets of information the South East Asia Bureau had gathered about Ahmad Bashir Khan, his wealth and hatred of all things Indian, his willingness to supply arms and ammunition to the dissidents in the Punjab.

And the Director of Public Prosecutions wouldn't have to look very far to find a motive for Graham Oliver's willing involvement. Contrary to what a lot of people thought, his ex-wives hadn't left him strapped for cash. Neither had asked for maintenance and if anything, Oliver had come out of each marriage slightly better off financially than when he went into it. He was motivated by the knowledge that in order to make himself look good, Vines had blighted his career by damning him with faint praise in his annual confidential report. If he was forever denied the chance of becoming a future Director General of the Service, Oliver was going to make sure that, if nothing else, he retired on an equal if not greater pension.

"What time do you make it?'' Immelmann asked.

Quilter peered at the luminous face of his wristwatch. "Twelve minutes to nine.''

"Funny, I could have sworn my watch had stopped.''

"Stop worrying, Franz. Henderson won't keep us waiting much longer."

*　　*　　*

Henderson changed down from third into second and went into the sharp left-hand bend. Driving on this particular stretch of road was hard work and he wished they'd rented a car with power-assisted steering which would have taken most of the drudgery out of it. Crans Montana didn't seem to be getting any nearer either; the lights they glimpsed every now and then still appeared no larger than the decorations on a Christmas tree. It was an illusion of course but it didn't stop him putting his foot hard down on the accelerator at every opportunity.

"This isn't Brand's Hatch," Alex reminded him calmly.

"I'd be doing twice the speed if it was," Henderson said and glanced into the rear view mirror.

"They're still there, Jack," she said. "You haven't lost them yet."

They were the flaxen-haired Louise and her partner, the strong silent type who had little to say for himself or to anyone else. The two Special Branch officers were dogging them now because Alex had insisted on coming with him and wherever she went, they were never far behind. But he wasn't complaining; the fact that Royles was in Crans Montana where Ahmad Bashir Khan happened to have a chalet was too much of a coincidence and there was such a thing as safety in numbers when you weren't too sure what sort of reception could be waiting for you. Other people had evidently felt the same way; in the two and a bit hours it had taken them to drive down from Nottingham, fellow officers had visited their respective homes and a colleague had been waiting for Louise and her partner at Heathrow with their passports. London had also laid on the Detective Lieutenant at Geneva who had introduced himself as their Liaison Officer.

Two more 'S' bends and suddenly the lights were much closer and looming directly above Crans Montana was the dark mass of the Gletscherhorn. They went on past the isolated chalets on the outskirts, a golf course on their left, and still climbing gently, entered the village. A variety of boutiques, sports outfitters, jewellers, a branch of Crédit Suisse, a mini supermarket, a disco, two bistros within a few yards of each other and directly ahead the Etoile Hotel and a small Kino showing *Out of Africa*.

"I think we'd better stop here," Alex said.

Henderson pulled into the kerb and eased the gear shift into neutral; moments later, the other Peugeot 305 slotted in behind them.

"What's the idea?" he asked. "Are we picking up reinforcements?"

"We should be. Royles is a key witness; he can link Beardsley with Khan and point a finger at Quilter. Without him, we don't have a case and there's a distinct possibility he may refuse to come back to England after what happened to his friend Charlie Freeman."

"You think Quilter did that?"

"He almost certainly hired the skinheads who called round to his flat in Belmont Court. Because Royles was one of the last to see Beardsley alive, Goodman thought London ought to know when he decided to leave Indus Tours and return home. Oliver passed the information on to Quilter and he did the rest once he knew you were trying to find him."

"So what are you going to do about Royles? Arrest him?"

"If necessary."

Glancing into his rear view mirror again, Henderson saw the Swiss Detective Lieutenant get out of the second Peugeot and move forward to greet the uniformed police sergeant who was standing on the street corner up ahead. After exchanging a few words with him, the Lieutenant returned to the other vehicle and the sergeant got in behind Alex.

"Bonsoir Monsieur le Sergent de Ville," Alex said and then lost him completely as she continued as though French was her natural second language. Finally, she turned to Henderson and told him to let the others lead the way.

"It's your show," he said.

Henderson gave the Peugeot driven by the taciturn Special Branch officer a head start and then followed on roughly twenty yards in rear. The road curved to the right and went on up a slight incline past a filling station, a small shopping precinct and a ten-pin bowling alley before levelling out. More shops, a café, a couple of pensions, a right and left turn in the centre of Montana and they were heading out of town towards Aminona. A good quarter of a mile beyond the end house, the leading Peugeot suddenly turned off the main road on to a narrow track. As he tripped the nearside indicator, his headlights picked out a notice board which said 'Private Road – No Thoroughfare'.

"Lights," Alex said tersely.

Henderson switched off the main beams and keeping the tail lights of the other vehicle in view, began to negotiate the switchback descent to the chalet. Royles was expecting him to come alone and he knew he couldn't afford to use the footbrakes.

$$*\qquad*\qquad*$$

The chalet faced due south, angled so that the entire frontage was never in shadow from sunrise to sunset. From the kitchen on the north-west side, Quilter spotted the headlights of a vehicle between the fir trees as it zigzagged down the track.

"Here comes our boy." Quilter checked his wristwatch. "Twenty-three minutes past nine – didn't I tell you he wouldn't keep us waiting for long?"

"You did, several times over."

Immelmann tested the suppressor to make sure it was locked on to the muzzle of the Manurhin assault rifle. To the uninitiated the attachment was a silencer but in reality there is no such thing as a truly noiseless firearm. There are sound moderators and suppressors which momentarily cause the emergent gas to swirl round before escaping, thereby reducing the velocity, but for all that each shot is accompanied by a hollow cough which is clearly audible at close range. But no one in Crans Montana would hear the shot that killed Henderson.

"Let's get with it, Franz."

"Jawohl, Herr Oberst," Immelmann said mockingly.

Immelmann went out into the hall and swiftly made his way up to the room above the front door. Shortly after they had broken into the chalet, he had placed a small chest of drawers in front of the window to provide a steady platform for his elbows when he adopted a fire position. Cocking the rifle, he pulled the butt into his shoulder and leaned forward, elbows braced on the chest of drawers. A light came on in the sitting-room below to his left and, between a gap in the curtains, a narrow beam played on the drive. He thought Henderson would find that reassuring.

Quilter walked into the hall and switched on the light above the porch. Although he could no longer see the headlights of the car from the front of the chalet, the night was still enough for him to hear the faint whine of the transmission. Knowing it was only a matter of seconds now before he came face to face with Henderson, he instinctively reached behind his back to feel the butt of the 9 mm SIG-Sauer automatic pistol he had tucked into the waistband of his slacks.

Was that one vehicle he could hear or two? Quilter listened attentively; the engine sounded uncommonly loud even allowing for the possibility that Henderson had changed down into second gear. Then the main beams played on the window to the left of the door as the car made a U-turn in the drive and there was no time for further speculation. The headlights were doused a split second before the driver cut the engine. Opening the front door, Quilter walked out on to the porch.

"Mr Henderson?" he asked loudly. But the man who got out of the car was a good three inches shorter and suddenly his voice deserted him at the crucial moment.

The target was less than twenty yards away and was illuminated by the light over the porch. Taking a deep breath, Immelmann lined up the sights with the centre of the visible mass, took up the slack on the trigger and squeezed off a single shot. Below him, the man he thought was Henderson went down, and stayed down flat on his back. The nearside front door opened, so did the offside rear, and in that instant he realised that things had gone terribly wrong. He thought he heard a woman scream as he put a round through the nearest door, then a figure with blonde hair fell out of the Peugeot and started to crawl away on hands and knees. Although like most assault rifles, the Manurhin SG543 could be set either to fully automatic or single shot, the change lever also had a third fire position which restricted a burst to three rounds, a refinement that was intended to conserve ammunition. Flicking to controlled automatic, Immelmann ripped off a burst, hitting the woman in both legs and the rump. This time when she screamed, he knew he wasn't imagining it; taking a fresh aim, he fired again. As he did so, a sliver of wood from the window frame lanced his cheek and he heard the crack of an automatic pistol. Downstairs, Quilter had retreated from the porch and was returning the fire, his automatic sounding like a cannon in the confined space of the hall.

Henderson had switched off the engine on the penultimate bend in the track, shifted into neutral, and coasted the rest of the way, gliding to a halt behind the chalet. As he got out of the car, his attention was arrested by a hollow coughing noise; seconds later, he heard the unmistakable crash of gunfire. Reacting swiftly, the police sergeant pushed him out of the way and ran towards the back door. In the best traditions of Hollywood, he drew his pistol on the run and used his left shoulder as a battering ram. Unlike in the movies, the door refused to give. He hit it again to no effect and was backing off for a third attempt when Henderson tried the latch and discovered it wasn't locked. In what was a moment of pure farce, the sergeant went past him like an express train and ended up doing a ballet dance before measuring his length on the polished tiled floor of the kitchen. Somewhat shaken, he got to his feet and opened the door to the hall.

Henderson was behind the sergeant and slightly to his right when he saw the gunman in a crouching position at the far end of the hall. Thinking Alex was still outside, he yelled to her to stay where she was and flatten herself against the wall for protection. Although the sergeant had the drop on the other man, he had been trained to effect an arrest whenever possible and he made the mistake of challenging the intruder.

Quilter didn't hesitate. With one police officer engaging him from the front and another about to from behind, he thought his chances of survival were about zero even if he were to obey the order to put his hands up. In one fluid movement he turned about and threw himself forward, firing twice while his feet were still off the ground. Hit in the stomach, the police sergeant went down on his knees and toppled forward so that the automatic pistol he'd been holding was trapped beneath his body.

Henderson was between Quilter and the back door; recognising him as he scrambled to his feet, Quilter grinned wolfishly and took a deliberate aim, his right arm fully extended as though fighting a duel. In that instant all the years of training counted for nothing as he forgot that he was silhouetted by the porch light directly behind him. The Detective Lieutenant crouching behind the Peugeot fired only once but that was enough; the bullet, partially deflected by the spinal column, shattered the heart before exiting high up on the left side of his chest. By the time Henderson reached Quilter, his eyes were already glazed.

Immelmann had heard the exchange of shots in the hall and knew the abrupt cessation was bad news. Quilter would have called out to let him know everything was okay, but this ominous silence could only mean that he had been hit. He flicked the change lever to repetition in order to conserve what little ammunition remained in the twenty-round box magazine and moved out on to the landing. From up above, he could just see the body of the police sergeant near the kitchen doorway and assumed that Quilter must be lying somewhere directly below him. But where the hell was Henderson?

"All right," he said loudly. "I'm coming out with my hands up. Okay?"

Henderson crouched inside the entrance to the dining-room on the right side of the hall where he could cover the staircase. He had armed himself with Quilter's automatic because it had happened to be readily accessible but he had no idea how many rounds were left in the magazine.

"Did you hear me below? I'm coming out with my hands up."

Henderson glanced to his left. Despite his instructions to the contrary, Alex had followed him into the chalet and was now lurking somewhere in the kitchen. He hoped she would stay there and resist the temptation to have another go at retrieving the pistol belonging to the dead sergeant.

"I'm coming out. Don't shoot."

"Then throw your gun down," Henderson told him in a loud voice.

Immelmann smiled. For a while it had looked as though Henderson wasn't going to be drawn but now he had him pinpointed. He moved quietly to the top of the stairs, then came down them sideways on to the dining-room and shooting from the hip.

A bullet smashed into the skirting board a few inches from where Henderson was lying, another chipped the door frame and a third passed low over his head. Then he saw the gunman's legs on the staircase and got off two quick shots before rolling sideways behind the inner wall.

Crouched in front of the refrigerator in the kitchen, Alex had an oblique view of the staircase and could see the gunman. He was tall, about six two, and resembled the description of Franz Immelmann which Special Branch had obtained from the Home Office and passed to Louise at Heathrow. Immelmann was feeling his way down to the hall one step at a time, his whole attention concentrated on the room where Henderson had gone to ground. She had already made one sally into the hall to retrieve the sergeant's automatic but had only succeeded in moving his body out of the way when Immelmann had called out from the landing above and she had been forced to retreat. The pistol was lying there out in the open barely ten feet from her but she would be dead before she could grab it. And any moment now, Immelmann would make a dash for the kitchen and that would be it. Alex looked round for a weapon. There was bound to be a selection of kitchen knives but in which drawer were they kept? Then her eyes fastened on to the copper-bottomed saucepans hanging from a row of hooks above the electric cooker and she quickly removed her shoes. Tiptoeing across the room, Alex unhooked the two heaviest saucepans and returned to her previous position by the fridge.

She took a deep breath, sidestepped into the open and wielding the saucepan in her right hand like an Indian club, took aim and let fly. The pan struck Immelmann on the right kneecap and he swung round to face her, lost his footing and sat down heavily on one of the steps. His rifle was pointing up in the air when he accidentally squeezed the trigger and blew a hole in the ceiling.

Henderson heard him fall, broke cover and crouching in

the doorway, opened fire. As he did so, Alex pounced on the automatic lying out in the hall, scrambled to her feet and holding the pistol in a two-handed grip, emptied the magazine into Immelmann at point blank range.

Then, apparently horrified by what she had done, she threw the gun down and ran towards the front door. Lunging after Alex, Henderson grabbed an arm and hauled her into the dining-room.

"For Christ sake," he panted. "What are you trying to do? Get yourself killed? The Detective Lieutenant is out there and he's likely to shoot first and ask questions afterwards."

"Sorry," she said shakily.

"You will be, love, unless you tell him the war's over."

Alex did exactly that in fluent French, in a voice that was still unsteady. It was a long time before the Swiss police officer believed her.

CHAPTER XXII

THE CLIPPING from the *Nottingham Evening Post* was dated the seventeenth of September and was almost a month old. Pamela Wagnall had forwarded it on to her with a brief note explaining that she hadn't known where to send the enclosed until receiving her letter. There was also one of Draycott and Draycott's compliment slips attached to the clipping which said:

'Dear Miss Drummond,

Leonard Simons thought you would be interested to see the attached.

I trust you are keeping well.

Yours sincerely,

James Young.'

The report was headlined 'PRIVATE DETECTIVE'S NIGHT OUT ON THE TILES'. It read: Mr Jack Henderson, proprietor of the GOLD SEAL INQUIRY AGENCY appeared in court today charged with Driving Under The Influence, Committing A Breach Of The Peace, Causing An Affray, Criminal Damage and Assault Occasioning Actual Bodily Harm. Giving evidence, Police Constable Cashmore stated that at approximately seven p.m. on Tuesday the fourth of August he went to Mount Street where he found the accused slumped over the wheel of his Ford Escort. His eyes were glazed and there was a strong smell of alcohol on his breath. After collecting his vehicle from the multi-storey car park, Mr Henderson had failed to stop at the barrier and had subsequently collided with a Montego on the opposite side of the road before finally coming to a halt on the pavement. When questioned by PC Cashmore, he had become violent and had attacked one of the ambulance men called to the scene of the accident.

Inspector George Richardson stated that on arrival at Sherwood Street Police Station the accused had refused to provide a specimen of his blood and urine and had smashed a pane of glass.

Mr Leonard Simons claimed that his client had been the victim of a cruel practical joke when, after being attacked and knocked unconscious by two unidentified men, he had been given whisky laced with a hallucinatory drug. No evidence was produced to support this contention and the accused was found guilty on all five charges. Mr Henderson was fined a total of six hundred pounds, was banned from driving for twelve months and was ordered to pay costs of two hundred and fifty pounds.

The clipping had brought Alex to Anderlecht and was the reason why she was now standing in a kiosk on the corner of Rue James Ensor waiting for Henderson to answer his phone. It seemed an age before she heard his voice on the line.

"Jack?"

"Yes, who's that?"

"It's me, Alex." She bit her lip, wondered how to continue, then said, "I've just seen the report of your case in the *Nottingham Evening Post* and I wanted to say how sorry I am."

"I was pretty sorry for myself too at the time."

"I'm also very angry with Walter Tindall."

"What's he got to do with it?"

His voice was still cold and she could picture him standing there in the hall or perhaps the kitchen, his jaw set in a hard line.

"He assured me the police were going to drop the case."

"Are you sure he exists, this Walter Tindall?"

"Of course he does, you've heard me mention his name often enough."

"I'm not denying that, only thing is, no one had ever heard of him at your place. As a matter of fact, the girl I spoke to when I dropped into Bell Yard gave me the impression that the Finlayson Trust itself was about to vanish into thin air."

Jack was right in a way. Godfrey Vines had been retired, Henry Uxbridge had been transferred to a low grade administrative job at the training school and the South East Asia Bureau had been absorbed by the Far East Department. The Foreign Office would take over the legitimate side of the Finlayson Trust and gradually allow it to die for want of funds. Walter Tindall had returned to the Security Service and would have been reassigned to some post where he was out of sight, out of mind, out of reach.

"Are you going to appeal?" she asked.

"On what grounds? Avery denies everything, the retired school-teacher who lives across the road now says she was mistaken in thinking he was the man she saw at my house and the estate agent says he doesn't remember him."

"They've been got at."

"Right. But I don't have a hope of reversing the decision unless you are prepared to testify, and you can't do that, can you?"

"I've signed the Official Secrets Acts."

"Which means you are effectively gagged."

"There must be something I can do . . ." She frowned, then the idea came to her that at least there was one practical way she could help him. "I know . . . the fine . . ."

"Forget it," he said harshly, "it's been taken care of. A week ago, some well-wisher popped an envelope through my letter box containing eight hundred and fifty pounds in used tens and twenties. There was no message of course but I know who I have to thank for it. Pity they can't do something about my disqualification but I suppose that would be a little too obvious."

"So how are you managing?"

"Sheila Luckwell chauffeurs me around. Business isn't as brisk as I would like but I expect it'll pick up." His anger faded, and with it, the harsh tone of voice. "How are they treating you? Will we be seeing your name in the New Year Honours List?"

"Absolutely not."

"What about Oliver?"

"You won't be seeing his name in the newspapers either."

The Foreign Office had been worried about the harm the incident would do to Anglo-Indian relations, the government had lost too many cases against former Intelligence officers to be sanguine about this particular one, and Century House had always had a strong aversion to any form of publicity. In the circumstances, it was hardly surprising that the Director of Public Prosecutions had decided there would be no trial. Instead, Her Majesty's Inspector of Taxes had been invited to investigate Oliver's financial affairs, a course of action which had been described to Alex as hitting him where it would hurt the most. Ahmad Bashir Khan was receiving the same kind of treatment with the Swiss and French tax authorities thrown in for good measure. The Home Office also had reason to believe that Immigration would discover some loophole in the regulations which would allow them to deport him.

"Where are you calling from?" Henderson asked. "Or aren't you permitted to tell me?"

"I'm stationed in Brussels."

The non event job they had given her with NATO was a form of rustication. In going to Henderson she had committed a major breach of security and while Century House had decided she could retain her vetting status, it would be a long time before they welcomed her back into the fold, if ever.

"Can you give me your address?"

Alex hesitated, stared at the rainspots on the glass, the onset of yet another autumn shower. She had already said too much for her own good and she wasn't entirely sure how she really felt about Jack. Then the meter started flashing and she rummaged through her purse, desperately looking for more coins.

"Total silence, I might have known that would be your answer," Henderson said quietly. "I had a long talk with Danny Preston the other day and he said something that I should have recognised much sooner. We were discussing the way my trial had gone and from there we got on to the subject of winners and losers and he said there were two kinds of people in this world – the users and the used. I guess you used me, Alex, and I'm a born loser."

She wanted to tell him that that might have been true in the beginning but there were no more coins in her purse and suddenly the line was dead and he was no longer there.

She left the kiosk and walked up and down in the rain looking for a bar where she could change a note and eventually found a café in the Rue de l'Aiguille. But he wouldn't answer the phone when she rang back.